THUNDER SNOW
MELISSA GUNN

ROSE KOWHAI PRODUCTIONS

ISBN ebook 978-1-06704-612-5
ISBN paperback 978-1-06704-613-2
ISBN hardback 978-1-06704-614-9
ISBN audiobook 978-1-06704-615-6

For Paul, who would have made it much grimmer

CONTENTS

AUTHOR'S NOTE

This book is written in New Zealand English. It may contain more 'u's and 's's than you're used to!

Chronologically, it falls between Storm Surge and Heat Wave in the Weather Gods series.

CHAPTER ONE

A NEW HOME

Freya joggled the old key until it fitted into the lock of the peeling, blue-painted door that led to her new flat. The flat was a ground-floor one, part of a row of brick and stone houses that lined the sides of the valley. Another door next to hers probably led to the flat on the upper level of her building. Across the road, tall trees shaded a similar row, slightly higher than those on Freya's side. The terraced valley was one of many in the city of Sheffield that Freya had just arrived in; she'd passed endless rows of similar ones on the bus from the station, some with street trees, more without. She would be living a fair walk from the nearest set of shops, but not unbearably so. The key grated in the lock a moment, then the locking mechanism caught and the door swung open onto a short, narrow hall lined with aged beige wallpaper. There had probably been a print on it once, but years and the passage of the flat's occupants had worn any pattern away. An open door off the hall revealed a tiny front parlour containing a battered couch and a dusty radiator.

Freya put down the cat cage containing Mr Fluffbum in front of the couch, and after closing both the front door and the parlour door, released the black and white cat from his durance vile. He gave a small meow as he stepped cautiously out and proceeded to sniff every surface. Then he leaped onto the couch, kneaded it into submission, and sat down. His eyes glowed yellow-green as he fixed them on Freya. He meowed again, more intensely this time.

"Yes, Mr Fluffbum, I'll get you some food really soon. As soon as I've looked at the rest of the flat, so I know it's safe, all right?" *Honestly, I wish 10-year-old me had come up with a better name. Still, it's his now.*

Freya was too excited to be taking ownership—well, rentership—of her own student flat to be overly concerned about her cat's unflattering name.

A second door down the hall promised another room, so Freya slipped through it, careful to shut the parlour door behind her. She would explore the rest of her new-to-her student flat and close any windows that looked like Mr Fluffbum could climb out of them. For the next two weeks, at least, the internet assured her she should keep her cat indoors.

Ten to one, he finds a window he shouldn't be able to get to and climbs out of that.

But some scares when he was younger had taught her that she had to try to keep him in. She didn't want to start off life at university by losing her beloved cat. And with any luck, a dish of tasty cat food should ensure that he stayed indoors for at least a few hours. She'd made sure to pack some, but it was inaccessible at the bottom of her backpack. Exploring could come first.

Freya found herself in a bedroom—the only one the flat possessed. She'd have to find herself a bed, the agent had explained, as there had been... issues... with the last one. Freya hadn't been brave enough to ask what issues could arise with a bed in a student flat. She'd seen photos of the flat before signing the agreement online, so she knew more or less what to expect, but seeing it in person was different. For example, she could see distinctive scars on the bare wooden floorboards that looked very much like those left by rootlets. A boarded-over hole in the middle of the room could well have been caused by a tap root.

Did some hapless demigod student discover their dryadly powers while meditating in bed one day? It certainly looks like it.

Freya bit her lip as her imagination ran riot.

Still, there's no proof. Perhaps they smashed up the bed, and the floor, some other mundane way. There could be a simple, everyday explanation.

Freya was in search of mundane explanations for a lot of things these days. That was why she was here, in an inland city, ready to attend a mundane university, and hopefully get a mundane degree to do mundane science. It sounded a bit dull when she put it like that, but Freya felt she'd had enough of the supernatural to last her a good many years. She'd applied at university towns well away from any were-havens she knew of, as well as away from the coast, and she'd been accepted by her second choice. It was a shame she hadn't been able to follow her friend Karim to York, but at least she was still in the North. Her mum's reaction had surprised her.

"Not near the sea? At least you'll be safe." Then she'd turned away. After some thought, Freya had decided that that was probably about her still-missing sister, Tammy.

Don't think about Tammy. There's nothing you can do.

Tears pricked her eyes despite herself, and she angrily blinked them away. Even now, with a new flat, a new town to explore, and a degree to pursue, thoughts of her sister threatened to overwhelm her. She looked out the window at the surprisingly sunny skies. No point in looking for her friend Lio. He only turned up with storms. And Aisha, her other friend, had stayed behind in their coastal town.

She cast another look at the floor and hoped she'd be able to afford at least a mattress to sleep on this week. The lack of complete furnishings had made this flat cheaper than many. That, and the agency's willingness to accept pets, had made it the only possible choice for her. She left the bedroom and found herself back in the hall, staring at a kitchen, which was definitely not large enough to swing a cat in. Not that she would, of course.

A late rose tapped on the window, and Freya leant over the small counter to see a short sloping lawn adorned with some small shrubs. The garden of the row of houses opposite her own sloped upwards from a stone wall which separated the properties. According to the agreement she'd signed online, Freya had shared use of the garden, but as the ground-floor flat, she had the easiest access. A small well of delight sprang up inside her, and she flung out her hands as though to share it with the world.

"This is great, Mr Fluffbum," she called to the cat. "We're going to love it here." A mew at her feet drew her attention. "Mr Fluffbum? How did you get out?" Freya bent and patted the cat anyway, eliciting purrs of pleasure.

A few steps completed her exploration, with the discovery of a clearly tacked-on bathroom with a half-bath and overhead shower taking up much of the space.

I guess bathrooms weren't a thing when this house was built. However, many hundreds of years ago that was. Or maybe it's just that they split the house up for single flats. Freya returned to the kitchen with her cat at her feet. When she stopped, he twined around her legs urgently.

"Yes, I know you're hungry," Freya said. "I'll find you some food soon. I'll have to buy more soon; I know you don't like the cheap kibble." Her usually unfussy cat had turned his nose up at the small packet of budget bits she'd kept at the top of her backpack. She opened the kitchen cupboards at random, finding mostly dust and cobwebs. But one cupboard held some elderly tea bags, their packet a little faded but still legible. The final cupboard stuck until

Freya found a knife from her bag and chipped away at the poorly applied paint that held it closed. It grudgingly opened with a firm application of her knife to the gap between door and shelf. Inside, Freya found a single tin of salmon-flavoured cat food. She read the label suspiciously.

"What do you know, Mr Fluffbum?" she exclaimed. "It's still good! Mum would call this a sign." She hesitated. "I think I do too," she said. "In any case, here's your lunch, puss!"

She lost no time in opening the can and setting it down for her cat. Watching him lick at the food gave Freya a warm feeling. This place could be home, it really could. All she had to do was unpack her few things, and find a bed. If she didn't manage that today, she could always sleep on the sofa, however uncomfortable it looked. She settled down on the single chair next to the cooker, where a tiny table provided a place to eat. Rummaging in her backpack for a snack, she came across her phone. The screen was black, and it wouldn't turn on, even when she held the power button down. Freya shrugged. She'd figure out the phone later, after she'd finished enrolling in her classes. Meanwhile... a piece of chocolate and an orange-chocolate flavoured oat flapjack meant only one thing. It was lunchtime.

"Well, Mr Fluffbum." Freya bit into her flapjack hungrily, leaving the chocolate to have as a luxurious second course. She swallowed her mouthful, enjoying the tang the orange lent to the otherwise sweet, chewy snack. "This is going to be home. I hope you like it."

CHAPTER TWO
A NEW PHONE

Freya inspected the proffered mobile phone doubtfully. She didn't really know the Hephaestus demi who was selling it, but that wasn't the only cause of her unease. It was also her conditioned response to avoid other demigods. For much of her life, she had been taught to recognise and steer clear of her fellow demigod and demigoddess descendants, relying on a collection of minor cues—modes of dress, names that related to gods, personal traits or physical characteristics. Although in her teens she had realised that she probably didn't need to fear other demigods (or demis, as they were known in her family) as much as her mother had told her, it was hard to overcome a lifetime of training.

On the other hand, her friend Karim had recommended Kessler, the mobile phone dealer, and the phone he was selling was considerably cheaper than anything in the shops. If there was one thing Freya had discovered she couldn't do without in the city, it was a phone.

"You won't find a better deal," Kessler said in persuasive tones. "My phones last longer than anything mundanes make. Bring it back if you have problems. Not that you will."

She considered Kessler and the phone once more. Kessler was tall, clean-shaven, all angular jaws, prominent cheekbones, and silvery eyes. His hands looked like they could have been used to stoke a furnace, calloused and with a myriad small cuts, mostly healed. There was little doubt of his Hephaestean origins in Freya's mind. There was the technical know-how, the work-worn hands... Apart from anything else, he'd approached the student bar from the engineering building. According to her mum, many engineers were also descendants of the Greek smith-god.

Freya bowed to the inevitable.

"All right," she said. "Do I need to do anything to get it started?"

"It's all good to go," Kessler replied. "Transfer me the money and it's yours."

Freya hesitated. "Do you take cash?" she asked.

Kessler lifted his eyebrows in surprise, and Freya hastened to explain.

"I don't have a phone at the minute. My Mum gave me her old one before uni started, but it died a few days ago."

Kessler whistled. "Wow, what dark ages have you been living in?"

Freya couldn't prevent her blush and a deep sense of embarrassment.

"I just...well, I haven't had enough money, that's all."

Kessler laughed. She could hear the disbelief in his voice.

"Well, since Karim has vouched for you, I guess cash is ok. Welcome to the 20th century," he said.

Freya opened her mouth to correct the century, then realised he was making a joke.

"Oh. Thanks, then." She pulled out the bent envelope in which she'd been hoarding cash from occasional stints at her friend Aisha's family cafe. "Here. This should cover it." Feeling a pang of loss, she handed over the cash. She'd have to forage to get enough to eat until her student allowance came through next week. Hopefully, she would find edible things growing in walking distance from her rented flat, since she now didn't have cash for trams or buses. Fortunately, she had bought an extra-large bag of slightly more expensive than usual cat kibble at the start of the semester, so her cat, Mr Fluffbum, wouldn't go hungry even if she did.

Kessler riffled through the wad of cash and handed back a ten-pound note.

"Here you go. Discount just for you, 'cos no-one should be without tech." He passed her the shiny black phone. "Pleasure doing business with you, Freya. See you round."

Stuffing the cash into a back pocket—*isn't he worried about being pickpocketed?* Freya wondered—Kessler sauntered out of the run-down student bar into the late-autumn sun.

Freya drank the rest of her lime & soda (the cheapest drink available since it was aimed at student drivers) and set the empty glass down with a sigh. Moving away from home was proving to be more of a culture shock than she'd anticipated.

I'd forgotten how lonely it is, not having a friend. Even Mum was company.

So far, she didn't really know anyone. Most people in her classes seemed to live in other suburbs, or perhaps they drove around. She hadn't seen them walking her way. The longest conversation she'd had in weeks was the negotiation for a new phone just now. And living in a city instead of a town meant that she'd have to go a long way to find wild edibles that weren't at dog height. Freya looked at the money in her hand. It would buy seven packets of pot noodles, one for each day of the week. Or three tins of baked beans. She wrinkled her nose at the thought. Maybe she should enliven them with wild autumn greens. That might be an improvement. But meanwhile... she turned on the phone and was relieved to see it glowed with the current time like any other phone would.

Unfortunately, that time showed her that she was five minutes late to her next lecture.

"Frigg! I'd better run." Slipping the phone into her own pocket, she hastened out. With any luck, she'd be able to slip into the back of the lecture theatre unnoticed.

Chapter Three
Late to a Lecture

Freya had forgotten that the only entrance to the lecture theatre for her afternoon class was down by the podium. The lecturer had already started speaking. The thin, grey-haired woman broke off mid-sentence with an indignant glare at Freya, who hunched her shoulders and scurried to find a seat. The only seats left were in the front row, which meant a short scurry, but one which left Freya feeling as though every eye in the room was locked onto her. She folded down the seat, which squeaked loudly in the silence, and groped in her bag for a notepad. Her ancient laptop had run out of battery earlier in the day and she hadn't managed to recharge it yet. The lecturer started speaking again as Freya scrabbled for a pen.

"As I was saying, it is vitally important that we make the most of each session. We have only a few days left before the study break, so today we'll be reviewing what we've covered this semester in preparation for your term test."

Freya's pen had run out of ink. She swirled it in circles on her notepad in the hope that the ink would magically start to flow again, but that had never been the sort of magic she possessed. When no ink appeared, she burrowed into her bag for another pen and came up with a pencil. A minute later, the lead broke. Resisting the urge to bang her head on the awkward slide-out table in front of her, she reached in desperation for her new phone. Perhaps if she recorded the lecture now, she could take notes later. She'd overheard other students telling each other about doing that. Freya found the voice record function and laid the phone casually on the table. Three minutes after that, the lecturer's flowing words once again came to an abrupt halt.

"No recording devices allowed in this room, young lady," she said, staring directly at Freya. Freya felt her cheeks burn and wished she could sink into the floor. Behind her, there was a rustling murmuration, as a hundred or so students shifted uncomfortably and covered their own phones. Freya hurriedly put her phone in her bag, and the lecturer resumed speaking. A tap on her shoulder startled her. Turning around, she saw a young woman with exceptionally curly hair holding out a pen. Silently mouthing 'thanks', Freya took it and turned her attention to her notes once more.

In the post-lecture chaos, Freya felt alone amongst the buffeting crowds. She wished she'd got into York, where Karim was, or that Aisha hadn't stayed home on the coast. Starting over again was proving harder than she'd imagined it would be, socially speaking. She angled sideways to remove herself from the crowd, trying to avoid eye contact. She jumped when someone tapped her arm. It was the curly-haired girl from the lecture.

"Oh, sorry, I forgot to give your pen back!" Freya exclaimed, conscience-stricken.

"Nah, it's only a pen. I wanted to ask if you want to join me and my friends. We're off to the pub. Maybe dancing after."

Freya hesitated. Dancing wasn't something she'd done a lot of in her life. And a pub visit meant spending money.

"Go on, it'll be fun," said the girl. "You looked like you were down in the dumps. It's not that bad here once you get used to it."

Freya still hesitated. Although the girl was acting friendly, Freya didn't usually jump into new friendships. However, she wasn't sure how else she'd meet anyone here. Perhaps this was the moment to stop holding back.

"Oh, all right then," Freya agreed. University was supposed to be fun, wasn't it? So far, she'd concentrated on getting a place to live and finding her classes. She could almost imagine Aisha encouraging her.

Go on, live a little.

Freya wasn't even sure what the lecture had been now that she'd left. Biochem? Organic chemistry? Biological systems? Hopefully, her notes would make more sense later. Though she was sure doing a university degree was the key to a better future for her, and she looked forward to the day she graduated, the actual minutes in a lecture theatre were passing at the speed of the now-vanished glaciers—and that didn't include assignments, tests, exams... She gave an internal shudder, and turned her focus to the external world. The girl with curly hair was walking alongside her, or perhaps half a step in front, leading the way to the student pub.

"I can't believe I signed up for this *on purpose*," Freya said to her new acquaintance, feeling greatly daring at making conversation.

"I know, right?" said the girl. "And we'll be paying for the experience into middle age, barring miracles. I'm Val, by the way."

"I'm Freya. Are you expecting miracles?" Freya asked.

Val laughed. "No, if I wanted miracles, I'd have gone in for theology. Or business school, I guess. I hear they manage the odd miracle."

"Seriously?"

Val winked. "They say one lecturer has the Midas touch. But he's probably in league with Plutus. You know, Greek god of wealth."

Freya felt her eyes bug out. "For real?" A demigoddess herself, albeit one with limited powers, she had been conditioned to hide what she was from mundanes, the assumption always being that people were mundanes until proved otherwise.

Val ducked away from the main crowd. A group of people followed her. She turned a corner into the shade of the old traffic over-bridge that cut the campus in half. Although Freya had been appreciating the sun, she followed, glancing back nervously at the trail of people.

"Of course, not for real," said Val. "If I were for real, I'd be telling you to watch out for that biochem lecturer, 'cos she has some serious bad power vibes. And the stats lecturer is probably a vampire, but my brother says he's careful about his victims and doesn't choose students, it's against uni policy. And the—"

"Stop!" said Freya, half laughing. "If you go on, I doubt I'll make it to any of my lectures. And I can't afford to fail."

Val snickered. "Didn't think you'd heard the rumours. It's all nonsense, really. You're not from round here, right?"

"Right. But surely most people are just, er, normal?"

"No-one is truly normal," said Val in a deep mock-serious voice.

Freya wasn't sure what to make of that. She looked at the rest of Val's followers, who had grouped themselves into a loose circle. *Better talk,* she thought, feeling cornered.

"How about you introduce yourselves?" she said. "I'm Freya. I've lived all over, but most recently, in a little village near the coast." She hesitated, unsure if she should tell them more about herself. "I've never really lived in a city till now." She was reassured when there were understanding nods from the group. They were a varied looking crew, all manner of skin tones and hairstyles. Freya thought that probably meant that they were unlikely to be a were-pack of any sort.

She didn't see any of the usual tells for werewolves at any rate. She relaxed a little.

"Well, you know me now," said Val. "I come from down South. Don't think I've ever been to the coast. Not up close, anyway—the Thames doesn't count. Isn't it dangerous with all the storms?" She didn't wait for an answer, but hurried on. "The dude on your right trying to hide under a hood despite it being the hottest day since we've arrived is Nesh, on account of him always being cold."

Nesh shrugged and looked sheepish.

"I was born for warmer climes," he said in an accent that assured Freya that he came from the same wet and usually chilly climate that she did. "But my parents thought Bristol was enough warmer than Skegness to count. Believe me, Bristol is warmer than this place." He shivered dramatically, and pulled his hood further down over his black, curly hair. Freya smiled at his self-deprecating introduction.

Val turned to the girl who stood in front of Nesh, a head shorter and dressed in shades of grey. A large white cartwheel symbol adorned her t-shirt. Her hair was short too, in a light brown pixie cut. She gave Freya a brief smile.

"Don't believe anything Val tells you about me," she said. "I actually do come from near here. But my dad's in London too these days, so I'll be going there during the breaks. I'm a biology major. I'm guessing you are too, since I've seen you in most of my classes. If you want to swap notes sometime, you're welcome."

"Way to bring the mood down, Jemima!" said Val. "We're on our way to have fun, not swot."

Jemima gave a small shrug. "There's no harm in friendly study, either," she said.

Freya got the impression that this was a continuing argument.

"Why don't you finish the introductions, and we can get on to the pub?" Jemima suggested.

"I'm only agreeing 'cos you're right this time," said Val.

"I can introduce myself," said a young man with tanned skin, who loomed taller than Nesh, but narrower and a little hunched, as though he wanted to be smaller. Freya caught herself admiring his dark eyes and elegant cheekbones as he talked. They reminded her a little of Karim or Aisha.

"My name is Manuel. I am also used to warmer climes, with better reason than Nesh there."

"Why is that?" Freya asked, although she reasoned that his accent placed him from beyond Britain's borders.

He broke into a smile.

"I come from South America," he said. "Much, much warmer than this grey place. And the boat trip here was terrifying. But the maths department here is good, so I will put up with the rain for a while, and try to forget that I have to go back by sea too."

"Are you sure?" Freya couldn't help but ask. "You haven't been here for winter yet, have you?"

Manuel shuddered. "No doubt I will suffer for my art," he said dramatically. "Although we have rain at home too."

"I keep telling you," said the short, blond, bearded man beside Manuel, "that mathematics is not an art, it is a science. Art is what I do." He tossed his head a little, dislodging a rogue strand of golden hair that had dared to fall over his eyes. A stray ray of sun glinted off it, making Freya feel quite dull in contrast to him, with her dark-blond-shading-to-brown hair completely failing to catch the light.

"Ben is in law," explained Val. "He claims that arranging words is the only true art."

The dark-haired, Chinese-featured girl who had yet to be introduced spoke up. "He'll learn. Probably."

"There *is* nothing to learn," Ben interrupted. "Using words to win an argument is the truest art form there can be."

The girl looked put out, her lips thinning. She continued to introduce herself without engaging Ben again.

"I'm Lin. I'm doing arts too, but history. Nice to meet you, Freya." She gave Freya a friendly smile. "Shall we go? We'll be lucky to find a seat in the beer garden at this rate."

She and Val led the way, and Freya followed, bemused.

Apparently, she had been adopted. She just hoped that that was a good thing.

CHAPTER FOUR

A NIGHT ON THE TOWN

Back in the same pub she'd vacated earlier, Freya cautiously took a seat on the end of a worn wooden picnic table. The rest of the group piled around it without ceremony.

"You're up first, Val," said Ben.

Val stood up, although she had only just sat down. "What's everyone having?" she asked. The group responded with a chorus of requests. Freya shrank into herself. How could she accept being part of a round of drinks when she couldn't afford to buy one herself?

Val's eyes were on Freya, expectant. "What'll it be then?" she said.

"I'm not thirsty."

"You can't come to the pub and not drink. Come on, what do you want?"

"Just a soda and lime," Freya replied, once again going for the cheapest drink.

"Are you sure?"

"Yeah," she muttered. "It's not pay week this week. And I had to buy a new phone."

"Hey cool. What sort did you get?" asked Val.

Freya shrugged. "Hopefully one that works. Unlike my old one, which my mum gave me after she had worn it out."

"Better than nowt," said Jemima.

"Don't go using Yorkshire on us," said Ben. "You know we don't understand it."

"You just did," said Jemima.

Ben shook his head disapprovingly, though Freya thought he could be teasing. He was sitting as close to Jemima as the pub seats allowed. Manuel sat on Jemima's other side, and Freya had found a space opposite them on the end of the picnic-table seat. She rather thought Jemima was uncomfortable with her spot; the other girl twisted and turned in her seat as though trying to find a comfortable position. Manuel shifted a little sideways, and she gave him a grateful glance.

"Anyway," Val interrupted. "You're welcome to your soda. But if you want something stronger, you can always buy next time."

"I'll stick with soda today. But I'll try to buy next time anyway," said Freya, anxious not to be standoffish. She sat back on the wooden seat, its worn edges digging into her thighs. Loud chatter filled the garden bar, punctuated by frequent laughter. The smell of beer and wine, both fresh and old, overlaid everything. She wondered if this was really a good place for her to hang out, given her dad's Dionysian origins.

I should be alright if I stay away from wine. Not that I could afford it, anyway.

Freya resigned herself to drinking soda for the foreseeable future.

Her companions chatted amiably to each other. At first the conversation was centred around the usual uni things: assignments, labs, complaints about lecturers or tutorials. The range of subjects taken by her companions surprised Freya.

"How do you all know each other if you don't have classes together?" she asked.

"We're all in the same hall," Ben explained.

"Oh, of course," said Freya, feeling silly.

"Did you go private?" asked Val.

"Yeah. It's much cheaper. And I have a cat."

There were understanding nods.

"Yeah, I miss my cat," Jemima said. "But she stays with my mum."

"I think I would starve if I went private," said Manuel, "But I may starve anyway on the food I am given here."

"You'll have to learn to cook next year," said Jemima.

"Plenty of time between now and then," Ben joined in confidently. "Besides, cooking is a low-wage skill."

Freya was silent, but she struggled to imagine a world in which someone her age couldn't cook. Ben's pronouncement seemed very classist. Once again, her unusual upbringing was making her stand out. Then again, perhaps Ben was the one who stood out.

"I like cooking," said Jemima. "Besides, halls food doesn't agree with me. I'll be glad to be out on my own. It's more adult, too, right?"

"I've got the rest of my life to be an adult," said Ben. "Why start before I have to?"

Val's return with the drinks interrupted the general laughter.

"Give us a hand, you lot," she demanded. "Or I'll drink it all myself."

There was a general rush to relieve Val of glasses, and she made a second trip to retrieve the remaining drinks.

Freya sipped her soda, enjoying the autumn sun on her back. It had been a hot summer, at least two weeks of heat wave, and the warmth had lasted into autumn, giving a golden glow to her first weeks at uni. However, before she was halfway through her drink, a cloud covered the sun. She shivered in the sudden coolness and looked up at the sky.

"Is there a storm forecast?" she asked.

The group looked at each other.

"Can't say as it's something I watch out for," said Ben.

Nesh shook his head. "You're the one with a new phone. Why don't you check?"

Freya ducked her head, embarrassed to be reminded. But she did pull out her phone and check the forecast. It was something to do with her hands, to cover her feelings.

"Oh, hey. There's a big one coming," she announced with some surprise. It had been good weather for so long she'd begun to wonder if perhaps her new university town was blessed with perennially fine weather. "It's even named."

The group rearranged itself to centre around Freya and her phone. She shivered a little, not liking the crowd, however friendly they were being.

"There's warnings and all," said Jemima. "Perhaps we should skip dancing this once."

"Oh no," said Val, "I was looking forward to going out. We're going to be inside, anyway. Why don't we just carry on?"

Ben nodded. "Yeah, a big thunderstorm will add excitement."

"Too much excitement if you ask me," said Lin.

Before the argument about dancing had finished, large drops of rain began to fall.

"Forget dancing," said Nesh. "I'm all for a night in."

"Party pooper," said Val.

"I'm not stupid enough to stand around in the rain, is all," Nesh said. He drained his glass and stood up. "Anyone else heading home?"

"I'm going home too," said Lin. "I hate getting wet." She, too, put down her empty glass and pulled a jacket out of her bag. "Let's go."

"How bad can a storm be, away from the sea?" Freya asked aloud. She wasn't at all keen to be caught out in a storm, but then again, her friend Lio usually appeared with storms. Given the mild weather since she'd arrived in Sheffield, she hadn't seen him. She checked the time on her phone. She had a while before Mr Fluffbum expected to be fed. Then she shook herself, displacing some of the raindrops that had already fallen. "But there's no point in sitting here in the rain having our drinks diluted. Where were the rest of you headed?" She hoped she wasn't imposing herself on these new friends—but they'd asked her to join them, she reminded herself.

"Centre of town, for those as are coming," Val declared.

"I'm up for dancing," said Ben. "Coming, Jemima?"

Val stood too. "Come on, you lot," she said. "I'm not doing a rain dance. Let's go dance somewhere dry."

Everyone drained their glasses in a rush.

"Very good," said Manuel. "A beer garden is better in a warmer climate. Lead on to warmth and dryness."

Following the reduced group through the slick, rainy streets and into an old building with a stone façade, Freya found herself in a dingy underground room throbbing with bass. Coloured lights strobed at random intervals, overlaying background dimness. Sconces that looked like they were dribbling metallic droplets adorned the walls without adding much to the lighting. The ceiling was covered with a mural that made Freya blush when she noticed it. She glanced at the bare concrete floor instead and hastily removed her attention from it.

At least I have shoes on. Luckily. I'd hate to touch that floor with my bare feet.

Around her, the group threw themselves into the music in a variety of idiosyncratic moves. Ben tried to get Jemima to dance with him.

Freya wasn't sure if Jemima wanted to or not. It was hard to tell as Jemima spun one way, then another, Ben's hand holding one of hers high. Val danced enthusiastically on her own. With a shrug, and the thought that perhaps this would be easier if she had drunk cider rather than soda, Freya tried copying some of their moves.

With the bass reverberating through her, it was more natural to move than not. Before long, she was surprised to find that she was actually having fun. She essayed a few moves of her own, swinging first her arms, then her hips to the music. Feeling daring, she tried a spin, but wobbled as she concluded it. She hastily stepped sideways to steady herself and found Manuel beside her. He too took a sidestep, then added some fancy footwork. She grinned at his evident skill and tried a simplified version herself. Fitting her footwork to the beat was harder than she'd thought it would be, but she enjoyed the challenge.

Manuel leant over to shout near her ear.

"You are a natural."

Freya smiled at the unexpected compliment.

"Thanks."

She continued to improvise to the beat, warming up as she did so. Swaying her hips from side-to-side evoked whistles that she was uncomfortable with, but before long, the whistler's attention moved elsewhere, allowing Freya to enjoy herself again as she stepped and swayed. The music changed, and she adjusted to the new song. Manuel danced between her and Jemima. Ben glared at Manuel whenever he got close to Jemima, but she smiled and kept dancing. Freya thought she should say something—she wasn't sure what. Perhaps something about Manuel's dancing, or maybe she should comment on the unusual décor. Then again, she'd have to shout to be heard. Before she could come up with a suitable topic, she noticed a strange phenomenon. All the dancers were forming a rough circle. Each group or couple edged away from the centre of the dance floor, still involved in their own response to the music. Manuel, too, had moved closer to the wall. Freya shuffled with him rather than stick out.

In the middle of the circle, spinning wildly in the space created, was Val. Though she wore jeans, a belt with hanging objects created a skirt of sorts around her waist. The objects were hard to see in the flickering lights, but from her own position, dancing with Manuel on the side of the room away from the bar, Freya thought they were glowing. She squinted. Were those… ponies? Val raised her arms as she spun, as though to accept the energy of her surroundings. And Freya thought perhaps there was some sort of actual energy transfer. A roar went up from the dancers as Val's hands pointed to the ceiling, head flung back, still spinning. The lights went black. The music stopped. The roar of the crowd turned to shouts of confusion.

Screams pierced the darkness for unbearable minutes, till someone shouted, 'shut up!' in a voice loud enough to carry. There was a shocked silence, before an irritated voice exclaimed 'go on then, haven't you all got phones?'. Freya felt herself grin as she recognised the speaker as her new acquaintance, Val. Moments later, beams of light lit the room, faces highlighted in piercing moments of brightness as people looked around.

"Nothing wrong here," Val declared. "Someone get the music back on." Sounds flared from someone's phone. "Not that. Show some taste," Val directed.

"Get your own music then," replied someone, presumably the music's owner.

Freya fumbled for her own phone. "Let's get out of here," she said in the direction where she thought Manuel was. "If it's going to be dancing in the dark to someone's phone, I could do it just as well at home. Besides, I need to feed my cat."

There was no answer from Manuel. Freya's brow wrinkled. Had he gone already? She found the flashlight and swung it around. Plenty of people, but none she recognised. Her heart sank. Had she been abandoned so soon? What had she done wrong?

Chapter Five
What Lurks in the Night?

Freya caught sight of the staircase she'd descended to enter the nightclub, faintly lit with tiny red lights, and made her way towards it, trying to ignore the yawning pit of rejection inside. Pushing her way through the crowd, she brushed against arms that were suspiciously furry. Someone or something sniffed loudly. There was a prickle on her arm that might have been claws. She shrieked involuntarily and scrambled away through the heaving crush of bodies.

I'm sure there are no weres here, Freya reassured herself. But her mind couldn't help but slip to the tales her friend Aisha had told her when she'd announced her university placement.

"All those old mines, Freya. There'll be cave trolls for sure. Goblins maybe. Probably darker things. Be careful, won't you?"

But so far, she had seen only humans. Val's warnings about the lecturers were the darkest things she had yet to come across. Bolstering her courage and drawing her shredded ego around herself, she slipped through the overexposed crowd and up the stairs.

The bouncers were still standing at the door. One nodded at Freya.

"Alright then?" he asked casually. Freya didn't feel she could reply with the usual 'Alright' in reply.

"You know there's no power down there, right?" she said instead.

The bouncer turned to her, streetlights gleaming on his leather jacket. Whatever power outage had occurred evidently hadn't affected those lights.

"Yeah, it happens now and then. Should come on again in a few. It's drinks on the house if it goes off for more than twenty minutes though, so no-one minds too much once they're used to it." He waved a hand at the darkened stairwell. "Going back down?"

"Er, no thanks," Freya said.

The bouncer shrugged.

"Suit yourself." He turned away and continued his conversation with his partner. From what she heard, he was complaining about the weather.

"Looks like another visitation from the polar vortex," he grumbled.

"Yeah, blimmen' Arctic weather," replied the second bouncer. "The weather gods never give us a break."

Freya went on high alert at the mention of weather gods. *Are they supernaturals?* She looked from one to the other. Neither looked especially hairy. Probably not weres, then. Although both were reasonably built, neither had that over-muscled look she'd been taught to associate with Herculean demis. Nor did they possess the military stiffness and adherence to protocol she'd expect from any of the various descendants of war-gods, who were often found as security guards. *No, they're probably just mundane humans moaning about their self-inflicted weather disasters again. That's probably not fair, though. It was our predecessors who gifted us this weather. Demis, weres and humans alike.*

Goosebumps peppered Freya's skin as a gust of sleet-laden wind whistled down the street, and she decided not to worry about the bouncers' origins. After the crowded warmth of the dance floor, and the last few weeks of summerlike heat, the sleet was a shock. Freya scrabbled hastily in her bag for her coat. Even that wasn't enough warmth. She buttoned up the coat, wishing it were twice as thick, or that she'd brought her cloak along too, and crossed her arms. The stone front of the building gave her a little shelter as she looked around for anyone she knew. This was exactly the sort of storm that Lio would swoop in with on the coast, but there was no sign of him here.

A couple more refugees from the club emerged from the doorway. One of them blinked at the sleet, turned around, and went back down the stairs. The other was Manuel. He brightened when he saw Freya.

"Ah, you didn't abandon us," he said.

He sauntered a couple of steps away from the bouncers, and Freya followed.

"I couldn't find anyone down there in the dark," Freya explained. "I was getting a headache with all that screaming." *See, you shouldn't jump to conclusions,* she told herself.

Manuel laughed. "All in a night out in this city," he said. "The electricity is very unreliable. I expect it comes of not enough sun."

"We've had plenty of sun," Freya protested. "Maybe not by South American standards, but awesome for the North of England."

"And yet here we are in the cold and dark," Manuel said.

Hard to disagree with that. "Are the others coming, do you think?" she asked.

Manuel consulted his watch, tapping it so it glowed in the dark. "They should be out in a minute or so," he said. "Once they have had their free drinks."

Sounds like it's not their first time here. A suspicious thought struck her. *Was Val shorting out the lights with that energy draw? On purpose?*

She didn't have time to pursue the theory, as another group of nightclubbers emerged, chatting and giggling. The red stair lighting flickered and was replaced by the brighter blue it had been when Freya entered the club. Cobalt light gleamed on Val's bouncing curls as she stepped through the doorway.

"Hey Freya. What d'you think, cool place, isn't it?

Freya laughed uncertainly, not really agreeing, but not wanting to sound stuck up, either.

"I guess. Warmer than out here, anyway."

Chapter Six
Just a Piece of Clothing

As the sleet continued, the city streets were becoming slick with watery ice. The group huddled in the lee of the stone building, avoiding the icy rain that lashed the area as much as possible. Freya was glad of the others' presence. While she had appreciated Manuel's looks, she didn't want to be alone with him. Not until she knew him better, at any rate. And there was some shelter provided by the bodies around her.

"How come it's winter out here already?" complained Val. "We haven't had autumn yet."

"I do not expect anything better in this country," said Manuel. "It is too cold in summer. It stands to reason that there should be even worse weather to come." He pulled another piece of clothing out of his bag—Freya thought it was a t-shirt—and draped it over his head.

"It's not that bad," Val said, apparently happy to ignore the goosebumps decorating her arms.

"I have not been warm since I arrived," Manuel said, crossing his arms and hunching even more than usual. "Nesh had the correct idea in staying home."

"It's a polar vortex breakout," announced Jemima. The others stared at her blankly. "Oh, don't look at me like that," she said.

"We've had them before. You know, when the weakening polar jet stream lets Arctic blasts get down to us further south."

"Here we go again," muttered Val. "Never a break from the bloody weathergirl."

"My mathematics tutor has mentioned this as an excellent example of chaotic modelling," said Manuel, sticking up for Jemima, Freya thought.

"Spare us the modelling talk," Ben said good-humouredly. "But let's get out of the weather all the same."

"No need for bickering," said Val. "I know somewhere else we can go." She pulled out her own jacket at last, shrugging it on as the sleet lightened and became snow.

Freya stilled in shock. The back of Val's jacket was emblazoned with a large pair of crows: the sign of the Wodenites, the descendants of Odin. Was Val some sort of demi? Why hadn't Freya recognised the signs? She unstuck her suddenly dry tongue with an effort.

"What's that decoration on your jacket, Val?" she asked, in what she hoped was a casual tone.

Val's reply was unconcerned. "Oh, the ravens? Some club my dad was in when he was young. I nicked the jacket when I came here. Reckoned I'd need it more than he did, him being down South and all. I like the look, don't you?"

Freya reminded herself that despite her Mum's oft-repeated fears, she herself had had no real trouble with Wodenites.

"It's a bit grim for me," she said. "But at least it's not a murder of crows."

Val's laughter rang out quickly. Too quickly? Most people wouldn't get that joke—that a group of crows was called a murder—so fast.

"Nah, only a conspiracy. I prefer ravens to crows, anyway. I'll stick with these ones being the ravens of thought and memory. They're more useful day-to-day," she said.

"Especially in exams, I'm guessing," said Ben. "Isn't that cheating, though? Besides, what's wrong with crows?"

Val paused to brush snowflakes from her shoulders and shook her head. "You're getting over-excited. It's just a piece of clothing. And one that's not quite warm enough for snow, at that. Anyway, as I said, I've got an idea. Let's get going." She ceased the increasingly futile task of brushing off snow and set off down the sloping street.

Freya hesitated before following. What if Val really was a Wodenite? And she really did need to feed Mr Fluffbum. But Val had denied the jacket being significant, and it wasn't late yet. Mr Fluffbum should be fine for a bit longer.

Val confidently led the way down the gently sloping street.

"Do you know where you're going, then?" Freya asked, doubt colouring her tone.

Val half-turned to look over her shoulder, an incredulous expression on her face. "Course I do," she said. "I've had weeks to get to know this place. What have *you* been doing with your evenings?"

"Studying, of course. That's what I'm paying for." *Do I sound like a nerdy swot? Probably, but it's true, I* am *paying for that.*

The ever-increasing snow muffled their voices. It was difficult to recognise the city streets with a thick coating of white, though the reflected light on snow made it easier to see.

"Does it normally snow like this inland?" Freya asked.

A step or two away from her, Manuel answered. "I hope not. Else I am going home sooner than I planned."

Jemima laughed, though there was a bitter note underpinning the sound. "Were you not listening to me earlier? This is the new normal, where there is no normal."

Freya wondered privately if there was some angry demigod involved somehow, but she didn't want to be like her mother, thinking that every storm was deity-driven. Jemima's explanation seemed perfectly sound, and in line with the bouncers' discussion, too.

"Should we be heading home?" she wondered aloud. "If the power goes out in the next place, I mean," she added, as Val turned a disbelieving eye on her. She hoped Mr Fluffbum wasn't too cold. Her student flat wasn't exactly luxurious, and didn't boast a heat pump or hydrogen boiler.

"You won't want to go home from the next place," Val assured her. "It's even better than the last one."

Given that the last place had lost power, and was probably inhabited by weres or worse, Freya wasn't sure how to take that. But she kept following Val, unsure of how to leave the group gracefully—and unsure of where she was. She hadn't spent much time on this side of the city.

A few minutes later, they crossed the snow-covered street. The wind howled through the open space, biting through Freya's outer garments.

I should never have left my cloak behind, she thought. *I'll have to sew a second one to get through winter here.* She had left her unfashionable—and worn out—cloak at her flat, thinking to make a fresh start on her wardrobe as well as her education.

Distracted by wind and cold, she didn't notice the double ridges in the road until she stepped on one and slipped sideways, revealing cold steel rails. She recovered her balance without accumulating too much extra snow, then realised the significance of the rails.

"Oh, we're still on the tram routes," she exclaimed in relief. Any of the tramlines would lead her to the central station and out again to her flat. She wasn't lost after all.

"Well, yeah, of course we are," said Val. "How else would we avoid the barghests?"

Freya stopped where she was, forgetful of traffic possibilities.

"You mean barghests are real?" she asked. *I remember hobs under the bed, but they were helpful. Barghests—big black slavering mythical dogs that portend death—are another thing entirely.*

"You won't find out if you stick around steel," Val replied cryptically.

Freya pushed a bit more snow off the tram track, eyeing it thoughtfully.

"So barghests are sensitive to iron?" she asked. "How much iron does it take? Or is it steel specifically?"

Val turned to face Freya, hands thrust deep in her pockets. She withdrew one hand to display several straight, shiny objects. Nails.

"Not too much," Val said carelessly. "And there's iron in steel, so either will work".

Somehow, Mum never mentioned that when she taught us mythology. I suppose if you want to keep your kids in line, telling them that a pocketful of nails or a bit of cutlery in your vest will let them ignore your wishes isn't a great idea. Or maybe she didn't know. It's not like there were barghests down south. Giant black cats, sure. Not so many rogue black dogs.

"Got any spare?" Freya asked. If there really were mythical, slavering dogs around, she wouldn't mind a bit of protection from them.

"Not enough to share," Val replied. "There's some sort of minimum weight requirement. You should be fine sticking with me, though. And it's not like there's a shortage of iron here in steel city."

Freya nodded, acknowledging the city's history of steel-making, but found herself calculating how soon she could get to an open hardware shop. She hadn't considered anything beyond weres and the like when she'd encountered that hairy body in the nightclub. But there wouldn't be anything open till morning.

"If there's so much iron around, that would keep barghests away anyway, wouldn't it?" she said.

"You'd think so, but I've seen several since I arrived," Val said. "That's why I have these. I wouldn't spoil the lines of this jacket for nothing."

Unexpectedly, Ben chimed in. "I heard it's because so much steel got removed in the wars, back when. There used to be more steel, less barghests."

Val shrugged. "No point in blaming ancient history for today's problems," she said.

Jemima, who hadn't paused when Val did, called back.

"Hurry up, you two. I want to be inside, dancing. Not outside doing a jig to keep warm."

Val and Freya hastened to catch up with the group.

"We're just about there," Val said, pushing to the front. "Right across the alley, and down to the river."

"Away from the trams, you mean?" said Freya.

"Yeah, but like I said, you're fine with me," Val said. She increased her pace, leaving Freya behind.

Before, you said we were fine if we stuck to the tramlines, Freya thought. *Which is it?*

She looked back at the tramlines with longing, but the desire to be part of the group was strong, too.

CHAPTER SEVEN
THE SAFETY OF STEEL

Resolutely turning away from the safety of steel, Freya hastened to catch up. If there were dangerous beasts further from the tramlines, Freya didn't want to encounter them alone.

"Where are we going?" she asked, trying not to slip on the steeply sloping street.

"To the river," said Val. "Or near it, anyway. There's a club down on the waterfront. Climbing walls, music, the works. We've been going there since we arrived. Now's the perfect opportunity to go again."

"Climbing walls?" Ben said. "Now you're talking. The usual place?"

"Of course," Val said.

Manuel was interested, too. "I wish I had known in advance," he said. "I would have worn something more suitable."

Val looked at Manuel's jeans and t-shirt consideringly. "What you're wearing isn't ideal," she said, "but you'll do."

"I wanted dancing," Jemima complained. "Climbing's fine, but dancing's better."

"Chill, girl, you can dance all you want. Hitch yourself up to a rope and you can do it midair," Val said.

Freya rolled her eyes, then wished she hadn't as she stepped on a particularly slick piece of pavement. She recovered herself, then joined the conversation.

"I'm not convinced about dancing midair," she said. "Are you sure about this place?"

"Climbing is practically compulsory in this city," Val said firmly. "And like I said, there's music too. No-one need miss out. I think it's a brilliant opportunity."

When no-one contradicted her, Val nodded firmly, and resumed her brisk stride.

Despite Freya's nervous glances into the shadowy side streets, there was no sign of any black dogs, supernatural or otherwise, as they traversed the dark streets.

Just as well, Freya thought. *Barghests are supposed to be an omen of death. Not something I want to encounter before some climbing excursion, no matter how many nails Val's got in her pockets.*

The snow amassed abundantly along the riverside as they walked. The water itself still flowed strongly, though the occasional patches of reeds and rushes had collected impressive piles of snow. Factories and apartments on the other side of the river provided a tall, blank face pocked with occasional squares of light. Even with the reduction of available energy that school history classes had taught her about, there was so many more people, and so many more lights than Freya was used to, in the smaller towns of the coast..

Freya was distracted from her new fixation on barghests by a fresh worry. She had so far avoided making herself known to the local river goddesses. Should she have done so earlier? She hadn't wanted to attract attention to herself, of course. But what if the deity was offended by her neglect? Glancing from her striding companions and back to the river, she heard a small plop, and saw streetlights reflecting off rings of water expanding from a point near the steep riverbank. A few seconds later, a broad brown head popped up in the centre of the river. Freya smiled at it. If the presence of otters was any indication—and she thought it probably was—she shouldn't fear this river's deity, despite the punishments the river had endured through centuries of industrialisation.

"Hello, Lady River," she murmured. Better not to make a formal announcement while in company. A river visit needed time, space, and privacy. Not to mention singing and a good thyrsus. Besides, she was trying to fit in here.

"What was that, Freya?" said Jemima, pausing a few paces ahead.

"Oh, n-nothing," Freya fumbled over her words. "I thought I saw an otter."

"Really? That's good spotting in the dark. I hear there are quite a few these days, even in the city. The place is thriving!" Jemima's voice was full of enthusiasm. She turned back to stand beside Freya and peered into the dark space that was the river. Faint reflections of light rippled on its surface from the windows of buildings on the far side. "What a shame. I must have missed it," she said. "I'll have to come back tomorrow morning, when I can actually see."

"You like otters, then?" Freya asked.

"Who doesn't?" Jemima said.

Freya half-smiled in the dark. "My sister isn't—wasn't—so keen on them," she said. "But she had extenuating circumstances."

"Well, I think they're awesome," Jemima asserted, clearly not interested in Freya's sister.

Freya sighed. She could have done with someone to talk to about her missing sister, now Aisha wasn't just down the road for conversation or distraction. While Freya had looked forward to striking out on her own, she hadn't realised how much she'd come to rely on having a friend.

A menacing growl disrupted her melancholy thoughts.

"Did you hear something?" Jemima asked.

"I wish I could say no," muttered Freya. Her eyes followed the river's path downstream. There was nothing to be seen but black walls and buildings that way. Upstream though... Was that a four-legged shape fading into the shadows of the bridge that crossed the river? She hesitated, not sure if she should run or pretend to have seen nothing. As she froze in place, the growl repeated. Glowing eyes appeared in the blackness under the bridge, much higher than Freya would have expected for a dog. It sure wasn't a troll, though. Not running towards them on four legs, ears flapping, streetlights glinting off bared teeth.

"Run!" Freya blurted. Jemima took off like a champion sprinter. But Freya hesitated, remembering how fast canines went on four legs—at least were-foxes did. She could only assume barghests had a similar turn of speed. In that case, there was no chance of getting away on foot. She'd have to summon help.

The stone streets were bare of weeds and grasses. Only a thin strip of park up ahead offered any vegetation for a thyrsus, Freya's version of a wand. She hastened towards it. As soon as her feet hit the snow-covered grass, she grabbed handfuls of whatever was in reach of her grasping hands; autumn-high grasses and hemlock straggling unmown near the fence that separated the river from the unwary. She used the toes of her trainers to draw a circle around herself in the snow and began the song her sister had taught her long ago. Peering into the snow-flecked darkness, she could see the barghest clearly now, a dark hound against white snow, terribly near. It growled no longer, but its eyes were fixed on her as it paced slowly forward.

Don't eat me, she thought. *Don't be a self-fulfilling death omen.* It was time to ask for help. *But is the river here the Don or the Sheaf? Better not risk the wrong name.* She knew that at least two rivers flowed through Sheffield, and she wasn't quite clear on the geography of the city yet.

"Come to me, Lady River!" Her shouted words were muffled by the falling snow, but she was sure she heard an increase in the quiet trickling of the nearby river. Darkness lapped at her feet as the water rose, melting the snow as it came.

"Are you all right, Freya?" Jemima's voice came from very close by. "I heard you shout. Did that thing get you?"

Freya blinked, then looked around wildly.

Where did the barghest go?

She couldn't see its glowing eyes anymore. No growls or glints of teeth. She put a hand out to steady herself and felt the cold iron of the fence under her hand.

Iron. Safety. Or did the river help too? As she peered into the shadows, hoping to reassure herself that the threat had passed, Jemima repeated her question.

"Are you OK?"

As icy water pooled around her feet, having melted away her protective circle, Freya discreetly dropped her thyrsus.

"I'm fine," she said. "It's gone, whatever it was." Under her breath, she murmured, "Thank you, Lady River." After all, she couldn't be sure if it was the presence of the iron railing, or the running water (that was even now ruining her best pair of shoes), that had saved her from the attentions of the barghest. She just hoped she hadn't revealed anything supernatural to the mundane Jemima.

"Hurry up, Jemima. Come on, Freya, we're just about there. I want to warm up, don't you?" Val's voice floated back to them through the swiftly falling snowflakes, and Freya left her concerns behind as she hastened to narrow the gap between herself and the iron-bearing Val. She barely noticed that Jemima was hurrying after her just as quickly. How had Val got so far ahead in the short time Freya had been attempting to fend off the barghest?

Chapter Eight
A Different Sort of Club

Val was waiting for them at the entrance to the promised club. The brick building towered darkly over the river, old chimneys rising at intervals—no longer allowed to be used, even if they were functional. It must be one of the many repurposed factories that dotted the city. Val and Ben were half lit by a beam of strong yellow light that streamed through the glass window of a single door. Freya gladly joined Val under a small overhang which sheltered them from the weather, though it was still bitterly cold.

Whatever this place is like, it will be good to get inside.

When the whole group had assembled, Val flung open the door, allowing light and music to tumble forth.

"Come on in, you lot," she said, leading the way.

Freya blinked in astonishment. She'd been expecting another nightclub, not least because of the throbbing bass beat that emanated through the door. But the interior of the building was lined with artificial rock walls in a myriad hues. Climbers dotted the walls—Freya saw one climber who surely was half spider, clinging to the underside of an overhang. Ropes connected the climbers to others standing around on a piles of vinyl-covered mats. The scent of chalk and sweat was so strong Freya could taste it.

"You really want us to go climbing?" she asked Val in disbelief.

But Val was nodding, a grin plastered on her face.

"Absolutely! You can't live here in Steel City and not climb. And without heading into the Peaks, this is the only way to climb. So here we are. Your new second home. Come in and stop letting the draught in."

Freya started forward when the rest of the group did, but baulked when she realised that everyone was stopping again to pay an entry fee.

"Can I just watch?" she asked the youth sitting at the reception desk.

"No spectators allowed on the floor," he said, clearly following a scripted response. "But belaying-only gets you a reduced entry fee."

Freya put a hand on the ten-pound note in her pocket. If she spent it, she would be living on foraged greens *without* instant noodles. Still, hopefully she'd find some nut trees this week; greens alone weren't exactly filling, no matter how healthy. If she had to, she could make acorn flour, but it took such a long time to process the acorns... and if there were dangerous supernaturals in the area, should she be out foraging alone? She didn't want to ask for charity handouts.

She thought about the barghest and its possible meaning. Perhaps it was just as well for her not to attempt climbing tonight. She glanced again at the overhang, where a lithe figure was clinging on with one hand and a hooked foot while reaching for a tiny dot on the far edge of the ceiling.

No way do I want to hang off that thing. You'd have to be descended from a monkey god to manage it, surely.

But there were other walls that sloped away from the floor, the artificial handholds reassuringly large.

That looks do-able. Not much like dancing, but achievable.

She looked around. Despite the pumping music, few people were dancing, either on ropes or off them. But as she looked, one song faded to a close, and another began. The new song was obviously more popular, as heads bobbed and feet shuffled on the mats.

Manuel, who had already paid and gone past the reception desk, looked back, and must have noted her hesitation.

"Don't you want to try climbing?" he asked.

Freya made a face. She was still recovering from her run-in with the barghest, and she had just realised that her shoes were leaking frigid water onto the surrounding floor. But that wasn't the problem. She squelched uneasily.

"I would like to, I guess," she said. "It's just a money issue." She glanced away, embarrassed to admit to poverty despite her long acquaintance with it.

To Freya's surprise, Manuel turned to Val, who was hovering just beyond the reception desk.

"Got any change?" he asked her.

"I can spare a quid or two," she said. "Can't have Freya's first climbing experience be a damp squib."

She advanced on the payment machine and, after muttering something to the desk jockey, waved her phone at it.

Manuel did the same, and a muted beep sounded from the device.

"You can go through now," Val said authoritatively. "Jack here will get us set up with gear."

The man sitting at the desk, presumably Jack, rose rather reluctantly to his feet with a noise of assent. "This way," he said. "You're a bit late, but there's still plenty of shoes and harnesses to go round. I'll give you all an induction."

Val snorted at the mention of an induction, but made no other protest.

"How are things going?" she asked him instead. "Many punters? How's the gear holding up?"

"Pretty good," Jack said laconically. "We had to change out a couple of ropes yesterday," he added. addressing Val with an odd formality. He strode off, Val keeping pace with him, Manuel, Jemima, Ben, and Freya trailing behind. He led the way into a small room which smelled overwhelmingly of feet and old sweat. Rows of pigeonholes containing rubbery-looking climbing shoes lined one wall, and an array of climbing harnesses were hung like dark webs on the other three walls, size labels above each wooden peg. A couple of wooden benches stood under the harnesses.

"Great," Val replied. "How about you set up Freya first. She might need a bit of time bouldering before going up." She turned to face Freya. "Unless you've climbed before?"

Freya shook her head. It was hard to imagine anyone in her family spending food money on something as frivolous as indoor rock climbing. Why climb something when you don't have to, anyway? Self-doubt flooded her even as Jack proffered a tiny-looking pair of shoes. What was she doing in a climbing gym, of all places? Was the possibility of friendship and acceptance worth it? And what if the barghest was a sign? Usually, she didn't put much faith in folkloric signs, since she knew they tended to be borne of misunderstood deities, shifters, or demigods, but the barghest had been unsettling in its own right. And what if she'd angered the river deity, calling for aid before having a proper introduction? Uneasiness gnawed at her stomach.

Perhaps mistaking the reason for her hesitation, Jack started unlacing the shoes.

"These look to be your size," he said. "And they are disinfected after every use, so you don't have to worry about catching anything disgusting. You'll need to take your socks and regular shoes off, though. Too risky wearing socks, your feet can slip right out of them. And no regular shoes allowed on the climbing floor. Especially not wet shoes," he added, glancing at her soaked trainers. "Here you go." He motioned to one of the benches, thrusting the shoes at her, and Freya perforce sat down. It seemed she would be learning a new skill tonight. Hopefully that wouldn't also lead her into trouble.

Come on, Freya, she told herself. You've survived worse by the sea.

It didn't help much, but Val's expectant look pushed her into donning first the shoes—just as tight and uncomfortable as they had looked—and then a harness, which made her feel like a trussed-up... something.

I wonder if river deities feel this constrained when weird things are built on them? That would explain a lot of grumpiness.

Freya stood up, and wincing as the tight shoes constrained her toes, followed the rest of her new friends into the barnlike climbing space.

Jack insisted on showing everyone how things were done, to Val's obvious boredom. But Freya listened closely, worried that the barghest earlier might have been an omen after all. When Jack was done, her fears were mostly quashed. There did seem to be a lot of safety features involved in climbing like this.

"I'll belay you, Jemima," Ben said, giving the pixie-like girl an eyebrow wiggle.

But at the same moment, Jemima took a step closer to Manuel.

"You can belay me this time, Manuel," she said.

Freya might not be clear on the politics of belaying, but there was no mistaking the fury on Ben's face.

"I asked first," he said belligerently, stepping between Manuel and Jemima, fists clenched. Although he was shorter than Manuel by several inches, the threat that rolled off him was intimidating. Freya could see the muscles in his jaw clenching. She took a wary step back. But before anything more could happen, Val made her presence felt.

"Don't start a fight, children," she said in a school-teacherish voice. "Not in here." She turned to Jemima. "*I'll* belay you after my climb.

You can do the same for me. Manuel, you look after Freya. And Ben, go cool off."

Ben shared his glower with Val for a tense few moments, then stalked off. Freya looked after him in concern.

"Don't worry about him," Val said. "He won't make trouble. Give bouldering a go first, then you can try an easy climb. You'll love it!!"

Halfway up an artificial rock face, holding in a sneeze induced by the copious amounts of chalk in the air, Freya wondered again what she had got herself into. One toe supported all her weight, while a tight pincer grip with forefingers and thumbs was all that kept her from plummeting into empty space.

If I bring my knee up above my waist—somehow—and move my foot to the right, can I reach the foothold? Or is it just inviting certain death? Sure, she was attached to a rope, and Manuel was holding on to the end of it, ready to halt any fall before she hit the ground. She still didn't feel exactly safe. The first part of the roped climb had been fun, she had to admit. There was a certain satisfaction in finding hand and foot-holds, rising above Manuel and Jemima's heads surprisingly fast. Ben was bouldering on another wall, and Val was higher than Freya, climbing a more difficult route, apparently. Jack had explained the route classification, but Freya had lost track at some point. She thought she was looking for the yellow holds. Or was it the orange ones?

"You're sure you do this for fun?" she called down. Her hands were sweating. She probably needed to apply more chalk from the bag attached to her waist, but she daren't let go of either hand-hold long enough to do so.

"Certainly, we do," Manuel called back. "You have reached the crux of the climb. The most difficult point. If you master this climb, then you will have beaten my first-climb score. I will owe Val a drink if you do not. Left a bit more with your foot, now."

Freya made a face. Who needed this sort of fun?

Still, I may as well try his suggestion. My hands are beginning to lose their grip.

She'd been clinging to this spot for some time now. Banging her knee painfully against the wall as she did so, Freya brought her free foot 'left a bit', which meant crushing her stomach uncomfortably.

Lucky it's a while since I ate.

But after a moment's panicked feeling about with her foot, she found the tiny foot-hold—*What if I had bigger feet, how does that work?*—and pushed upwards. Her foot slipped, and she thumped onto the wall, the impact pushing the air from her lungs with a whoosh. For a moment she hung from two finger holds, the chalky, sweat-smelling wood hard against her face. Her breathing accelerated. Though she was technically safe (wasn't she?) with the belay rope there specifically to prevent a catastrophic fall, the feeling of her fingers slipping was almost as terrifying as the barghest had been earlier. She scrabbled for another foot-hold and found it. Panic gave her strength as she pushed up from the hold.

She realised as her body pulled her hands upwards that if she didn't release her grip, she'd soon be crouched in a seriously awkward position, if not actively falling. She let go with her left hand—*remember, maintain three points of contact at all times, Jack said*—grasped the next hand-hold (a tiny affair that was mostly made of the screw that held it to the wall, and was red, not yellow), pushed upward with her toe, and slapped her right hand on the shelf that marked the end of the climbing wall. With a shock of triumph, Freya saw she had made it to the top. The blackness of night was only an arm's length away on the other side of a skylight. She shivered, her body reacting oddly to the mix of delight and terror.

Voices reached her from below.

"Way to go, Freya."

"Great climb."

"Are you ready to come down now?" That last was Manuel, belaying her—or holding the rope that kept her safe, as she would usually have said.

Down sounded good, however satisfying the success of her climb. She wouldn't have said she was afraid of heights, but it certainly didn't feel safe up here. She looked around in preparation for her descent. Val had already reached the top of her own climb, and was, as she'd suggested earlier, dancing to the background music as she let herself down on her own rope, bouncing off the wall with her feet, and generally making extravagant moves. Freya felt her lips twitch into a smile as she watched.

No way am I going to try that.

Freya saw Val reach the ground, unclip herself and help Jemima set up to start her own climb. Ben sauntered over, still radiating anger, and laid a hand possessively on Jemima's rope. For a moment, Freya thought the rope grew dark, like the feathers on a crow's back. But surely she was imagining things; it must be just the way the shadows fell. Val practically snarled at him to leave off, and Ben backed away, out of Freya's sight-line.

Focus on your own problems, Freya.

It wasn't so easy to let go of her hand-holds, lean away from the wall and hold the rope, which was tied firmly to her harness. It had looked straightforward when she'd been shown how the system worked on the ground, but up here, just letting go felt like an act of recklessness.

The only way to go is down, she told herself, and leant back. The world spun, dizzying, till she realised that she was still safely attached to a rope, feet against the wall, less uncomfortable now that her weight was off them. Though the harness dug into her in strange places.

"You can come down slowly," Manuel called. "This is your chance to dance."

Dance? Not likely.

But as Freya stepped her feet carefully down the wall, she found herself tapping it in time with the music. Maybe Val had a point after all. This wasn't dancing, exactly, but there was a curious sense of euphoria in being not weightless, but suspended, somehow detached from responsibility. She relaxed into the descent, and her eye was caught by the skylight again.

Funny, she thought. *It should be covered with snow, like everything else out there.* But it wasn't. A dark rectangle in the ceiling, only the edges showed evidence of snow. Even that wasn't a smooth white. Black lines in groups of three marred the frosty rim.

A bit like... yes, like the marks bird claws make.

Still. She wasn't anywhere near the window now, and anyway, surely a snow-free window wasn't going to hurt anyone, however odd it was on a snowy night. Unless... what sort of bird flies around at night in a storm? Surely nothing mundane. A niggle of worry invaded her feeling of euphoria, but she pushed it aside. Midair was not the time to worry about weirdly clear windows.

She looked down again, and was startled at how close she now was to the ground. Grinning faces looked up at her, and as she struggled to get her feet lower than her harness-encased rear, friendly hands pushed her shoulders up, so she didn't hit the mat-covered floor in quite the ungainly fashion she'd expected.

"Great first climb, Freya," Val said. "You're a natural."

Freya felt a grin spread across her own face as she received more congratulations. That hadn't been so bad.

Out of the corner of her eye, Freya saw something black flutter near the ceiling. Before she had a chance to look at it, a shout interrupted the warm glow she was feeling.

"Hold tight!"

She clutched frantically at her rope before realising that the shout wasn't directed at her.

You're on the ground, Freya, why would you need a rope now?

Looking wildly around, Freya saw Jemima clinging halfway up a wall. No problem there, surely. But as her eye picked out more details, she realised that the rope which should be attached to Jemima's harness was dangling below her, a frayed end in Val's hands.

"Hold on, there," called Jack. "I'm coming up with a new rope. Everyone, get those mats underneath her! Clear the walls!"

"I thought you said the old ones were swapped out?" Val demanded, even as she dropped the useless rope in favour of pulling the nearest mat underneath Jemima. Around her, climbers descended as fast as they could, and those not belaying pulled more mats to the potential fall zone.

Jack was strapping on a harness of his own. His feet were already jammed into tight climbing shoes—a different brand to the rentals, Freya noticed in an abstracted way.

Jack finished tightening his harness straps with quick, savage yanks, and dusted his fingers with chalk before replying to Val.

"All the ropes were in perfect condition this morning. It should have been *fine*."

He threaded another rope into his harness and strode to the wall where Jemima clung.

"Stay where you are. I'm on my way up with a rope," he called.

He turned to Val. "Belay me?"

"Of course." Val didn't seem surprised to be asked, and she roped herself up with what seemed surprising efficiency, to Freya's eyes.

"Why isn't someone else belaying Jack?" she muttered to Val, once Jack was well on his way, moving swiftly up a climb parallel to the one Jemima had attempted.

Val almost snarled her answer, startling Freya with her ferocity. "Joe should be doing it. But Joe *always* skips his turn. Too busy having fun on the upper walls." Her eyes returned to follow Jack's surprisingly quick passage up the climb, which Freya thought looked like a much harder one than hers had been. She assumed Joe was the climber she had seen on the overhang when they came in. He was still up there, swinging from hold to hold, apparently oblivious to the drama lower down the wall.

Unexpectedly, a flash of lightning lit up the window for a moment, highlighting jagged edges of glass and broad, dark wings as a bird flapped away through it. Somehow, the skylight had broken. How had no-one noticed a bird that size inside the gym? Thunder rumbled so close it shook the climbing gym.

"Alright, what idiot called on Thor?" Val demanded, as though that was a perfectly reasonable question, yanking the rope through her belay device to keep it taut as Jack took a couple more quick holds. "Thunder snow doesn't just happen."

"You'd be calling on your god too, if you were the one up there," Manuel said.

"I'm sure she's not affiliated with Thor. She's a biology major," said Val.

"And can biology majors not descend from a weather god?" Freya didn't realise she'd spoken until the words were out of her mouth. She shut it hastily, hoping no-one thought through the implications of her words. But then, did she need to worry? Val seemed to consider supernatural things as nothing out of the ordinary.

"Not good ones. They're all in physics or meteorology. And Jemima is a good one."

"You know I can hear you, right?" Jemima called down from her precarious perch. Freya could hear the strain in her voice. "And I'll have you know that I'm taking a paper in meteorology as part of my degree. Thunder snow is happening more frequently now because we're getting more warm air masses, whether or not some mythical being is involved. Which it won't be, because '*mythical*'."

Freya was impressed. She didn't think she'd be able to argue climate theory *or* theology while clinging for her life to a couple of broken climbing holds, let alone put that level of sarcasm into air quotes. Jemima was also fulfilling Freya's assumption that she was thoroughly mundane.

"Also, I 'd like to finish that paper, so if Jack could hurry up with a rope to get me down..." Jemima sounded as though her teeth were gritted, and even from here, Freya could see how desperately her fingers were clenched on the holds.

Only a few seconds later, Jack arrived beside Jemima. Freya saw his lips moving but couldn't hear what he said. He attached some piece of equipment to her harness, hooking her to a small metal anchor point that Freya hadn't previously noticed. Some of the obvious tension left Jemima once that was done. Jack continued past her, towards the ceiling where the belay ropes were looped through pulleys. His progress slowed as the difficulty of the climb increased.

"Why is she just hanging there?" Val wondered aloud. "She should be able to help herself a bit, at least."

Manuel, freed from belaying Freya, pointed wordlessly at the holds below Jemima or rather, at the loosely swinging remains of holds. One of her toes was poised on the tiny top of a foot-hold that hung upside down. The other was simply pressed against the wall.

No wonder she's holding on so tight.

"How in Woden's name did that happen?" Val swore. "Although at least that's within the bounds of possibility. That rope!" She broke off and shook her head.

Freya glanced at her in surprise, not having expected Val to swear by a god even if her dad *was* a demi. Especially since she'd just objected to Jemima calling on Thor. Val didn't notice, her attention fixed above.

Right, that's what you should be focused on too, Freya told herself. *Demigod or no, you're supposed to focus if a friend is in trouble.*

Nevertheless, Freya's attention wandered again while Jack climbed higher. As she watched, Jack reached the ledge at the top of the climbing wall, hauled himself onto it, and after a few steps along it, secured a new rope, which he lowered to Jemima. Freya wasn't sure how Jemima was supposed to attach it, but any rope had to be better than no rope. And perhaps that metal anchor would hold her there while she did so. Jack started to climb down towards Jemima, following another route that would take him close to her.

Maybe this is all going to turn out OK, Freya dared to hope.

She was sure something weird was going on. It was surely improbable for the rope to have frayed, as well as the holds breaking. Jack finally reached Jemima's side. He attached himself to another anchor point, using some piece of equipment that hadn't been in Freya's basic safety briefing. That done, Jack leant across to Jemima and helped her thread the new rope through the carabiner that attached to her harness. She slipped as he gave a final tug on the knot, and the watching group gave a collective gasp, but Jemima stopped, held to the wall by the equipment Jack had attached. Jack grabbed Jemima's new rope and pulled her sideways so that she could reach a new set of holds. Moments later, Jemima was gently descending to the ground, followed by Jack. Manuel and Val crowded around Jemima when everyone was earthbound again. Val gave her a hug. Manuel did too, then offered to buy her a drink.

I'm glad she's down safe. But what am I expected to do here? I only just met her this afternoon. I can't be expected to hug her. And I can't afford to get her anything. Freya settled for giving Jemima a quick smile when their eyes met.

"Glad you're down," Freya said. Jemima gave her a nod.

Freya's gaze slipped again to the skylight. The broken, jagged-edged skylight.

What sort of bird breaks out of a climbing gym through a skylight? Or into it, I suppose. But she remembered seeing a bird flying *out*.

Even as she spotted the breakage, she felt a swift, cold breeze sweep her cheek. Snowflakes whirled in, settling briefly on the landing pads before the warmer environs of the climbing gym melted them into tiny, icy puddles. The well-lit room was suddenly brighter as lightning flashed, illuminating every skylight with actinic blue. Thunder shook the building so soon after the lightning that Freya thought the storm must be right above them.

"Joe!" Val's bellow startled Freya almost as much as the thunder had. "Get that window covered!"

Funny, Freya thought, *Val's acting like she owns the place, not like a lowly student. Maybe if I acted more like her, I'd feel more confident, too.* She couldn't actually imagine herself doing that, though. *Besides, if I bellow at someone, the chances are they'll misunderstand me. Or I'll accidentally summon a flood or something.*

Up near the roof, Joe looked like he was casting around for something to cover the broken skylight, finally acting like he worked for the gym. He swung himself from one route to another, catching himself on handholds that Freya could hardly see. Freya shook her own aching arms and wondered how often you had to climb to do it so effortlessly. More often than someone would cover her entry fee, she was sure.

He's nowhere near the window, so I guess he *didn't break it.*

Joe paused for a moment to look around, then abseiled down rapidly. Now he was at their level, Freya could see he was tall and lean like Jack, wiry arm muscles revealed by his tank top, bunched from the climb.

"There's no way to secure the window without a cherry picker," he said as he approached, apparently addressing Val. "Jack will have to get a glass guy in tomorrow. Get a bucket to catch the snow for now."

Val glared at him. "Have you ever tried catching snow in a bucket, monkey king?"

"Nah, but it's the same principle as rain, isn't it?" Joe winked at her, unfazed by her name-calling.

Val folded her arms, a frown gathering on her forehead. She was clearly not amused, even before a stray snowflake landed on her head.

Joe was trying not to grin, a hint of mischief showing in the glint of his eyes and the set of his lips. But his voice was all business—faked seriousness?—as he replied.

"All right, I'll see if Jack's got a tarp or something stashed somewhere. We can cover the floor at least."

He wandered off, leaving Val brushing at her bare arms as a flurry of snowflakes landed on and around her. It was getting cold in the gym, the warm air escaping through the broken window. Freya abruptly wondered what had happened to the glass. Surely, someone would have noticed it falling into the climbing gym. She looked around at the floor. No glass shards decorated the piled-up mats. The only thing she could see out of place was a single black feather, partly obscured by fast-melting snowflakes. She shivered, and not just from the cold. The glass must have burst outwards with the force that hit it.

First the barghest, now a crow's feather. Maybe this city isn't as safe as I'd thought. But is the feather a message from an Apollonian demi, or from one of the Morrigan's descendants, or just from a crow that got in the way of whatever broke the window? Maybe the crow broke the window? But in that case, what was it doing inside?

Freya wasn't sure how she was supposed to tell which demi might be involved—her mum had told her the myths, but without, in this case, any practical magic to go with the theory. Climbing gyms hadn't featured heavily (or indeed at all) in her practical theology lessons. She glanced around. Jemima had been led to a sofa near the reception desk. Manuel had an arm around her and was offering sympathy. Joe and Jack were still rummaging around for something to cover the window, to judge by the loud thumps that were emerging from the gear room, liberally interspersed with Val's instructions. But... Ben. Where was he? He was not on the bouldering wall, and now Freya came to think of it, she hadn't noticed him since before Jemima fell.

CHAPTER NINE
AFTER THE FALL

Without really thinking about what she was doing, Freya turned away from Jemima and her support crew. It surprised her that Ben wouldn't be there to offer sympathy to Jemima—they'd both been fully accepted members of the group, and Ben had been trying to cosy up to Jemima most of the evening. Perhaps he hadn't seen the fall?

But how could he have missed it?

Freya peered around the big room. The music was still pumping, but most of the other climbers in the gym had vanished, presumably not allowed back on the walls after a rope had frayed. Jack was back at the reception desk, receiving a harness and a pair of climbing shoes from another departing climber. As Freya watched, the climber turned away, shaking his head, and headed for the exit.

Perhaps Ben's gone home already.

Freya walked over to the desk, picking up her feet quickly as the tight shoes she still wore constrained her feet. *Note to self: never walk in climbing shoes.*

Jack looked up as she arrived at the desk. He looked harried and strained, but he gave her a smile as she appeared.

"Well done on surviving your first climb," he said. "Have we got you hooked?"

When Freya didn't immediately say yes, he hurried on.

"It's not usually like this," he assured her. "I've worked here for three years with no major accidents. Tonight was—"

A growl of thunder overlaid his next words, so Freya didn't hear them clearly.

Jack glanced irritably at the broken skylight, still letting in snow. The flakes were coming faster now.

"Look," he said, catching Freya's eye, then looking back at the skylight. "I've got to close early. We can't stay open with a hole in the roof. Or with ropes fraying. And it sounds like the weather's closing in. Usually, I'd encourage a newbie to do another climb, so here's a voucher for your next time." He filled out a small piece of paper and handed it to her. "Now, if you'll hand in your gear, I need to get the rest of you lot out of here so I can get some repairs in before we're flooded in snowmelt." He muttered something else under his breath. Freya thought she caught Val's name, but she wasn't sure what he'd said. He turned to another customer to receive their gear.

Oh well, looks like climbing's over. After what happened to Jemima, I'm not sure if I want to come back.

She remembered that she'd been planning to ask about Ben. She waited till the customer had gone before enquiring.

"Has Ben already gone?"

Jack looked back at her, his hands full of mesh shoe bags.

"Blond guy? No idea, sorry. He didn't check out with me."

"Oh, OK." *Maybe he's in the gear room.*

She headed that way—she had to take off her harness and shoes anyway. She wasn't relishing getting her own soggy gear back on.

The gear room was packed when she got there. Jemima, Val and Manuel were all in there, along with a few other climbers she didn't recognise. Their shouted conversation was a mix of complaints about the weather, ribbing each other for perceived climbing faults and successes, and most of all, astonished comments about Jemima's fall. Along with the stench of sweaty shoes, it was overwhelming. Driven by necessity, Freya found enough bench to perch half a butt-cheek on, and sat down to remove her shoes. She was wiggling her toes in appreciation of their freedom when Val's feet appeared in front of her. Freya looked up. Val's expression was serious, her blue eyes chilly as she looked down at Freya. She leant closer, in order to speak to Freya semi-privately.

"If there's something you know about tonight's accident, tell me now," she said.

"What? I don't know any more than you do," Freya sputtered. "I've never even been climbing before!"

Val unbuckled her harness and hung it on one of the hooks labelled 'size medium' before stooping down to Freya again.

"You don't have to be a climber to see that that was not a normal accident. I've been climbing here since I arrived in the city, not to mention for years before that, and *nothing* like it has ever happened in all the years I've been climbing, anywhere."

Freya felt the weight of accusation in Val's eyes. "I have no idea about it, I swear."

"Jack says you were asking about Ben. And I saw you pick up that feather." Val's eyes shifted their focus from Freya to the bench beside her, where the crow's feather lay.

What is she accusing me of? It's no crime to pick up a feather.

"I wondered why Ben didn't come to check on Jemima, that's all," Freya said aloud. "I thought you guys were all friends."

Freya thought Val's features softened a little. "Yeah, I thought so too. And I'll follow up with Ben when I find him. Just—you should know that it's not a great idea to go picking up black feathers."

Jemima leant closer as Val said this. "What, because of the mites? Yep, I have to agree with you there. Bird feathers can be foul, Freya.

No pun intended." Jemima seemed to have recovered from her mishap, at least outwardly.

Val raised her eyes heavenward. "Yeah, I suppose that's a possibility too. Just leave that one where it is, Freya. Though the damage may have already been done."

"There's a bathroom just past the café," Jemima suggested. "You can wash your hands there. Get rid of any pests."

Freya looked from one to the other with some amusement.

Now there's a clear disconnect in communication.

"All right, I'll do that right after I've got this harness off. OK?"

"Here, I'll unbuckle it for you," Val said. "Wouldn't want to get mitey fingers on Jack's nice harness, would we?" The sarcasm in her voice was strong enough that Freya was surprised Jemima didn't protest—until she noticed that Jemima's fingers were shaking as she tried to remove her own harness.

"Here, I will help you," Manuel said to her.

"Thanks."

Freed of all climbing accoutrements, Freya did visit the bathroom to wash her hands. Demigod message or bird mites aside, her fingers felt sticky from the mix of chalk and sweat, and sore from gripping the handholds. The air was chilly out in the main gym as she returned. The queue of exiting climbers was gone. Jack was measuring a large piece of plywood with Joe providing minimal assistance.

"It'll be a right job getting it there," Joe protested to Jack as Freya passed them. "And it's not like *we* own the building. Can't you just call someone tomorrow?"

"You know Val's dad owns the building," Jack said. "She'll never let any of us live it down if we let the floorboards get damaged or owt."

That's one mystery solved, I guess. If Val's dad owns this place, no wonder she's protective of it.

Joe's lips thinned, but he didn't disagree.

Although she'd repaired more than her fair share of holes in roofs, Freya didn't have any of her friend Karim's handy ointments with her—and even if she did, their use would surely provoke too much comment, even if it had been possible to get at the skylight. Feeling that there was nothing useful she could contribute to the conversation, Freya re-joined the group in the changing room. She felt strongly that the night was at an end, and she'd be happy to be home, snuggling in bed, with Mr Fluffbum on her feet. But first, she had to get home. With barghests and crows on the loose, she didn't want to walk home alone. The thought chilled her already cooling body. She shivered.

"Is anyone heading out towards the moor road?" she asked the room at large. All eyes turned to her, and Val shook her head.

"We're all in halls, remember. We'll be heading up the hill, not along the valley."

"Oh." She tried again. "Can I come with you that far?" Freya hated the uncertainty and awkward hope in her voice, but there had been far too many strange occurrences tonight. She didn't want to be out in the weather, alone.

Once again Val was the spokesperson.

"Sure. It looks like it's getting nasty out there."

Relief flooded Freya, though she knew she'd still have a way to go after they separated at the student halls.

"Er, great. Thanks." Realising she had yet to put her shoes back on, she retrieved the sodden things from their cubby. It took her a few tries to undo the laces—she'd just pushed them off her feet earlier, and the icy water made them difficult to undo. Reluctantly, she squidged her feet into them.

Ugh. Next time, don't call on the river when trying to escape barghests. Unless there's really no other option, I guess.

"You still got those nails?" Freya asked casually. She'd been able to more-or-less forget about the barghests while she was inside climbing, but the prospect of returning to the dark, possibly grimhound-infested streets was not attractive.

Val shrugged on her jacket and jingled the pocket at Freya in answer. She turned to Jemima, who was standing by the door with all her outdoor clothes on. "You all right to walk home now?"

Jemima gave Val a shaky smile. "Walking is no problem. Lucky we've only a hill to climb and not a wall though."

Val walked over and patted her on the shoulder. "We'll get you back on the horse in no time," she said. "For now, let's conquer that hill." She looked over her shoulder at Freya. "Ready? Feather left behind?"

Freya stood up.

"Ready." *No need to comment on the feather, surely?* Unwilling to leave a piece of evidence behind, but mindful of mites, Freya had washed the feather and replaced it in her pocket.

CHAPTER TEN
SNOWED IN

The doorway was snowed in. It took the combined efforts of Val, Manuel, and Freya to push the door outwards, displacing a large snowdrift as they did so. A gust of icy wind greeted their efforts, and Freya shivered again. Going out wasn't attractive.

"This is a bit much," Jemima said, looking out at the thickly falling flakes beyond the covered alcove that held the door. "It's not even winter yet."

"How did everyone else get out?" Freya asked. It hadn't been *that* long since the other climbers left.

"There's a back entrance too, but it would take us the wrong way. Ben must have left a while back, before the snow built up." Val said. "Even he would have had trouble with that door."

No footprints, either, Freya thought but did not say. *Maybe Ben went his own way. Did he follow the crow somehow?*

"I hope Ben got home all right," Jemima said in a slightly worried voice.

"He'll be fine," Val said impatiently. "He knows what he's doing."

"This is much too much," Manuel complained. "Rain is one thing, but snow!"

Jemima flicked him a quick smile. "I'd be complaining of the heat in your country. But this isn't normal for us either. We'd better get home so we can keep warm. I'm betting on a snow day tomorrow, and I don't fancy spending it here." She did not look back into the climbing gym. Freya suspected that she'd be avoiding it for longer than Val planned.

"Nothing for it but forward," Val declared, and led the group out into the swirling haze.

Freya followed close behind, not wanting to get separated in a snowstorm, let alone in an unfamiliar area of town. She wished again that she'd brought her cloak. Still, the sooner she got home, the sooner she could get warm.

The walk along the riverside was deeply covered with snow, and Freya was soon numb. She started to fall behind as her feet stumbled. She wasn't sure if it was just her imagination that painted black canine figures in the shadows, and she didn't want to find out.

"Wait," she called, her voice weaker than she'd planned. "Wait for me."

It was Jemima who heard her and tugged the others to a stop.

"We'd better link arms," she said. "We don't want to lose each other in this mess."

Freya gratefully did so, feeling the warmth of inclusion more than actual warmth as Val took one arm and Jemima the other. They trudged along in silence. Freya came to herself enough to note that the river was no longer flooding.

But surely it will flood again when all this snow melts. Maybe I should stick to higher ground for a few days, wait till the river's in a better mood, before I make formal introductions.

They turned uphill, away from the river. Val perked up when they reached the tram lines.

"This is more like it," she said, although all of them were struggling in the snow. "Not a barghest in sight, and we're back on the rails."

"I don't know what this bar-thing is that you're talking about," Jemima said, "but I can't wait to be at home. I think I pulled all the muscles in my arms back there. It's a hot shower for me."

"No baths in halls then?" Freya asked, happy to stay away from supernatural topics.

Jemima shook her head.

"Not enough room. It's a shame. I like a good bath."

There were murmurs of agreement, muffled by snow. Now they were away from the river, the snowflakes flurried more than ever. Sudden gusts of wind blew snow into Freya's face, and she grimaced.

Too much snow for autumn. Any snow would be too much for this time of year.

Something was twanging at Freya's senses. Despite Val's pocket full of nails and the iron tram tracks, she was sure something more than snow was out there in the night. She glanced sideways at Val, who despite her cheerful words, was walking faster than before.

We're definitely not out of the woods yet. She couldn't help but smile at her own thought, since they were deep in the heart of a stony city, barely a tree in sight.

"I hope they have snow ploughs or something along the tops," she said, thinking of her own route home, and hoping to distract herself from her unease.

"They're not likely commissioned for the year," Jemima said. "I'm sure the drivers have other jobs the rest of the time, and no-one would have expected this much snow in October."

A gloomy silence followed her statement. No-one disagreed.

After a few minutes trudging, Val said, "I didn't expect it of Ben." She left the sentence hanging, as though they all knew what she meant.

I guess in a way, we do. Except no-one saw anything at the gym. At least I didn't, and I am sure if anyone else did they'd have spoken up.

"Ditching us, you mean?" she asked hesitantly.

Val looked at her sharply as they passed under a streetlight. "Ben usually waits for us, yeah," she said. She must have decided to be circumspect about the supernatural now. Perhaps she'd noted Jemima's repeated insistence upon mundane explanations. "Perhaps he was still in a snit with Manuel," she said. But before they could discuss the issue any further, Val tugged the small group to a stop. "There's something up ahead," she said, her voice flat.

"I don't suppose there's a tram due anytime soon?" Freya asked, half joking. It was unlikely that trams would operate in these conditions.

"I hope so," said Manuel. "A tram would be very welcome."

"A tram would be great," said Val, "but that's not what I mean." She pointed ahead.

Freya had seen it too now. Not a barghest this time, but a congregation of crows, black feathers stark against the snow.

They covered the street ahead.

CHAPTER ELEVEN
A MURDER OF CROWS

"That's unusual behaviour for crows," Jemima said. "They should be hiding in trees for the night. I wonder if that thunder scared them earlier?"

As though in answer to her words, thunder echoed around the sky. Freya had hardly seen the lightning that preceded it through the thick snow. The crows didn't move, except to flick their wings a little in response to falling snowflakes.

No, I don't think they were scared by the thunder.

"Could it be that someone left food out for them?" Manuel asked.

"Yes, that seems possible," Jemima said, giving him a smile.

Freya eyed the crows warily. They could be just birds, of course, but Val's reaction to her merely picking up a crow's feather suggested otherwise, as did the birds' indifference to the thunder.

Never underestimate possible supernaturals, especially when the supernaturals in question have sharp beaks. Lots of sharp beaks.

There were at least twenty of the big birds, and every one of them watched Freya and the others.

"Any of you bird whisperers?" she asked.

"Not a skill my dad taught me, unfortunately," said Val. "You'd think he'd be keen on befriending crows, as well as ravens, but he's always been particular."

"I'm fine with bird watching, but it's usually me watching the birds, not the birds watching me," said Jemima.

"I avoid birds, if possible," Manuel said. "I bet Ben would know what is wrong with them. He's always throwing things to the crows."

Freya looked around. It was some time since they had passed the last side street. The crows were mostly at ground level, apart from a few which perched on the iron railings in front of a tall stone building. Snow had drifted in between the railings and the building, so the crows' tails left little dints in the snowbank. Their feet had pressed into the snow in a chaotic pattern, exposing the tramlines in some places.

So, steel doesn't stop crows, Freya noted. *Still, crows have to be better than barghests, surely.*

"I wish Ben had told us he was heading off," Val muttered. "Ben going AWOL then these crows appearing does not look good."

"Does he go off on his own much?" Freya asked.

"Sometimes. It's hard to tell on just a few weeks' acquaintance, but I thought he was trustworthy," Val said. "A bit glib, mind you. Not that I'd expect anything else from someone taking law."

"Never mind Ben's subject choices," Jemima said. "We need to get past these birds and get home. I'm freezing! I bet they'll just fly off if we run at them. Come on!" Jemima broke free of Val's quick restraining arm, dragging Manuel with her as she ran at the flock. The birds hopped out of her way, then closed ranks behind her and Manuel. Jemima came to a confused halt in the middle of the road, surrounded by corvids.

"This is crazy," she said. "They must belong to a zoo or a circus, or something. It's totally not natural behaviour. But they're not hurting anyone. Come on, guys, we can just walk through them."

She turned to continue uphill. None of the birds moved. "Come on, out of my way, crows. I'm much bigger than you," she said, taking a step forward, bringing Manuel with her.

"Are you sure this is a good idea?" he asked, as the crows failed to move.

"Of course it is, they're just birds," said Jemima, waggling a foot at a crow who was disinclined to move out from underneath her step.

"I'm not so sure of that," Val said softly.

"What are they then?" Freya asked, matching her low voice. Perhaps that would keep the crows calm.

"Your guess is as good as mine at this point," Val said, "But I'm willing to bet that Ben's got something to do with them. There was that feather in the gym."

Apparently she's forgiven me for touching it.

"And Manuel's seen him feeding them." Val called in a louder voice, "Jemima, Manuel, just come back. We'll find another way."

Jemima ignored her. Manuel looked back for a moment, but a tug from Jemima kept him moving forwards. She and Manuel were almost all the way through the crows now. She took one more step, the last before the snow stretched uncovered ahead. At that moment, the entire flock whirled into motion, flapping into the air, and swirling around Jemima. She screamed and covered her head as they began diving at her. Freya wasn't sure if they were actually making contact with those wickedly sharp beaks, but they were getting very close to Jemima and Manuel as they swooped and flapped. Manuel swore in what Freya assumed was Spanish, although it could have been Portuguese, and waved his arms around, but it didn't have much effect. A couple of the crows still on the ground hopped back a pace or two before taking to the sky to join in.

"Run," Freya yelled. "Find an open shop or something."

Jemima must have heard her because she began to stumble forward, and shortly disappeared with Manuel into a dark doorway.

"Come on," Val said grimly. "We're going to have to get through them too. May as well go now while they're distracted."

They don't look especially distracted. More like focused. But I don't know any other way home from here.

Freya gave a mental sigh, shrugged her shoulders, and then pulled off her coat and draped it over her head. It was colder that way, but she felt better with the fabric draping hoodlike over her face. It might give her some protection from the crows.

"Alright," she said. "Let's go."

Val obviously thought Freya's idea was a good one, because she hastily stripped off her own jacket and covered her head in the same way. The ravens on the back of her jacket appeared to shift in harmony with the fluttering crows.

"You're sure you know nothing about crows?" Freya asked as they strode towards the flock.

"Crows are definitely not my speciality," Val said evasively. "Duck!"

They'd reached the centre of the action, and more than one bird was taking offence at their presence. Freya crouched as a crow dived straight at her face and twisted sideways as another hurtled towards her from the left. A third followed suit, and Freya was harried towards an alleyway she hadn't seen beyond the snowdrifts. Ducking under the surprisingly hard blows from black-feathered wings, she scurried for the opening. A beak grazed her hand just before she reached it.

Fenris's teeth. That hurt!

She put the scratched hand to her mouth to ease the pain, then remembered Jemima's prognostications about bird mites. *Who knew how much worse bird beaks were than their feathers?* She snatched her hand away again swiftly and dived into the alley.

A few paces into the narrow street the crows eased their attack, perhaps not liking the confined space. They turned their attention to Val, who stumbled in a few moments later.

Freya slowly straightened up from her protective hunch, expecting to be swooped on at any moment. But when she looked out towards the main road, the crows were gone, leaving only claw prints and a few scattered feathers.

"Are you alright, Freya?" Jemima asked from further along the alleyway. She and Manuel must have used it as an escape route, the same way that Freya had done. Perhaps the 'doorway' had actually been the entrance to the alley. Jemima was bleeding a little from a scratch on her forehead, but apparently otherwise unharmed. The red brick walls of the alley were punctuated by occasional doorsteps, presumably leading to apartments in the three-storey buildings on either side of it. On another day, there might be rubbish collected in such a narrow place, but tonight the snow had fallen thickly enough that the ground was covered with a clean layer of white, only slightly trampled by footprints. The far end of the narrow street opened onto a back lane, not as well-lit as the main street they'd been following. Manuel sat on one of the stone doorsteps nearby, muttering in his mother tongue.

Val stalked up to Jemima and stood with her hands on her hips. "You got any undisclosed leanings towards corvids we should know about?" she asked.

At first, Jemima's already small form seemed to shrink before Val. But as Val spoke, Jemima rallied, standing taller. She looked at Val as though she were crazy.

"Come on, Val, I thought you were a friend. But tonight's got me wondering. First you start spouting woo-woo nonsense about mythical creatures while I am dangling from a stupid, broken rock-climbing wall without a rope—a rope which I personally heard you say was reliable—and now you're accusing me of being in league with *birds*? Birds which, you'll note, have just attacked me. And for your information, no-one I have ever met counts crows as birds when it comes to birdwatching. They're too... too human, I guess. I am *not* having a good night, and you are *not* making it any better with this crap."

Well, I am officially impressed. Again. Not that she knows what's really going on. Actually, neither do I. But she sure is firm in her stance on the universe, thought Freya.

Val was clearly nonplussed. Perhaps she was too used to being the boss of those around her to appreciate being stood up to, or perhaps the weirdness of the night was getting to her too. It took her a few moments to come up with a reply.

"Look, I'm sorry you had an accident at the gym," she began.

"Sorry doesn't help! I am mentally scarred. I doubt I'll ever go climbing again!" Jemima declared. "And I'll be lucky if I don't end up with a crow phobia too, and those things are *everywhere*." She paused for breath, and Manuel stood up behind her.

"I'm not sure that I will escape the crow phobia either," he said. He was bleeding from several scratches. Perhaps being taller, he had attracted more crows' beaks or claws. "And I think we might consider climbing elsewhere for a while." He laid a hand on Jemima's shoulder. "I am sorry," he said to her, "but I do not wish to give up climbing entirely."

A slow clapping noise echoed in the narrow confines of the brick-walled alley.

Freya whipped around towards the sound. Ben stood at the far end of the alley, clapping in an exaggerated manner. His hair was still perfectly styled despite the snow, and over the casual clothes he'd worn earlier, he wore a thick coat with dark lapels that glinted a little—not quite like fur, or fabric... more like feathers. His expression was the thing that had changed the most. Instead of being affable, approachable, or friendly, his face now showed a sort of supercilious disdain. And his eyes... were they black and shiny like those of a bird? Or was it just the light? The difference in his appearance was so great as to make him a different person.

"Good one, Manuel," Ben said as he approached. Freya now saw that a ragged-ended rope was slung crosswise around his body, over the coat. He held a bow of some sort in one hand. "Very gentlemanly of you. But I would suggest that no-one in this group is going climbing again soon."

Val puffed up, visibly offended. "What do you mean, none of us is climbing? My dad depends on that gym running. *I* depend on it. How else will I pay my uni fees? And where did you spring from, anyway?" Her eyes narrowed in suspicion as they fell on the rope. "Where were you when Jemima fell?"

Ben gave an ostentatious yawn. "So many questions!" he said in exaggerated surprise. "But I'm afraid answering questions is not what I'm here for. I'll thank you all for coming this way," he continued, gesturing down the alley in the direction he'd come from. "At the very least you can get out of this snow, which I must say has been most inconvenient. If I find one of you has been stirring up Thor or Taranis, I'll be seriously annoyed. Not that it will matter to you, of course."

Freya took a cautious step backwards, then another. *I'd prefer rogue crows to a rogue demi. But avoiding both seems like the best option right now.*

"Stop right there, Freya," Ben said, ducking around Val, Jemima, and Manuel to grab her arm. "You're too new to know anything much, but you've seen too much tonight for me to let you off. Down the cellar with the others you go." He pulled her towards the rest of the group, who hadn't moved. Perhaps they were as stunned by Ben's change of attitude as Freya was.

Freya tried to twist out of his grip, but he merely tightened his fingers. They felt like bars of steel on Freya's arm. Or possibly claws. Bird claws. She gave a slightly hysterical gasp of laughter. "You can't be serious," she said.

"I am usually serious," Ben replied.

"You're mad," Jemima declared.

"Not mad. Just following orders," Ben replied cheerfully. "And if you knew whose orders, your mundane little mind would be blown, so I'll leave you to guess. Well, you won't be able to, but perhaps Val will." He gave Val a sunny smile that was utterly incongruous, given their current situation.

"You're Apollonian, then," Val said to Ben. "I should have realised that when the crows showed up and wouldn't listen to me." She paused. "Or is it the Morrigan you're with?"

So, Val did try to control the crows. I thought she might be able to, Freya thought, focusing on Val rather than Ben. *But is she a Wodenite, or something else? I've never heard of Wodenites with pony charms. I wonder what Val is short for? The daughters of Odin are Valkyries...*

"What do you mean, Val?" Jemima demanded. "Ben's from Nottingham, you know that."

Ben made shooing motions with his hands, indicating they should start walking. "Go on, Val," he said. "Dig your hole deeper, why not? You might as well tell Jemima all about the world she's been missing." He pushed Freya towards an open coal chute a little way along the alley, using her to make the rest shuffle in the same direction.

Val glared at him, but gave a half-hearted explanation to Jemima. "There's another side to the world beyond simple biology, chemistry and physics," she said.

"And law, don't forget law," Ben said.

Val shook her curly head. "Apollonians are so hooked on law," she complained. "The rest of us have better things to worry about. But what Ben is trying to get me to explain is... well, you know people believe in all sorts of gods, right?"

Jemima nodded uncertainly. "I suppose so. Some do, anyway."

"Well, every one of those gods was—I guess—believed into existence. And then people forgot about them, or moved on to new gods, but the old ones were still there, and had children with humans, and... well, you're the biologist. What happens when you get mixing of populations?"

"A variety of parental traits appear in the offspring, with traits manifesting at variable levels according to Mendelian principles," Jemima responded, as though quoting a textbook. "But this is crazy. Gods aren't real."

"What if they were?" Val encouraged her. "Their offspring would be demigods, right? If they, er, mixed with humans. And their offspring would have, as you say, a mixture of traits. Different inherited abilities and affinities. So here we are." She gestured towards herself and Ben, then more hesitantly to Freya and Manuel. "I'm sure about me," she added. "Less so about Freya and Manuel."

"Well done, you'll pass your exams yet," interrupted Ben in jeering tones. "So you know, Jemima, the variation in traits in this case means that *I* have more powers than her, or him." He pointed to Val and Manuel.

Val blew out an indignant huff of breath. "You do not," she objected.

"What do you know about it?" Ben said. He made a casual gesture with one hand, and about half the crows reappeared in midair and glided into the alley to surround Val and Manuel.

Manuel glowered at Ben, but stepped away from the crows. Freya wasn't sure what he made of this whole situation. Lightning lit up the alleyway for a moment, thunder following on its heels. The snowflakes, which had eased off a little, drifted down thicker than ever, even in the narrow confines of the alley. Ben glanced up uneasily, but continued to speak as soon as he could be heard over the thunder.

"I'm not yet sure what Freya here is like, but indications so far are that she isn't a threat to me. Right, Freya?"

CHAPTER TWELVE
BETTER TO BE UNDERESTIMATED

The scarce light in the shadowy alley didn't show Freya much of Ben's face, but enough of his expression was visible that Freya could see him grinning at her. Smugly. Freya shot him a look of pure dislike, but she thought it was probably not a good idea to argue demi-powers at this moment.

Better to be underestimated. If I must, I'll call in the river, but best not to do that twice in one night, let alone twice before an introduction. At least I know Ben's not the one behind the thunder snow. But who is? And why do none of these people care about letting mundanes know about the demi-world? I thought we were supposed to be hidden.

"Cat got your tongue?" Ben taunted. "Never mind, it's not like you had much of interest to say anyway."

It was Freya's turn to gasp with indignation, but Ben ignored her and turned back to Jemima.

"Now, Jemima. I know you're just a lowly mundane, but you seem to be well acquainted with weather phenomena. Tell us about what happens when thunder and snow mix." He waved at the crows, who flapped at Val, hustling her closer to the coal chute. Ignoring Freya, he advanced towards Manuel and Jemima.

I can't believe he got the plural right for phenomena, Freya thought. Although law... I suppose words are part of his daily life. You'd think a lawyer-in-the-making would be more law-abiding, though, not the sort of person to reveal supernaturals to mundanes and shove other demis into coal holes. Think, Freya. If Ben's an Apollonian demi, he'll have some sort of Apollonian traits. Let's see… Apollo had a lyre and was associated with the sun, herd animals, and with law and guilt. Ben doesn't act like the musician-type; he's hardly sunny in disposition… but he's doing law. So that leaves… herding animals or applying guilt. I suppose the crows were herded, in a way. And they are messengers of Apollo. But if he's also a descendant of Morrigan, that could explain his inner darkness. She's got all sorts of negative associations with war and death and the like. Plus, the crow thing. But who is guilty of what, that makes him think treating a bunch of students as hostages is a good idea?

Jemima, who must have been searching her memory, suddenly blurted out a string of facts. "Thunder and snow don't usually fall together. When they do, it's because of a clash of cold air and warm, moist air meeting. But you don't care about the weather, do you?" she ended in a rush.

Ben gave her a considering nod, as though he were a judge in court. "Very good, you can keep your weathergirl status."

Jemima glared at him.

Ben stepped closer to Manuel and said something to him that Freya couldn't hear. Even in the low light, Freya could see Manuel go pale.

"You wouldn't!" he half-growled.

"But I would," said Ben. "No point in this whole performance otherwise."

"I'll remember this," Manuel said in a voice that rumbled a note or lower than his earlier light tenor.

"But not for very long," Ben said, with another of his unpleasant smiles.

What secret is Manuel hiding? I thought he might be a demi, the way Val was talking, but that doesn't seem quite right.

Freya didn't have long to wonder though, because Manuel leapt at Ben, transforming as he did so into a long-legged, red-furred wolf-like beast, with enormous ears.

"What is *that*?" Freya asked involuntarily. "It's not a fox." *Thank goodness.* She took a step away from Ben, anxiety at the unexpected appearance of an unknown were-beast making her heart beat faster. She felt like she couldn't get enough air. *Not a were. I can't handle any more weres.*

"I don't believe this," Jemima gasped, a hand over her mouth partly obscuring her words. "Maned wolves are almost extinct. And they come from South America. What is one doing in the north of England?"

Freya's breath came faster, matching her heart rate as a bubble of hysterical laughter forced its way out of her mouth. "Would it be better if he was in South America?" *Mundanes are so weird. She's focusing on the species? Never mind that the maned wolf before you is your friend who's just transformed.*

"Well, yes," Jemima said. "There are some in zoos in Europe, but none near here. I'd have visited them. What I want to know is where has it come from, and where has Manuel gone?"

"Now you've done it," Val said, apparently to Manuel, though maybe to Ben as well.

Manuel clearly couldn't reply. Ben didn't try. He was too busy fending off the maned canine that was Manuel, who was snapping at Ben's raised arms, leaping about on stilt-like legs. "No, you don't," he said. He unslung the rope from over his shoulder, pulled an arrow from a quiver that Freya hadn't previously noticed, and in seconds was holding a bow and arrow trained at Manuel's new form. Manuel cringed away from the arrow, whining.

"What are you *doing*?" Val hissed at him. "Manuel's a friend!"

"Your friend, maybe, not mine," Ben said. He released the arrow.

Despite her fear of weres, Freya felt time stand still.

"You idiot!" Val yelled as Jemima gave a wordless cry of protest.

Manuel turned away as the arrow struck him, and it buried itself in his shoulder. He yelped and tried to bite at the arrow with his teeth. Jemima rushed to his side. "Don't pull at it," she implored. "It will need a vet, special tools, all sorts." Tears streamed down her face, but she glared at Ben all the same. "You bastard. How can you treat an innocent animal that way?"

"That's not an animal. That's a were. A filthy desecration of the demi world. No-one wants or needs animal-human hybrids. The very idea makes me sick," Ben said. Ignoring Freya and Jemima, he bent over Manuel and yanked the arrow out, evading the were's sharp teeth as he did so. "Barely worth an arrow," he said carelessly. "It better not be broken." He glanced around, apparently only now noticing that the three women were staring at him in open-mouthed horror.

"Come on, don't tell me you like beasts," he said.

"That's not a beast, that's my friend," Val said through gritted teeth. "And whatever species he is, that's also your friend Manuel."

"I don't know how it got here, but you can't just go round *shooting* animals. Especially not endangered ones," said Jemima, oblivious to Val's words or misunderstanding them.

Freya felt all eyes turn towards her. Apparently, she was expected to express her outrage—or something.

What do I say? Manuel is part of the group. And not liking weres doesn't mean wanting to hurt them.

"I don't like weres, but I like demis who shoot their friends even less," Freya said.

"See, Ben? Wrong choice. I won't be including you in any rounds next week, that's for sure. Or getting you discounted entry at my dad's climbing gym. And I'll thank you for releasing those crows so we can get home," Val said.

"Temper, temper," Ben admonished her in a mocking voice. He continued more thoughtfully. "Although I did like the climbing gym. Maybe my mentor can set up a rival establishment."

"That is *it*!" Val straightened her shoulders, eyes flashing like lightning. "You do *not* get to act like this. I don't care who your 'mentor' is." She turned on the spot in the snowy alley, first slowly, then faster, faltering only as the oddly muffled thunder rolled around their heads. "I wish I knew who was causing that," Val said, still spinning. "And no, Jemima, before you speak, I am sure it's not just a new weather phenomenon. You're smart, I know you are—you beat me in the last in-class bio test. Look around and think about what's been happening." Val stopped talking and spun faster.

Ben folded his arms and stood back with a superior look on his face. His attitude surprised Freya; he'd been nice enough in the pub.

I guess it's hard to judge someone from just one drinking session with them. She thought uneasily of the darkness on the rope when he'd argued with Val. Perhaps it had been more than just a trick of the shadows?

Jemima, who had been looking with disbelief from Ben to Val to Manuel—still huddled on the ground in the form of a maned wolf—turned at last to Freya. "Is this really the way things are?" she asked, her usually confident voice diffident. "It all seems very unrealistic."

Freya shrugged a little helplessly. "Sorry," she said. "We're not supposed to tell mundanes about the supernatural. I don't know why they've dragged you into this, whatever 'this' is. Wrong place, wrong time, perhaps? But yeah. My experience is that this really is the way the world is." She felt uncomfortable telling such an obvious mundane even that much, but she supposed with Val being so open about the demi-world, Jemima would have found out, eventually.

Jemima looked down at Manuel, who she'd been patting absentmindedly, as though he were a stray dog that needed calming. She took her hand away and Manuel whined a little.

"I still don't believe it," she muttered. "The structural changes alone are too big."

"If it helps, biology still conforms to the usual rules," Freya said. "At least when nothing weird is going on. Physics, less so."

Jemima gave a shaky laugh. "Just as well I'm not taking any physics papers then. Though isn't that supposed to be the basis of everything else?"

"So I've heard. But then I'm not taking physics either. Maybe it's quantum or something," Freya said.

"Yeah, sure. Blame it on quantum."

A sharp increase in the wind which blew through the alley caught their attention. Manuel pressed against Jemima's thigh. Even as a maned wolf, he was tall and leggy. Blood matted his coat where it streamed from his shoulder wound.

"Perhaps you could apply pressure to that wound, Jemima?" Freya suggested. Since Manuel appeared to trust Jemima the most, it made sense that she should be the one to administer first aid.

Jemima bit her lip. "I hate blood," she muttered. But she pulled her sleeve over her hand and pressed Manuel's furry, wounded shoulder. He whimpered, but held still. Meanwhile, Val turned so fast she blurred, and her skirt of ornaments, which Freya hadn't noticed while they were climbing, flared out again. Ben nocked another arrow and took aim at Val.

"Look out, Val," Freya blurted.

Val raised her arms above her head and gave out a pulse of energy. Snowflakes blasted in all directions. Ben's arrow, loosed at the same moment, was flung wide and clattered off the wall of the building behind Val before falling into the coal chute. Ben gave an incoherent roar of rage and threw himself at Val. They both fell to the ground, rolling as Val tried to evade Ben's clutches.

"You're going to—" Freya cut herself off as the inevitable happened: Val and Ben both tumbled into the open coal-chute that Ben had been trying to get them into. There was a muted series of bumping sounds, followed by a loud thump and a cry of pain.

Chapter Thirteen
Home Go the Hunted

"Val, are you ok?" Freya and Jemima both rushed to the edge of the chute. It was too dark to see anything inside. "Val?" Freya didn't feel inclined to enquire after Ben's wellbeing, given the way he'd spoken and acted. Val's display of power had been impressive, but in Freya's experience, impressive power didn't mean being impervious to earthly harm.

A faint groan reached their ears.

"Is that you, Val?"

"I think so." Val's voice was wavery, a far cry from the bubbly tones she usually employed. "Have any of you got a flashlight app? I can't see a thing down here."

"I have." Jemima nudged Freya out of the way and toggled on her phone while Freya was still swiping through the unfamiliar screens of her new phone. They both peered down.

The walls of the coal chute were dark with the soot of centuries of coal use, but the underground space it led to appeared to be mostly empty. An old bed frame and some miscellaneous sacks caught Freya's eye as Jemima shone her light down. Then Val's smudged face appeared at the end of the chute. The blue-tinged light made her look even paler than usual.

"Hey guys," she slurred, "glad you could make it. Fun night, right?"

Jemima and Freya glanced at each other. "She must have hit her head," Jemima whispered.

"Yeah," Freya agreed. "But what about Ben?"

"'S'okay," Val said. "He's here too."

"Is he threatening you?" Jemima asked practically.

"Well, he's breathing."

"I don't think breathing counts as threatening," Freya said. "At least, not usually."

Jemima snorted, not quite a laugh.

"Think he's asleep," Val said. "He's snoring." She giggled, an uncharacteristic sound.

Jemima and Freya's eyes met. Freya shrugged. "That sounds safe enough," she said. "Can you climb up?"

"'m good at climbing," Val confided. "But I need a rope."

"The ropes are all back at the climbing gym, Val. Unless you can find whatever Ben had along with that horrid bow," Jemima said.

Val disappeared from view, and a string of unidentifiable noises emerged from the coal chute. Her face reappeared at the base of the chute, grinning. "Found a rope," she announced. "Here, I'll throw you the end." Despite Val's odd behaviour, she coiled the rope up in a workmanlike way, and tossed the coil up through the chute. Her first attempt resulted in the rope slithering back down. Muffled curses floated up, but she soon managed a more successful throw. Freya caught the rope but handed it to Jemima.

"I have no idea how to secure this," she said. "How about you?"

Jemima grimaced. "I'm only middling at knots. I always get them to check mine at the gym. Manuel could help, if he was here." She looked around as though expecting Manuel to appear from a doorway. Her eyes slid over the maned wolf that was licking morosely at its wound, as though not associating it with Manuel.

Well, he's certainly not in prime rope-handling form. At least he doesn't seem to be bleeding out, either.

"Let's start with something heavy," Freya said, returning to the problem at hand. She cast around the alley for inspiration. There were open windows higher up, but they were well above her reach. Her eye fell upon the solid metal bars that secured the windows on the lowest level of the brick building opposite, a little above her head. "Perfect!" she said. "Do your best with the knots, Jemima. The only knot I know is a granny knot, so you're probably ahead of me there."

"We'll just have to hope the screws hold," Jemima said, squinting dubiously at the way the bars were fastened to the wall. "But I can't see anything better."

Freya jogged up and down on the spot in an attempt to keep warm, while avoiding Manuel on general principles—who knew what an injured maned-wolf-were would do if approached? And how much humanity a were retained in its animal form?

Jemima doled out the rope that Val had thrown up to them. It just reached across to the window bars, but didn't leave much leftover for securing it. Halfway through tying the rope on, she exclaimed. "Hold onto this, will you, Freya? My hands are half frozen. I can't keep a good grip on it."

Freya untucked her hands from under her arms and held the rope in place while Jemima jigged around for a few moments, rubbing her hands.

"Thanks, I'll finish it now. Are you still with us, Val?" Jemima said, taking over at the rope again.

Val replied in the affirmative, and gave the rope a tug, but added, "I think Ben's waking up. He stopped snoring a moment ago."

"I don't think we should leave Val down there with him if he's awake," Freya said. "Are we ready to go?"

"I think so," Jemima said, giving the knots a final once-over. "Away you go, Val," she called.

"I've tied the rope around my waist," Val called back. "This is the first time I've wished I went dancing in harness." The rope went taut, rubbing a little against the edge of the hole that led down to the old coal repository. It slipped sideways, and Val cursed.

"I think we'd better hold the rope as well," Jemima suggested. "From the sound of things, Val won't be up to much climbing, and I didn't see any handholds in that chute. Besides, I don't like the way it's rubbing the edge there. It could fray." Her voice held a hint of a quiver. "You know, this rope looks kind of familiar. Like the ropes in Jack's gym."

"More like Val's gym, from what I heard." Freya took hold of the rope in both hands. Jemima placed her phone at the edge of the coal hole, angled it so that the flashlight still shone inside, then also grasped the rope.

This is *the same rope as the stuff in the gym,* Freya realised. *How did Ben get it?* But the needs of the moment pushed the thought out of her head. She and Jemima heaved at the rope. Val uttered a few curses, but her form filled up the coal chute, inching towards them.

"Hold on a mo," Val said after a minute. She rearranged her limbs. Freya realised she had wedged herself into the chute so she wouldn't slip back down again. "Alright, give me a bit of a pull, but not too much. It's slippery with snow or worse in here. And I don't think anyone's scrubbed this place since they last used coal a few decades back. Wish they had."

Jemima and Freya obliged her with a slow and steady pull on the rope, and Val half crouched, half walked her way up the chute. She slipped a few times, her weight jerking the two women forwards. At last, her head emerged.

"This'll be tricky," she remarked. "I think my arms will fall off if I pull myself any more. And I'll fall on my face if I don't."

"You hold the rope, Freya. I'll give you an extra pull up, Val," Jemima decided.

Freya braced herself to take more weight and gave Jemima a nod. Her feet slipped a little on the snowy ground, and her hands burnt from how tightly she was gripping the rope, but she set one foot against the brick of the building. After that, she didn't think she'd give way.

Bending down to reach Val, Jemima put a hand under her arm and pulled. Nothing happened. "Come on, Val, give me a hand. You're really close," Jemima coaxed.

Freya tried pulling the rope herself, with no obvious effect.

With a flash of red fur, Manuel was beside the coal hole. He grasped Val's collar in his teeth and yanked at it, long legs splayed at the very edge of the hole, shoulders braced against the wall of the building on the other side to Freya's foot. Jemima gasped again but kept hold of Val.

"Hey, I like this top," Val complained. But she was now half out of the coal hole, and as Jemima, Manuel and Freya all pulled, she emerged fully, sprawling onto the trampled snow. "I suppose I'll forgive you," she panted, "since there was no chance of a dance down that hole."

Jemima patted her back. "That's more like the Val I know," she said. "Did you hit your head down there?"

Val hauled herself upright and nodded. "When I fell in. There was old furniture and stuff down there, but it wasn't conveniently arranged for anyone to fall onto." She turned to Manuel, who was standing to one side, shivering in great quivers that shook his skinny body. "I guess you don't shift much," she said to him.

His large black eyes opened wider, and he shook his head. The heavy fur around his neck was no longer erect, and he looked miserable. Blood and saliva flattened the fur on his left shoulder.

"Or at all?" Freya guessed.

Manuel dipped his head. Given the length of his dark-furred legs, that brought his head almost, but not quite, to Val's eye level. Freya wondered how Val could stand to be so close to the were's fangs, though she supposed they weren't especially large. For a wolfish thing a metre tall.

Still too large.

"Well, this is interesting," Val said. "I've never met a were who didn't shift regularly. How about you shift back so we can talk about it, Manuel?"

The maned wolf just stood there, head drooping, snow accumulating on the darker ruff that topped his shoulders.

"Can you stop talking to the wild animal as though it's Manuel?" Jemima said. "It's weird. And it still needs a vet to look at that arrow wound. It must be very used to humans, to just stand there; it must have come from a private zoo."

Val turned her bleary gaze on Jemima.

"Girl," she said, "you and me need to have a chat very soon." She turned back to Manuel. "Your problem is way out of my comfort zone. But I'm not going to do a Ben on you. Speaking of which, I am colder than a monkey's backside right now. Let's get back to halls. I am sure we can sort out whatever it is, away from Ben."

"Inside is good," Jemima agreed. "And I can set you straight about animals and humans."

Val rolled her eyes. "Yeah, sure," she said.

"What about Ben?" Freya asked.

"What about him?" said Jemima.

"Well... I guess he deserves to be left in a cellar, but what about the mentor he mentioned? Couldn't that be a problem for us?"

"Don't borrow trouble, Freya," said Val. "We're not home yet, but we're not being attacked by a homicidal ex-friend, either."

"And those crows have disappeared," said Jemima.

"I guess," Freya agreed. The alleyway walls still felt close, and the night, usually a time when Freya walked with her cat, felt dangerous.

What happens if someone with even more power than Ben turns up? And I've got further to go than just to the student halls. Are there still barghests around? I don't want to end up as barghest fodder. But closer to home is definitely better.

CHAPTER FOURTEEN
A QUESTION OF NAMES

The trek back up the hill, past the university and on to the halls of residence, was free of incident, barring the odd slip on paths made slick by wet snow. Fresh snow continued to fall, but it wasn't nearly as heavy as it had been. Occasional cars passed them, sliding around on the slippery streets. Freya tried to tell herself that the exercise of walking kept her warm, but didn't convince even herself.

"Imagine if we had soft, powdery snow instead of this icy stuff," Val complained.

"Imagine if we had no snow at all in October," Freya countered, thinking of every other October she'd known.

Jemima refused to be drawn into the friendly argument. She walked a little apart from the others, and glanced frequently at Manuel, who was walking on all fours between her and Val. Freya felt bad for the girl, who all too clearly didn't want to believe the demi-world was real.

Maybe I should distract her.

Manuel padded up beside them, so Freya dropped back to walk beside Jemima, letting Val lead the way. Although Val *had* hit her head when she fell into the coal hole, she refused to seek medical help, claiming that she had hit it on Ben, and he wasn't nearly as hard as the wall or floor would have been. Freya figured that getting her somewhere she could rest was probably the next best thing.

"Do you live on the same floor as Val?" Freya asked, as they negotiated a steeper slope, clinging to hedges, fences and brick walls to avoid slipping down again.

"Yes," said Jemima. "She's in the room next to mine."

Freya grabbed a branch in the beech hedge she was currently using as a prop, accidentally shaking snow onto herself as she did so. "Ugh. I mean, good. If she got concussed when she fell, Val should have someone check on her."

Jemima looked doubtful. "I don't know that she'll take well to that," she said. She slipped a little, but managed to turn the slip into a slide to the edge of the hedge, where she too grabbed a branch.

"Sure, but better than her having some sort of medical emergency and no-one realising," Freya encouraged her.

"I suppose when you put it that way..." The regular sluff, sluff sound of Jemima's feet hitting the snow assured Freya that she was still right behind her. "Look, about all that stuff Val was talking about."

"Mmm?" Freya reached the end of the beech hedge and switched her handhold to the top of a brick wall, which stretched ahead in a series of decreasing-height levels.

"Frankly, it sounds made up," Jemima said. "But I can't deny that Manuel disappeared, leaving us in the company of a ridiculously docile, singularly out-of-place *maned wolf*, which is not behaving at all the way the ones in documentaries do."

Maybe she doesn't want to be distracted after all.

"And earlier, there was that insane black dog-thing. And I can't see how it's related at all, but there is just no way both the rope and the handholds at the gym could all have given way like they did. I'd never go climbing if that sort of thing happened!"

Freya reached the end of one section of wall and started on the next one. Her hands were lower down than before, making it more awkward to shuffle along—she had to bend her knees a little with each step. She took a moment to look back at Jemima, who had paused at the junction between beech hedge and brick wall, with an introspective expression on her face.

Ah, she's putting the clues together. I thought she'd picked it up earlier, but now she's working it out in a more sciencey way. If that's a thing.

Jemima looked up and met Freya's eyes. Freya instantly looked away, not ready for a deep and meaningful staring session.

"What I want to know," Jemima said, "is if any of that stuff is real, or if this is some crazy reality TV show with insanely good special effects."

"Er. Well, unfortunately, I've never met anyone that good at special effects," Freya said. "And I don't do reality TV either."

"I thought not," Jemima said. "But I didn't want to believe it. So, what are you?"

"Not a were," Freya said firmly.

Jemima started moving again, so Freya swivelled round with care and did the same.

"This is all new to me," Jemima said. "Fill me in on the details a bit, will you? I'm assuming that you mean Manuel is a were-wolf. Or were-maned-wolf, I guess. They're practically vegetarian, you know," she added in an apparent *non sequitur*.

"Good?" Freya said. *That's one point in Manuel's favour, I guess. Though I'm still not a fan of weres of any type.*

"Yes. Definitely good. Val thought you were something different, too. Something like Manuel?"

Freya shuddered at the idea of being mistaken for a were. "I'm nothing like him," she said sharply. "Just your common or garden demigoddess." She winced at how odd that sounded. "And I try not to do anything weird," she added. *Not that that works out often.*

"That's something, then," Jemima said. "But I don't want to be blindsided by someone like Ben again. I would never have guessed he could be that vicious. I was *worried* about him." Jemima appeared puzzled and sorrowful. Thunder growled overhead, not so close as before, but too close for comfort. Snowflakes started to drift down again, fluffier now.

I'd be happier having this debate indoors, too. I hope Mr Fluffbum isn't scared by the storm. Thinking of her cat alone at home, Freya tried to move faster. She ran out of brick wall, started to cross an open driveway and promptly slipped painfully onto one knee. "Ow. Is there any way to the halls which doesn't involve going straight up a hill?"

"Sorry, no. Do you not go this way to get to your flat?" said Jemima.

"I usually go through the council gardens. Downhill, mostly. There's not much up here to draw me." Freya managed to cross the driveway and catch hold of an overgrowth of Japanese knotweed, which was obscuring whatever wall or fence had previously existed underneath it. "Though I have to admit, there's plenty of foliage here."

"I haven't visited the gardens yet. I've been going out to the moors on the weekends," Jemima said. "Ben came too, sometimes. That's partly why it's such a shock, the way he acted. I thought he was a friend," she added.

"Well, I haven't known Ben long enough to know what to expect, but I'll definitely be avoiding him in future. Val seems alright though," Freya tried to inject some enthusiasm into her voice, a difficult task when pulling herself uphill in a snowstorm.

"Yeah, Val's great," Jemima agreed. "She's always got new ideas. I'm just not convinced about this latest one. I mean, belief doesn't will things into existence. There's got to be a scientific explanation." She crossed the driveway faster than Freya had managed, and without slipping. The fresh snow was building up now, less slippery than slush.

Freya paused, hands full of knotweed stems. "I don't know exactly what she is," she said. "And she's obviously been taught differently to me. But I'm here to get away from that sort of thing if I can. I *want* to focus on scientific explanations. Maybe there's a good reason for some people being different, like Val and Ben and Manuel. Maybe science just hasn't figured it out yet."

Jemima caught up to her while she spoke, and clung on to the knotweed next to Freya. "That sounds better than belief to me," she said. "I can work with that." She looked ahead at Manuel's reddish fur and Val's hand resting lightly on his ruff. "Although it's a stretch for weres to exist," she said quietly.

Freya patted her on the shoulder. "You'll get used to it." She sighed. "And I know Val wants to have a talk with you herself, but have you noticed the way the thunder and snow comes and goes with your emotions?"

Jemima's eyes grew round as lightning lit up the clouds, thunder on its heels. Then she shook her head. "Coincidence," she said firmly.

"Maybe," Freya said. "I'm all in favour of a mundane explanation. But... maybe check your ancestry." She started walking again; the road levelled out after the knotweed hedge, and she could see a tall building with the university's logo on it in the near distance. "Is that your building?" she asked.

"It is," Jemima said. "And I'll have you know that my ancestors are very ordinary Celts and the like, nothing weird."

"Ah." Freya kept herself moving this time as she mentally worked her way through the various gods, goddesses and mythical beings that she'd studied as homework all her school life. "Could be Taranis, then," she said at last.

"And what's that when it's at home?" Jemima asked, an edge to her voice.

Freya walked the final few metres to the entrance of the halls before answering. She could see Val in the entrance lobby, beckoning her to come in, but turned to Jemima to answer before opening the door. "Taranis is the Celtic god of thunder," she said.

"No relation," Jemima said firmly, reaching the shelter of the building just as thunder rolled around the sky once again. "And I think Val should have known better than to tell you my real first name."

Freya blinked in surprise. "Your real name? I thought Jemima was your name. I don't think Val said anything else," she said.

"She must have, for you to come up with that idea," Jemima insisted. "My first name—which I don't like, by the way—is Tara."

Chapter Fifteen
Checking in at the Halls

Freya entered the lobby of the halls of residence just in time to be showered with water droplets, as Manuel shook himself beside Val then whimpered in pain.

"Ugh."

There was some sort of receptionist in the lobby. She glared at Manuel.

"No pets allowed," she proclaimed in a nasal voice. "You'll need to remove that... dog... pronto."

Interesting, the pause she puts around 'dog'. I guess she can see Manuel isn't one.

Val turned to the receptionist and set to work.

"Oh, he's not a pet, he's a stray. But he'd die out there. It's snowing! And he's injured, look! Can't I take him to..." She paused for a moment, perhaps thinking of a suitable place. "To the rubbish room? Just until the snow stops, and then I'll take him to the pound. Please?"

The woman glanced outside. Even in the dark, the snow was clearly falling thickly, piling up beyond the entrance of the building. Manuel turned a little so that his injured shoulder was clearly visible in the receptionist's desk light. It had bled more during the walk home, Freya saw. It looked awful.

"I'll stay with him to make sure he doesn't make a mess," Val added.

Manuel pricked his large ears forward and looked beseechingly at the woman. He didn't want to be left outside.

"Oh, very well. But make sure he's gone by dawn," the woman agreed.

"Thanks, I'll make sure of it," Val said. She gave Manuel's head the sort of ruffle Freya had seen people giving their favourite dogs and walked towards the elevator.

"Coming up, Freya?" she asked. "You should warm up before heading out again."

"You'll need to sign her in as a guest," the receptionist reminded Val. "And the rubbish room is down the stairs, not up the elevator." She gave Val a stern glare.

"I'll do it," Jemima said, stepping toward the reception desk.

Freya didn't really want to stay out longer—there had been too many things happen tonight already—but she couldn't deny that she was chilled through. Perhaps a pause inside was a good idea before heading home.

After Freya was signed in as a guest, the four of them entered the stairwell. The door swung automatically closed after them.

Val leant back against the wall as soon as they were out of sight. "Nevermore," she said dramatically.

"What?" Jemima's brow wrinkled as she tried to work out what Val meant.

"Nevermore shall I climb any more stairs," Val explained. "It's because of the crows, get it?"

"No," Freya said.

Val sighed. "That was probably the first and only time I get to use that line, and it's wasted. It's Edgar Allan Poe. Why don't I know more English lit students? Anyway, I'm pooped. Exhausted. Done. Give me a hand, will you?"

Remembering that Val had had some serious bumps that evening, Freya moved forward to support her. Jemima hung back, looking with concern at Manuel's shoulder. He returned her gaze, gave a small nod, and they set off up the narrow stairs, Manuel giving a heaving jump on every other step.

"Just as well I'm only on the second floor," Val said, as they heaved their way up, stair by stair.

"Yes, or you'd be bunking down in the rubbish room where Manuel's supposed to be," Jemima agreed, her breath coming in pants. She must have accepted that Manuel's was the were-maned-wolf, Freya noted. She nodded, with no breath to spare. Val wasn't light, though she was still on her feet. "You weren't really going to leave him there, were you?" she added, glancing down at Manuel, who was clearly finding the stairs hard going with a shoulder wound.

"Course not," Val said. "Though I might get one of you to go down and bang a door or so for verisi-si-" She hesitated, perhaps experiencing some effects from her concussion. "I mean, so it sounds like we took him there."

"I'll be warm through by the second floor," Freya said. She was panting too, although she'd thought she was fit these days.

If she'd had extra layers of clothing, she would have stripped them off by the time they reached the required floor. Val directed them along the hall to her room. She unlocked it and staggered in under her own steam. Freya closed the door behind them. The room was small enough to be crowded with the four of them, and it quickly grew muggy with their combined warmth and breath.

"I'm going to lie down for a bit," Val announced, taking off her corvid-decorated jacket. "Freya, you'd better see if you can get Manuel to shift. Otherwise, Miss Bossy downstairs will have a fit. I don't want to have to take him to the pound."

"They'd probably feed him the wrong diet," Jemima agreed.

Freya wondered if she was joking.

Manuel gave a whine. He obviously didn't like the idea of going to an animal rescue institute, either.

Freya stared at the were in consternation.

"I don't know how to make a were shift," she said. "And I need to get home to my cat before he freezes. Or more likely, starts destroying the couch."

Jemima looked worried again, out of her depth. Val lay down on her bed, shoes and all.

"Think of something," she ordered. Then she closed her eyes and appeared to fall asleep.

I guess she really did need to rest.

Freya looked at Manuel helplessly. *How am I supposed to get a were to shift? It's not like I'm one.*

"Think about how you did it in the first place?" she suggested.

Manuel cocked his head on one side, then leapt at her.

Freya screamed involuntarily and ducked sideways.

Manuel missed her by a whisker and thumped into the wall. He whimpered again.

There was a muffled curse from the other side of the wall, as whichever student lived there was awoken by the thump.

"Sorry," Jemima called.

Manuel bounded to his feet, still all maned wolf.

"Don't try that again," Freya ordered, her voice more shrill than usual.

Manuel leapt sideways instead, knocking over a pile of textbooks that Val had left stacked on the floor.

"I don't think leaping about is key," Freya told him. "You were pretty stressed when you shifted, right? Maybe it's an emotional response thing."

I feel like a psychologist now, Freya thought. *All 'tell me how you were feeling when you did that thing.' Still, the sooner he's shifted back, the sooner I can leave. And we'd better get him shifted before he wakes up any more students.*

"Think of what Ben was doing then," she said aloud. Manuel growled, his head sinking below his shoulders as the dark mane of fur there stood on end.

"I hope that bastard wakes up feeling like an ice block," Jemima said. "That rope he had; I think it was the rest of my climbing rope. The one that broke. I need someone really calculating to help get the better of him." Thunder muttered outside, present, but not as loud as before.

Smart thinking, Freya thought. *Appealing to Manuel's most human side. At least, I assume maned wolves aren't into maths.*

Manuel's growl shifted pitch as he straightened up and became substantially less hairy. Also, substantially more human-shaped.

"You want calculating? I'm your man," he said in a voice that echoed his recent growl. "Maths by major, mathematician by nature." Then he snatched at Val's bedclothes as he realised he'd shifted into nudity.

"Sorry, ladies," he added in his normal voice. "Who stole my jeans?" Then he winced and put a hand to his shoulder. Apparently shifting didn't magically heal arrow wounds.

Freya and Jemima glanced at each other and burst into laughter.

"I didn't see where they went," Jemima said. "You're my first were." She shook her head. "This is insane. I can't believe it's real."

"Too real for me," Freya said. "But now you're all safe and human, more or less, I'm going home."

Jemima looked out the window. "Are you sure?" she said. "It's not great walking weather."

"I know," Freya said. "But my cat needs me. And I often go walking at night."

Jemima looked sceptical. "He's a cat. Surely, he'll be fine if you leave him inside for one night?"

Freya watched the snowflakes flurrying through the dark sky for a few moments. It was so very tempting to stay where she was, safe and warm inside.

"Probably. But... it's been a rough night. I really want to be at home, in my own bed. And Mr Fluffbum—my cat—is a bit of an Houdini, but he hasn't been outside in this city yet. You're supposed to give cats at least four weeks inside, you know, when you move houses. I don't want to give him a reason to escape my flat, and have him get lost trying to walk home."

Jemima looked at Freya, then out the window, weighing up something. "OK. Well... now that Manuel is himself, perhaps he can keep an eye on Val. I'll see you home. It's probably not safe to go out alone."

"Then it wouldn't be safe for you to return alone, either," Freya pointed out. "Don't worry about me. I'll be fine."

"I may not be used to this weather, but I am sure none of us should go out alone in it," Manuel said. "I will ask the halls manager to check on Val. Once we have more clothing on—" He glanced down at himself. "Better winter clothing on," he amended, "then the three of us can go, leaving Jemima and I to return together. Agreed?"

"What about your hurt shoulder?" Jemima protested.

Manuel felt at his left shoulder with his right hand. A pained expression crossed his face, but his hand came away from the wounded area clean. "I am no longer bleeding," he said. "I'll live."

"It's agreed, then." Freya smiled at Manuel, surprised to be feeling grateful to a were. But it did seem much the best plan.

Five minutes later, Manuel and Jemima returned to Val's room, where Freya had been keeping watch on Val—a boring job enlivened only by Val's light snoring, once Freya had removed Val's shoes and found a blanket to put over her. Freya felt her heart lift unexpectedly at their return. Manuel had another pair of jeans on, indistinguishable from his previous pair, topped with a wool jumper and an anorak. Jemima was laden with clothing. They were trailed by Nesh, one of the other guys from the pub who'd chosen to go home rather than out dancing. It felt to Freya as though it had been years since she had sat in the sun in the student tavern, rather than mere hours.

"Good news," said Manuel. "I ran into Nesh in the corridor. He's going to look after Val. So we don't have to bring the halls people into this."

"Anything that keeps me inside and warm," Nesh said with a disarming grin. "Plus, it should get Lin on my good side."

Freya suspected that if Lin, one of the other students who'd decided against going out clubbing, had wanted to be onside with Nesh, she'd have made that clear by now. Still, she didn't know the girl. Perhaps Nesh had a chance.

"Good luck with that," Jemima said, clearly agreeing with Freya's unspoken thought. "It will take more than a bit of nurse-maiding to win her over. Especially when you're looking after someone else."

"Small steps," said Nesh. "Besides, it shows off my warm and caring personality." He gave Freya a wink, then pulled out the wheeled chair from in front of the desk that filled one wall, spun it once and took a seat facing Val. "Right," he said. "I'm good. You can head out if you're set on experiencing that crazy weather firsthand."

Jemima hefted the winter coat she had unfolded from over one arm. She pulled a knitted hat out of a pocket, followed by a pair of gloves. "OK, I'm ready for anything. Anyone got something Freya can borrow? I only brought one set of woollens to halls."

"Borrow Val's things," Nesh said, swinging a leg lazily. "You can bring them back with you."

"Won't she mind?" Freya said.

"Nah, she's always lending out her stuff. So long as it gets back to her, she'll be fine."

Freya still wasn't convinced. "I'd rather borrow stuff from someone who isn't unconscious."

Jemima, who'd been adding layers of clothing while they talked, finished pulling on her gloves. "Ask Lin," she said. "Or no, anything of Lin's will be too small. Nesh, why don't you offer Freya some of your winter clothes stash. You're always wearing too many layers."

"But I need all my warm gear," Nesh grumbled.

"In here?" Jemima asked acerbically.

"Lending your warm things to Freya will show Lin what a kind heart you have," Manuel noted.

"Oh, all right then. But you guys have to make sure she knows about it."

"But of course," Manuel agreed.

Chapter Sixteen

A Walk in the Park

Freya felt ridiculous when at last she exited the halls. She was much warmer, true, but Nesh was considerably taller than her, and his warm jacket hung to her knees. She had to keep pushing back his woollen cap as it slipped over her eyes.

"You're sure you don't want to wear this hat, Manuel?" she asked again.

"No, I am warm enough, thank you," he assured her. "Just sore."

Freya suspected he might be laughing at her, based on the glint in his eyes, but at least he wasn't openly mocking. That didn't seem to be his style, anyway.

"Let's go," she said, biting back several uncomplimentary replies. It wasn't his fault he was a were... no matter how much that fact unnerved her. She remembered the grisly hole the arrow had made in his shoulder and grimaced. No-one deserved that sort of treatment.

Jemima and Manuel flanked her at first, until the path grew too narrow, when they fell into line behind her.

"How far do we have to go?" Jemima asked. "Oh, that didn't come out right. I mean, how far is your place?" She suppressed a yawn.

Freya was reminded that Jemima had already had run from a barghest, had a terrifying fall, and an altercation with a demi who'd previously acted like a friend that evening. And that wasn't counting

"""

the dancing. For that matter, she was exhausted herself. *None of us are in great shape for a night-time trek. Maybe I should have stayed at the halls. Mr Fluffbum would probably have been all right. But it's getting colder.*

"I'm not sure how long it will take in this snow," she said. "Maybe fifteen minutes? It's not too far." Freya hoped she wasn't wildly underestimating the time it would take, but she was glad of the company. She didn't usually walk about so late, at least not without her cat. She probably shouldn't walk alone *with* her cat either, she reflected, but the habit was hard to break.

Ploughing through untrodden snow with every step, she was glad not to be alone this time, and gladder still of the borrowed layers. Though the wind seemed to have died down for now, it was still bitingly cold.

Maybe I'm just not used to the cold after that long hot spell we've had, she reflected. *What are the chances that Jemima's not a demi after all? It would be nice to have a friend who is mundane. Mundanes have so few complications.*

They had reached the edge of the public park—the last obstacle before they reached Freya's flat—before she realised there was one thing she was missing from her outfit.

Nails! I don't have any iron, steel or anything. But I've been safe till now without it. Maybe it's just an odd fetish of Val's that she likes to carry them. And maybe the barghest was just a local fluke. Freya glanced around. They would have to leave the tram tracks to go through the park. But the alternative was to go almost twice as far around the edge of the park. *No, we'll take the park path. It'll be fine.* She crossed her fingers inside her voluminous sleeves.

Freya strode onto the path that wound down the gentle slope towards a small bridge over a winding brook, hoping a confident stride would deter anything that might be out in the night. The path was only visible because of the clumps of bushes on either side, and the brook appeared as a wavy line through the snow. Tall trees surrounded the park, and usually, a grassy lawn took up the rest of the space. Tonight, everything was white, the lines of bushes softened by snow. Those branches not protected by leaves were highlighted with a layer of white frosting. Freya found her eyes playing tricks on her as the lights from surrounding streets dimmed and brightened in unexpected moments thanks to trees tossing in occasional gusts of wind. Shadows shifted, and it was hard to focus on the path as she became more unnerved by the thought that something was hiding in those bushes, or maybe even stalking behind them. *Stop that!* she told herself. It didn't really help. She crossed the small bridge, thankful it was almost flat, so wasn't too slippery, then stopped.

"Jemima, Manuel, there's enough space for us to walk together here," she said, wanting to be sure of the location of her companions. It wouldn't do to lose them in the snowy park.

There was silence. Freya's half-formed fears leapt into full-blown terror.

"Jemima?" *I should never have trusted a were.*

But Freya realised her leap of mistrust was unearned when she saw Manuel and Jemima a little way back up the slope. Manuel was standing between Jemima and a huge black dog with glowing eyes.

Frigg! Another barghest. What do I do now?

As Freya started to run back towards the pair, a gust of wind slammed into her, nearly throwing her to the ground. Icy particles flung themselves in her face, forcing her to squint her eyes closed. She gritted her teeth and kept going. Thunder exploded practically above her and she covered her ears.

I would put money on someone around here being a thunder demi. But is it Jemima or Manuel? Val thought Jemima might be one, but I suppose a were could have demi heritage as well.

Freya didn't have any more time to ponder who was or was not a demi. As the thunder ended, the snow began again, harder than ever. In a few strides, she could barely make out Jemima or Manuel. The barghest disappeared completely.

"Are you okay?" she panted as she reached the pair. She skirted around to Jemima's side, keeping the other girl between herself and Manuel.

Jemima had her fists tightly clenched and a layer of snow on her woollen hat. Her eyes were wide and flicked here and there. "I'd be OK if that awful dog hadn't turned up again. Can you see where it went?" She turned all the way around, trying to spot a black dog on a dark and stormy night.

"No idea, sorry. I thought it was going to leap on you when that thunder happened. Perhaps it was scared off?" Freya hazarded.

Manuel nodded slowly. "I believe you may be correct. But if that is so, it will not be gone for long. We should move. Also, it is getting colder." He gave a dramatic shiver. "Did you know that humans can experience lung damage in as little as fifteen minutes at zero degrees?"

"I didn't know that. I wish I still didn't," said Freya. She wrapped her arms tightly around herself. *I suspect that demigoddesses have the same freezing time as humans. Unless they're an ice demi, perhaps? But since I'm not... Brr.* "I'm sure that's without clothes or something," she added.

"I'm still more worried about dangerous dogs on the loose," Jemima said.

"Fine. Can you see the path anymore?"

Jemima shook her head slowly. "It's too dark here. All I can see is snow. We should never have come through the park."

"It's usually the fastest way," Freya said, defending her choice of route and trying not to sound whiny. She fumbled in her pocket with hands made clumsy by the cold. Surely... Yes. She pulled out her new phone, and this time managed to find the flashlight function. Its white beam highlighted snowflake after swirling snowflake. She angled it towards the ground and saw her own footprints rapidly filling with snow.

Think, Freya. You came uphill from the brook. So going downhill, you'll reach the brook again. That's in the right direction, at least. And running water might help ward off the barghest too.

"Come on," she said. "I think I know which way to go."

Chapter Seventeen
Not Quite a Trackless Wilderness

It was hard work slogging through the snow, even though the fury of the blizzard calmed a little after they got going. It was harder still figuring out which way the ground sloped when they could barely see it. Freya tripped over bushes several times, and the layers she wore became damp as snow got up her sleeves and down into her shoes. It even swirled past her face into her hood, where it melted in cool trickles.

Jemima and Manuel seemed to have similar problems, though with his longer legs, Manuel was able to step over those bushes that he saw in time. After some experimentation the three kept their arms linked, Jemima in the middle, Freya taking the lead, so as not to lose one another. Freya expected the barghest to reappear at any moment, and the thought kept her heart racing.

She found the stream by stepping into it. Her damp shoes were instantly soaking wet. "I know where we are," she said. "And the good news is that we shouldn't be able to lose this landmark."

"What's the bad news, then?" Jemima asked warily.

"We're probably all best to walk in the brook," Freya said. "We can't get lost that way." *Unless the local water deity gets annoyed, of course.*

"No way am I getting myself wet in this snowstorm," Manuel stated flatly. "The heat transfer coefficient would be insane."

"Won't the stream bed be slippery?" Jemima said, more practically, to Freya's mind.

Freya knew they both had good points, but she didn't want to keep wandering in the cold and dark all night. But, her wet feet were rapidly becoming numb. And some water deities objected to people walking in them. She *had* introduced herself to the water spirit in this brook when she first arrived, and he had been surprisingly polite—but he would probably not be one to appreciate being trampled on. She hauled herself out of the stream. More snow lodged in the top of her trainers as she did so. No doubt it would turn to ice in her shoes.

"Give me a better idea," she said, standing on one foot and trying to angle her trainer so it drained. It didn't work terribly well.

"Surely we won't get lost if we stay beside the brook," Jemima said.

"It's rather hard to see it. I know, I just fell in," Freya said. "With all the snow around, the banks blend in."

"I'm open to anything that gets us away from that dog, wherever it is," Jemima said. She glanced behind her, as though it would appear there. "Except walking in the stream. Can we keep moving, please?"

Freya was equally keen to move, but an idea struck her. "I want to try one thing first," she said. "Stay there. Actually, come upstream a bit. There should be a bridge."

Keeping the brook on her left, she moved slowly upstream, using the sound of it as much as anything to keep close, but not so close that she walked into it again. The other two followed her, though not without grumbling. It didn't take too long to find what she was looking for, fortunately. A short way upstream, they came to the bridge she'd been crossing when the barghest appeared. It was dispiriting to see how little ground they'd covered, but she stepped onto the bridge and rubbed away snow from the railing.

As I thought. It's got steel handrails. That should help keep the barghest at bay, if running water doesn't. But we can't stand around by the bridge all night. And the brook is in the middle of the park. We'll have to leave it behind to get home.

"Come on up," she said. "I'm going to go a couple of metres upstream—don't worry, I'll stick by the brook—and see if I can get some help so we can get to my place safely."

"Don't be stupid, Freya. *We're* walking *you* home, remember?" Jemima joined her on the bridge, but protested her plan.

Freya ignored Jemima's outburst and jumped lightly off onto the right-hand bank of the stream—*one step closer to home*—before beginning to trudge upstream. "Just stay there, alright?" she repeated.

"Freya!"

Freya quickened her step, not wanting to be stopped. She only went a few more metres before reaching a handy weeping willow hanging over the brook. She ducked behind its trunk—although it was still leafy, she wanted to be well hidden while she called on the river spirit, and the trunk would do a better job as a shield than flimsy leaves. Actually... She snapped off a few long twigs and wove them together, more by feel than anything else. The darkness would definitely hide her, Freya decided. She turned off her phone's flashlight. She used a wet trainer to draw a circle around herself, then waving the willow wand, sang quiet and low. *Low with bubbly bits*, she thought, as she pictured the stream in her mind. She adjusted her song, though it was hard to sing 'bubbly bits'. She tried quick variations in tone instead.

Definitely not time to join a choir, she thought wryly as she sang.

To her immense satisfaction, the resident brook spirit appeared before her, almost invisible in the dark but for the glimmers of light from the snow refracting through it.

No kobolds or grindylows here. Thank goodness.

She whispered a greeting to the water deity, mindful that Manuel and Jemima were close by.

It bowed to her, a welcome change from previous water spirits who had given her sarcastic answers, or demanded obscure payments.

"I need protection from a barghest," she explained. "Any ideas?"

The brook babbled something incomprehensible.

"Slower, please," Freya whispered.

Instead of answering in words, the brook spirit collapsed back in on itself with a splash.

"That's hardly poli—" Freya began to say, when the brook developed a series of ripples.

An otter appeared almost at Freya's feet, towing something in its mouth. It spat it out, turned around, and dived back into the brook without even a splash, before Freya could bend down to see what it had brought. *A chain! It looks like an old carpark barrier.* The links of the chain disappeared into the brook; it had clearly been too heavy for the otter to drag all the way out. But when Freya pulled on it, well over a metre of solid steel links appeared, only slightly slimed with algae.

"Oh. This is perfect!" she said aloud. "Thank you!" *This must be the most polite water spirit I've ever dealt with.*

She couldn't help but wonder if she would have had such a good result with the much larger but more constrained river Don, or the similarly maltreated river Sheaf. Then again, the larger rivers would have much more power. She smiled to herself as she imagined what sort of steel the Don might have brought her. A string of old shopping trolleys, perhaps? Though that would have been harder to use. She pushed aside images of Manuel and Jemima squeezing into a single trolley to avoid the advances of a barghest. It was fairly clear that Manuel was more interested in Jemima than in her.

And that's a good thing, I don't need any complications here. Freya told her internal voice to hush and wound the chain into a more portable loop and hitched it up over one shoulder. "I'm on my way back, Jemima," she called.

"About time," Jemima replied, her voice only a little muffled by snowfall. "Hurry up. The water level keeps going up and down in this stream. It's not natural."

Freya grinned to herself.

Not natural at all. And Jemima's pretty observant. I wonder if that's normal for mundanes? Or for not-really mundanes who've been raised as plain humans? If she isn't mundane, when did her family lose their knowledge of the supernatural?

"Also, I am getting cold, standing still," Manuel added. "Perhaps I am already suffering lung damage."

"I hope you survive it," Freya said drily. "Try covering your mouth with your scarf, that might slow the damage. People have lived in this climate, or something like it, for centuries. It should be possible."

"But I am from a tropical zone. I'm not acclimatised yet," Manuel moaned.

"You're complaining about the weather, that makes you practically a native already," Jemima commented.

Freya snorted her laughing agreement and started back towards them, following the crushed snow trail she'd left on her way upstream, her footprints not yet covered over.

After a minute or so she could see the dark shapes of Manuel and Jemima standing on the bridge. As she scanned the area, she spotted another dark shape. Watching them from behind a large snow-covered lump that was probably a shrub, but could equally have been a piece of statuary or a stone wall, was the barghest. Its eyes glowed, somehow reflecting starlight that wasn't there. A chill went down Freya's spine. At least it wasn't attacking right now, but was it being kept at bay by the steel? The brook? She didn't want to experiment, but if they were to get home, she had no choice.

That's why you called the brook, remember?

"I'm about ready to move," she said. "I thought we'd better..." *I can't say what Val told me about iron, can I? Not that talking to a mundane stopped Val, but it still doesn't seem right, when Jemima's origins aren't certain. I wish I had Aisha's ability to tell demis and weres from mundanes. Then Manuel wouldn't have surprised me.*

Inventing an excuse on the spot, she continued. "I think we'd better rope ourselves together, so we don't lose each other again. I found this chain. That should work." She shook the chain a little to emphasise its presence. It was heavy, and made annoying metallic sounds close to her ear, but surely it wouldn't be so bad once all three of them were holding it?

She was close enough now to see Jemima's expression of disbelief, verging on terror.

"You want us to *chain* ourselves together for a walk in the park?"

"Not exactly," Freya hastened to say. "We can hold on to it. I could barely see you just now. If I hadn't been following the brook, I'd have lost you again." *That much is true.*

"It is a good idea," Manuel said. "Very common for mountain climbers, though usually a rope is used rather than a chain."

Manuel's endorsement clearly counted.

"Oh, all right then," Jemima agreed, although there was a tremor in her voice. "Pass over an end. Though I've had enough of ropes and climbing for one night. Probably for ever."

"Climbing's not usually like that, is it?" Freya asked.

"No," Jemima agreed. "It should *never* be like that." She shuddered visibly.

"Good to know. We won't go climbing this time round. Promise."

Jemima gave Freya a half-hearted smile. "I'm holding you to that," she said.

"You take the middle. Tallest person last, and I should lead the way since we're going to my house." Freya didn't want to point out that it was Jemima that the barghest was targeting, assuming it wasn't her.

Although, she supposed it could also be targeting her, and Jemima kept getting in the way. But why would either of them be subject to harassment by barghest? And besides, she'd been alone several times now without the barghest attacking her.

This thunderstorm seems to be more than just a climatic inconvenience, the way it comes and goes. I'd put money on Jemima being a demi. But even so, Jemima's not the sort of person you'd expect to be visited by a harbinger of death. Nor is Manuel. Even Val would be a more likely target.

First step, get home safely. And to do that, we need to not get lost in the snow.

Chapter Eighteen
The Chains That Bind

She wrapped the chain around her wrist, then passed one end to Jemima. Jemima struggled for a couple of minutes, trying to do the same, before giving up and simply grasping the chain with her glove-covered hand.

"That'll do, won't it?" she said, passing the remaining chain to Manuel, who stood close enough to shield her from the wind-blown snow. Manuel efficiently threaded the chain through the belt loop on his jeans.

"Your method should work as well as mine," he said to Jemima, giving her a bright smile.

Freya found herself wishing he'd continued to show special attention to *her*. It wasn't that she was especially attracted to Manuel. She just felt left out, especially since she was so far from her closest friends now that she was attending university in a new city.

Feeling like the third wheel of a group is never fun. Try to feel happy for them anyway, Freya told herself. *You have friends. Elsewhere.* It was still an internal struggle. *Remember Karim,* she told herself sternly. Then she wished that Karim had written more in his email than simply the details of the best mobile phone purveyor in South Yorkshire. The lack of detail had made his message feel impersonal, rather than the letter full of longing for her which she secretly wanted to have received. *I guess that's why I'm feeling on the outer. It's nothing to do with Manuel or Jemima, really. I just don't belong here. Yet. Focus on the present, Freya. Karim always does.* The last thought didn't really console her, but the reality of being out in a storm did help to focus her mind.

"Right, now we won't lose each other," she said. "Let's get going. Upstream should work for now, but the exit to the park is... sort of west. That way." She pointed in approximately the right direction. She hoped. "The only problem is, there's a fence all around the top end of the park, so we'll need to go through a gate. That means we should leave the brook about halfway up the park, otherwise we'll have to spend longer out here."

"Let us move, then," Manuel said. "I cannot take these temperatures much longer."

Jemima nodded.

Freya set out upstream, past her willow-framed hiding spot. She found it wasn't as easy as she'd hoped it would be to walk while chained to others. Every time she stumbled, she pulled Jemima. Every time Manuel or Jemima stumbled, they pulled her. Freya got colder and colder. She felt her irritation grow as they continued in a push-me-pull-you manner. Thunder continually muttered around the edges of the sky, matching her feelings—*or perhaps*, she thought, *matching Jemima's feelings. If she's appreciating Manuel's gallant behaviour at all, it's not coming through in thunder.*

Freya lurched as she put her foot into a deep hollow, rendered invisible by snow, catching herself on the snowy ground with her gloved hands. The chain between them pulled tight, yanking Jemima's sleeve off her shoulder.

At the same moment, a massive streak of lightning forked down a short way ahead, striking a tall tree that stood by the edge of the brook. Freya stared up in disbelief as white lightning ripped down the length of the tree's trunk, crackling wildly. Ozone filled the air, wild and dangerous. There was a burst of flames as the tree was set alight. The associated thunder shook Freya and her friends like an earthquake; there was no three-second wait after the lightning for that sound. The smell of burning wood invaded Freya's nose, and she felt herself tremble with the power of the electrical storm. It was almost as though its wild power was a part of her. Snowflakes melted on her cheeks and dripped off her nose and eyelashes. The moment was somehow visceral, making Freya feel intensely alive, aware of every hair on her body, every snowflake falling on her face, every shrub and tree nearby. The image of the tree being struck by lightning was imprinted on the back of her eyelids.

"That was... something," she gasped incoherently after a few moments.

Recovering a little from her open-mouthed shock, she realised she should check on Jemima and Manuel. Jemima had been pulled to her knees by Freya's fall. Manuel had caught up with Jemima, perhaps balancing his fall with a stride of his long legs, and his hand was extended as though to offered her assistance, but both he and Jemima stared at the flaming tree with a similar expression to the one Freya felt on her own face.

"That was insane," Jemima muttered. She bit her lip, perhaps realising how close they had been to being electrified by the storm themselves, but her gaze softened as she saw Manuel's outstretched hand, and she gave him a small smile which he returned with a blazing one of his own. Looking on, it was hard for Freya to see Manuel as a dangerous were in that moment. Even her bubbling jealousy of Manuel's obvious admiration for Jemima seemed a small and petty thing compared to the awe-inspiring moment when the lightning seared the tree.

"Crazy," Freya agreed. "Just... wow. Um. Are you guys OK?"

"I am fine," Manuel said. "Although the chance of being that close to a tree struck by lightning is somewhat less than six per cent. At least, that is the chance of any given tree being struck. You would have to have good population density data to work out the probability of a person being nearby at the time. Ah... Are you intact, Jemima?"

Jemima pulled herself to her feet with Manuel's assisting hand when he paused in his statistical burbling.

"We need to get indoors, fast. Six per cent is not a low enough chance for me. And I do *not* like this chain," she bit out. "It's cold, it's heavy, it's not working for me. And how are we supposed to follow the brook past *that*?" She pointed at the now-flaming tree. Snowflakes fluttered onto her outstretched arm, and she shook them off irritably. Apparently, Jemima manifested her shock at the lightning strike as anger, despite her earlier smile for Manuel. Thunder growled again, although Freya didn't see any lightning with it.

We need to get her calmed down, or there's likely to be more... weather. The heat of the tree's burning warmed Freya's cheeks even at this distance—a pleasant sensation compared to the biting cold. She wondered, briefly and wildly, if they should go closer to the fiery tree to warm up. *Probably not. No matter how tempting the warmth.* She understood all of a sudden how difficult it must have been for people her parents' age to give up their fireplaces when the climate regulations went through. Not that everyone had, of course. Heating was too important, even with climate change. Perhaps more so, given the wild fluctuations in weather.

Imagine having a tamed fire spirit in your living room. The power of it would draw you in just like this. The heat of the fire almost pulled her towards it. There wasn't much wind, and the smoke from the burning tree grew thicker, acrid and stinging in Freya's eyes. Even so, she couldn't stop looking at the tree. *What if we'd been a few steps closer? We could all have been electrocuted. Jemima's right, we do need to get inside fast. Somehow. And get away from that tree before I run towards it.*

Snowflakes fell gently, inexorably around them. The shoulders of all their coats were white with the chilly flakes. The side of Freya that was further from the fire grew cold, and colder still. *I'm not shivering, though. Shouldn't I be shivering?*

"I don't know that we *can* follow the brook anymore," she admitted. "Let's strike out for the wall instead. We're probably at a good point to do that, anyway. But I don't have any idea how we can keep together without the chain." She really didn't want Jemima, or herself, exposed to that barghest. She wasn't sure how a barghest would react to Manuel, as a were, but she didn't want to find out. And getting lost was a real possibility, although they'd managed with linked arms earlier. Frostbite was even more likely given the amount of snow on the ground and in the air.

"I will stay looped to the chain, and you can too. Perhaps Jemima can hold on to me instead of the chain," Manuel suggested. "That way, she will not get pulled over unless I fall, which is unlikely." Freya had to admit he had a point—so far, it had mostly been *her* doing the falling. And surely if Jemima was that close to the iron chain, she'd gain some protection from barghests.

"I suppose that might work," Jemima said, losing some of the irritation from her voice. She looked Manuel up and down as though inspecting him, then gave a short nod. "OK, we'll give that a try," she said. "I think if we go perpendicular to the brook, we should be going in the right direction."

"Now you are speaking my language," said Manuel, the smile evident in his voice.

"Always the mathematician," Jemima said, a smile softening the tease.

"Always."

Trying to quash the feeling that she was once again being left out, Freya turned her back on the stream, keeping the burning tree on her right, then struck out cross country. She didn't mind being left out if the alternative was cosying up to a were. Even if she was working hard to keep that were safe.

At first, the light from the flames helped, letting her see otherwise hidden branches and other obstacles. But as they moved away from the brook, the flickering flames played tricks with her eyesight, and she found herself trying to step over things which weren't there, or stepping short when her foot struck something under the snow.

"This is a nightmare," she muttered aloud. "I just want to get home. Surely that wall should be coming up soon?"

"We are going better than before, at least," Manuel said. "Perhaps thirty per cent more efficiency per step, I would estimate."

Jemima snorted with amusement at Manuel's statement.

"Oh, great." *If Manuel is that mathematical all the time, Jemima is welcome to him.* Freya wasn't in the mood for efficiency calculations. She glanced behind her to check on the position of the lightning-struck tree. It was only just smouldering now, hard to see through the snow. "Fenrir's teeth, when will this storm die down?" Hoping she was still heading in the right direction—*how big could a park be, anyway?*—she led the small group onwards.

"I'm getting tired," Jemima said some time later. "I thought this park was long and narrow. How come we haven't crossed it yet?"

Even her voice sounds tired. I feel the same. And shouldn't I be able to feel my feet?

The cold brook water must have frozen her trainers. Freya wriggled her toes to make sure she still could, and pain lanced through them.

We've got to get out of this cold.

Freya looked around again. She could no longer see the burning tree, but she couldn't see the fence that should surround the park, either.

"We must have got turned around," she said. Even to herself, she sounded defeated.

"Perhaps we should simply pick a direction and go," said Manuel. "Eventually we will reach the edge of the park."

"Or we'll go in circles again," Jemima said. "It's pointless. We should just... I don't know. Huddle and stay where we are."

"We'll freeze if we do that," Freya said. "I'm half-frozen, even though we're moving. Aren't you?"

Reluctant agreement emerged from Manuel and Jemima. Peering at them—there was very little light in the park now that the tree was no longer burning, although the white blanket of snow on the ground maximised what little light there was—Freya thought Jemima's lips looked dark with cold. So did Manuel's. She looked around, searching for a direction, and a flicker of darkness against snow caught her eye.

Oh no, not more barghests. Or crows?

But the flicker came closer, and it didn't move like a bird, or even a dog. It came through the deep snow in stages, pausing to gather itself and then leaping again.

"It is a cat," Manuel said in a surprised voice.

"It is," Freya agreed, smiling with mixed relief and horror. *Mr Fluffbum wasn't supposed to be outside yet—he could have gone anywhere. What if he'd been hit by a tram? Or frozen in this storm? Or started walking back to the coast? But I'm so glad to see him. Thank goodness I didn't stay in the halls.*

She knelt down, and Mr Fluffbum's black and white form leapt at her as she did so.

"What are you doing here?" she asked him, catching him mid-leap and bringing him close for a hug. Her cat glared at her and blinked twice before shaking off his front paws, one at a time. Icy particles speckled Freya's face.

"I suppose you got too hungry, waiting for me," she said, half-laughing, although she wondered how Mr Fluffbum had escaped. And if he was too cold. And if he was hungry. Cat-guilt was complicated. She rose and turned to the others. "My cat has come to meet me! We can follow his tracks home if we're fast enough." *I'd better make the most of his escape, after all.*

Two pairs of eyes blinked at her. Neither of them were the cat's.

"Come on, this is exactly what we needed. What's the problem?"

Jemima pointed. There were crows perched on the snow in a ring all around them.

"Oh, no, more crows!" Freya groaned aloud. She spared a hand from holding her cat to tug her snow-encrusted hood further over her eyes.

Mr Fluffbum's tail lashed in irritation. Freya thought she could hear a growl low in his throat. Or was that more thunder muttering around the edges of the sky? She put him down as he began to struggle. The cat crouched and gave a little wiggle, as though ready to pounce.

"Leave them," Freya urged her cat. "They're nearly as big as you are."

Ignoring her words, the cat launched himself at the nearest crow, which flapped backwards with an indignant squawk as several kilograms of cat barrelled into it. The circle of crows broken, Mr Fluffbum stalked towards the next bird, ears flattened. The next nearest crow half-raised its wings and stepped towards him. He gave the crow a glare, his fugue growing louder. The crow stepped backwards, apparently a quick learner.

"We'd better make the most of Mr Fluffbum's efforts," Freya said to Jemima and Manuel. She had to grab their hands and tug to get them moving, but they reached the ragged edge of the crow circle before the insulted crows could get themselves back in place. One bird cackled at them, its caws almost words to Freya's ears. She shook her head and followed.

The sooner we get out of here, the better. I can't take talking crows on top of everything else.

Chapter Nineteen
Homeward Bound

The snow was still falling heavily, and every footstep felt like an enormous effort as they followed Mr Fluffbum. The cat travelled in leaps and bounds rather than shuffling through the snow as the humans were obliged to do, and once or twice they had to cast about for the soft indents made in the snow by his paws. Every so often, he paused and looked around as though to be sure they were still following, his eyes glinting green in the darkness. Freya pushed her too-big hat off her eyes, again, dislodging clumps of snow that had settled there.

Despite the difficulty of travel, they reached the fence that bordered the park surprisingly quickly.

"Knew we were going in circles," muttered Jemima.

Close to the iron railings, Freya felt safer. Surely no barghests would appear now? Although the cat could easily have slipped through the rails, he led them along the fence line until they reached a gate. The four of them stepped through it, at least three of them experiencing a sense of relief as they did so.

"Out of the park at last. Where now?" Manuel said.

Freya looked around to get her bearings. Everything looked different in the snow, but after a few minutes she recognised the chip shop across the road as one she'd frequented for Friday night treats since her arrival.

"Oh, I know where we are. It's not far at all now," she said. She led the way up the hill, round a corner and further uphill. Finally, they approached the house Freya was renting. The bottom part of it was hers alone: one bedroom, a kitchen, bathroom and a tiny living space. It was more space than she'd expected to have as a lowly student, and the rent took up most of her student allowance. It was worth it to be able to have Mr Fluffbum with her. Plus, he wouldn't have appreciated being left behind with her mum. Let alone with her sister's children, who spent half their time with Freya's mum, and the other half in fur-form with their father's family. Freya wrinkled her nose, not wanting to remember her own family's were-associations.

Mr Fluffbum wove around her legs as she fumbled through her pockets for the key, which burned icily in Freya's hand, then he leapt inside before the door was fully open.

"How did you get out, anyway?" she asked the cat rhetorically. "You were supposed to be safe indoors. Thanks for rescuing us, though."

Jemima and Manuel nodded mutely, apparently too cold and tired to talk, or otherwise disinclined to talk to cats the way Freya habitually did. Freya abruptly felt self-conscious. *Should I be talking to my cat aloud? Does that make me too weird?* Then she gave a mental shrug. There were far weirder things going on tonight than talking to her cat. She might as well carry on.

Freya closed the door on the outside world with relief. It was good to be inside, out of the storm. Her ears felt hot from the temperature change, even though the heating wasn't on in her apartment. They all shed their snow-encrusted outer garments with relief, quickly filling the few hooks by the front door. Freya dragged her trainers off with difficulty. Underneath the outer layer of snow, ice crackled as she moved her feet. Her socks were still wet though, smelling dank as she peeled them off. *Everything* smelled dank as the snow they'd brought inside melted onto the floor.

"I'll put the kettle on," Freya announced, feeling very adult. "And the heating."

Jemima nodded enthusiastically, and they all traipsed down the hall into the tiny kitchen.

"I am beginning to understand this country's endless enthusiasm for hot drinks," Manuel said. He stood as close as possible to the kettle without getting in the way of the steam. "Although not the choice of drink," he added as Freya fished tea bags out of a packet and moved him out of the way in her search for cups. Despite his lack of enthusiasm for the drink, he didn't object to having a mug of hot tea placed in his hands.

"It's too dangerous to go back out tonight," Freya declared once they were huddling in the living room, draped in blankets from Freya's bed. Jemima had borrowed spare clothes from Freya, which hung long over her arms and legs, but nothing Freya had would fit Manuel. Mr Fluffbum condescended to sit in Freya's lap, providing her with a spot of warmth.

Manuel nodded. "Yes, we have had too many odd encounters tonight. And I do not want to go out in the snow again. It is much too cold."

"It's only a storm," Jemima said. "Though I agree, a snowstorm like this is hazardous."

Freya bit her lip. Should she say something about the barghest? Apparently, Jemima was too steeped in mundane traditions to recognise supernatural dangers when they chased her through a park. She'd been on the verge of accepting the supernatural earlier, but the moment had clearly passed. Or perhaps she just didn't want to admit it aloud.

"You're welcome to stay here tonight," Freya told them. "You'll have to fight over the sofa though. I don't have a spare bed."

"Thanks," said Jemima. "I'm willing to risk a hard floor rather than go out again tonight."

"No need to risk it," Manuel told her. "You are welcome to the sofa."

Jemima gave him a grateful smile. "Perhaps we can have an end each."

Freya cast a doubtful eye over the small sofa, but refrained from commenting. *I don't have anything better to offer.*

"I'll let Val know we made it safely here," Jemima said. "If I can charge my phone, that is," she added when she pulled it from a pocket and discovered that it had gone flat. "I don't think it liked the cold."

Freya found the charger for her own phone and offered it to Jemima, who nodded in thanks.

"I will tell Nesh," said Manuel. "Val may be asleep, after all."

"And Nesh won't be?" asked Freya.

"No, Nesh does not believe in sleeping before the early hours," Manuel said. "Besides, I am sure he will be taking care of Val, if only to impress Lin." He began composing a message on his phone.

Jemima knelt on the floor beside her phone, waiting for it to gain enough charge to start. Freya felt as though she should be making conversation, but as the room began to warm up, she struggled to keep her eyes open. It had been a long, long night.

"I need to sleep," she said, gathering herself to stand. "The bathroom's that way." She pointed. "You can keep the blankets. Do the best you can with the sofa cushions." She was tired enough to risk the crime of moving a sleeping cat. Besides, surely Mr Fluffbum would be more comfortable on the bed beside her, rather than on her comparatively bony knees. The cat protested with a disgruntled yowl, but followed her to the door of the room. "I'll give you an extra treat," she promised him, "since you got us out of the snow."

Mr Fluffbum meowed in response, looking up at her enthusiastically. She fished a few bits of cat kibble out of the bag and put them on his plate, where he crunched contentedly.

"We'll be fine," said Jemima. "'Night."

Manuel gave a wave.

Relieved to be home, safe, and shortly, warm—*there's nothing like a cat as a portable hot water bottle*—Freya retreated to bed.

Chapter Twenty

A Chilly Morning

Freya shivered when she slipped out of bed early the next morning, leaving Mr Fluffbum curled up on the remaining blankets, a white-mittened paw pulled tightly over his black ears. She pulled on a thick pair of socks and her cloak before venturing out into the kitchen. It was cold despite the heating she'd switched on last night, and the house smelled of damp clothing. She'd woken up earlier than expected, chilly and edgily aware of the presence of others in her flat.

I should take my cloak everywhere, Freya mused as she refilled the kettle. *If the weather's going to be this unpredictable. I could have done with it last night.* The view out of the kitchen window caught her attention as she waited for the kettle to boil. The snow still dusted every outdoor surface, thicker than icing sugar. *More like a thick layer of marshmallow.* The usually plain back garden had acquired a magical appearance with its layer of snow, everyday bushes becoming beautiful mounds.

The boiling kettle called her awareness from the view, and she made a cup of tea as she usually did, then hesitated over whether she should make more.

She poked her head into the living room. Jemima and Manuel were both squeezed onto the sofa, Manuel's long legs draped over one end.

Fur-trimmed jackets and blankets covered them both, and the damp smell of melted snow had invaded the room. The sight bothered Freya, not because she was jealous now, but because Manuel's long legs as a human reminded her of his leggy appearance as a were. Sure, he wasn't a werefox or regular werewolf, but he was still a were. And if there was anything she'd learnt from her past, it was that weres weren't to be trusted, even if they acted nice. She shook her head at herself.

Why let a were stay in your house, if you don't trust him? What about mundanes? Can they be trusted? Or demis who haven't realised what they are yet? She tried to avoid thinking about the weres she was related to these days.

"Morning all," she said, mostly to stop her intrusive thoughts.

Groans arose from the sofa. Jemima turned over, pulling the blanket over her head, and thus off Manuel. Manuel stirred and fell all the way off, hitting the floor with a thump that had Freya wincing in sympathy, were or not. He rubbed his backside for a moment before rising.

"Thank you for letting us sleep here," he said. "But I think that next time I will try to make it home to my own bed." He yawned and stretched his arms over his head, then winced at the pull on his injured shoulder. "It is going to take a while for my muscles to recover."

Jemima sat up and rubbed her face. "It would have been too cold if you'd stayed on the floor," she reassured him. "Freya, don't you heat this place at all?" She put a hand over her lips as her mind caught up with her mouth. "Sorry, I'm used to halls. The heating is part of the cost there."

"It's OK," Freya reassured her. "It *is* cold this morning. It's not usually this bad, but there's still snow on the ground outside."

Jemima grinned weakly. "Usually I like a snow day," she said. "Somehow, I can't quite whip up the enthusiasm this morning."

"Perhaps if we have a snowball fight, it will help?" Manuel said. "I have always wanted to have one of those."

Jemima hesitated a moment, then nodded enthusiastically, much more like her usual self. "You're on," she said. "Coming, Freya?"

Freya had a moment's hesitation, too. She couldn't remember the last time she'd done something as carefree as having a snowball fight. *Why not? It's daylight. There shouldn't be any risk from barghests now.* She set down her tea and followed Jemima and Manuel out the front door, closing it carefully behind her. She still wasn't sure how Mr Fluffbum had managed to get out last night—however helpful his escape had been.

Enough snow lay on the ground for some decent snow play. Several groups of people were already out, making snowmen or shovelling morosely, more or less depending on the age of the participant.

Freya's group flung snowballs indiscriminately at one another for a while, then Jemima and Freya teamed up against Manuel till he cried for mercy, pleading a sore shoulder. Next, he and Jemima teamed up on Freya until *she* pleaded for a halt. She couldn't remember being this playful in years.

"This is crazy, but so much fun," Manuel said when they'd ceased pelting each other with snow. "I think I might need some more of your English tea now, however."

"Good idea," Jemima agreed. "Freya, can we impose on you for a brew before we head home?"

"Of course," Freya agreed. Her first instinct had been correct, after all. Tea must always be offered. The group retreated inside again. Although the exercise of snow play had warmed them up, the meagre sun which peeked through the clouds this morning wasn't warm enough to keep them outside.

"I can't believe this weather," Freya muttered as she closed the door once more. "What happened to autumn?"

Freya started making more tea while Jemima retrieved her phone, which had been charging overnight. Apparently, she hadn't managed to start it last night. Manuel vanished into the bathroom with a towel to dry off.

"Finally," Jemima said, as the screen lit up. "I thought last night's storm had done for it." But when she read the accumulated messages, she gave a choking gasp. The sunlight coming through the kitchen window abruptly cut off, and thunder grumbled around the house.

"Are you OK?" Freya asked in concern.

Jemima held up a hand before covering her mouth again—this time, to stifle the sobs which emerged. Finally, she looked up at Freya.

"I have to go home," she said. "There's been... a... a death in the family." Her voice cracked as she spoke, and her face crumpled into misery.

I don't know her well enough to give her a hug, but I'm sure that's what she needs. "I'm so sorry," Freya said. "Is there anything I can do?" She offered Jemima the cup of tea she'd made, not knowing what else to do. Jemima took it, but held onto it rather than drinking. Her fingers pressed into the mug so hard they turned white.

"I need to get home," she reiterated. "Mum will be in shock."

I think Jemima's the one who's in shock. Freya patted her awkwardly on the shoulder.

Manuel reappeared in the doorway. He was smiling when he entered the room, but his expression disintegrated as he took in Jemima's change in demeanour.

"What is wrong?" he asked.

Jemima silently turned her phone towards him so he could read it. He was still a moment, then offered Jemima a hug, holding out his arms silently. She moved into his embrace gratefully.

I'm glad someone could do it, Freya thought wryly. *I wish I knew better how to do that sort of thing. Social interactions are so hard. Is that because we moved so much growing up, or something else?* She didn't know.

"We will get you to your family," Manuel said. "Won't we, Freya?"

Freya nodded firmly. "Absolutely," she agreed. "Let's get you back to the halls first. You'll need clothes."

"Right," Jemima said. "Right." She seemed to be at a loss. Freya wondered who in her family she'd lost.

"And then a bus or a train to... where did you say your mum was? Is the rest of your family there too?" Freya asked.

Jemima shook her head. "Mum's out in the Peak district, but it's Dad. Dad who's gone. My aunt sent the message. She said it was an accident of some sort." She choked back a sob before returning to practicalities as though they were a life raft in her emotional storm. "There's usually a train to London around midday. I can get Mum to meet me on it if I get the stopping train."

"We'd better get you over to the halls before the weather traps us again," Freya said. "How about you message your mum while I feed Mr Fluffbum, then we can all go over together?"

Manuel nodded. "That is a good plan," he agreed. "Only, please, let us not take a short cut through the park today."

Freya could only agree.

The journey back to the halls they'd left the night before was considerably faster, and all done by road. Freya found herself crossing to the far side of the road to avoid the park entrance. But when she passed coal holes in older buildings, she shied away from them, too.

Several cars had slid on the icy roads, and there were notices at the tram stops saying the trams weren't running.

It seemed that Manuel soon tired of the novelty of snow in daylight, especially since it kept threatening to rain, the droplets closer to ice than water.

"How can it be this cold and not snow?" he complained.

"It's good that it's not snowing again," Freya said. "Visibility is good." They were on the last stretch up the hill towards the student halls, and there had been a welcome lack of barghests. Jemima had been silent for every step of the way. The sky was filled with ominous clouds, but there had been surprisingly little thunder.

Barghests are omens of death, Freya thought. *Do they go away once the death in question has been... what would you call it, omenised? Portended, I suppose. Maybe it's simply not around because it's daylight now.* She couldn't help but wonder about the connection between the sudden onset of barghests and the death in Jemima's family. Although Jemima had also had a near-death experience last night. Freya shook her head. It was too hard to tell. At least the only crows they'd seen during daylight had been solitary and hadn't bothered them.

Jemima's phone pinged as they arrived outside the halls of residence building.

"Val's up and about," she informed them in a more or less normal tone. "Let's go inside and meet her."

I guess she's not prepared to talk about her dad anymore.

A different receptionist was on duty that morning, a dark-haired, dark-skinned man. "Make sure you sign in, duck," he told Freya. He obviously knew that she didn't belong.

Manuel bade them farewell as he headed to his room for a much-needed shower and change of clothes.

"Do not leave without seeing me," he told Jemima.

She nodded at him. "I'll let you know when I'm off," she assured him. "I've not got a ticket yet."

Upstairs, Val greeted them enthusiastically at the door to her room, apparently recovered from her head injury of the night before. Her enthusiasm dimmed when Jemima told her that she would be leaving on the next London train, and could Val help her pack, please.

"What's wrong?" she demanded.

"My dad's dead," Jemima said bluntly. "Sometime last night."

Val laid a hand on Jemima's arm. "Oh Jem, I'm sorry," she said. "What happened?"

"An accident," Jemima said shortly. "Black ice, they said." She rubbed her eyes with a clenched fist. "He was supposed to come visit me next holidays. We were going to go birding, see some ring ouzel, grouse and maybe hen harriers on the moors. We had *plans*."

Freya remembered Jemima had said she usually spent the holidays with her dad. She hovered near the door, at a loose end.

"Is there anything I can do?" she asked, as Val escorted Jemima to her room and began packing a bag with her, leaving the door open. Freya followed behind and hovered in the doorway.

"No," Jemima snarled. "There's nothing anyone can do." She grabbed clothes apparently at random, hurling unmatched socks and summer dresses into a suitcase. Val quietly removed the more unsuitable selections as Jemima moved on to another drawer.

Freya drew back in surprise at Jemima's tone. *She's upset,* she reminded herself. *Of course she's not going to speak nicely to you.*

Val paused in her clothes-sorting, told Jemima to keep going, and joined Freya in the doorway. She pulled her a few steps away and hissed at her. "If you want to help, you could look into the workings of Apollo in this town. The high level of barghest activity last night would be pretty much explained, if Jemima's dad was important in some way, so we don't need to worry about that."

"How is that?" Freya asked, unsure of Val's reasoning and surprised that she'd been aware of the barghests.

"They were obviously portents of Jemima's dad's death," she said, as though it was clear to anyone with eyes. "They went for her first, didn't they?"

Freya nodded slowly. That much was true. "So?"

"So, barghests can appear as a warning of the death of someone important. As I see it, the barghest is more or less explained. Especially if Jemima gets her possible demi-ness from her dad. But Ben's actions are not. I don't want to fall afoul of any cults when I'm just starting out on my degree."

Freya sighed. Like her, Val thought the barghest had been there for Jemima. Or for Jemima's dad, anyway. But booking a train or packing a suitcase sounded like much easier options than an exploration of the demi-world in an unknown city. Especially an unknown cult. However, she supposed that Val was right: they couldn't leave Ben's actions unexplored. He was still out in the city somewhere and could strike again.

"I suppose I can do that," Freya agreed, albeit reluctantly. It felt a bit useless to be assigned to research, rather than doing something practical. At least she'd be doing *something*. She decided to start her research by talking to someone familiar. "Can I use your room?" she asked Val. "I need a bit of privacy for a phone call."

"Sure, go ahead." Val tossed her the key and went back into Jemima's room herself. Jemima had paused in her packing and was clutching a t-shirt with the same cartwheel pattern on it as the one she'd worn yesterday. Tears dribbled silently down her cheeks. Val rested a hand on Jemima's shoulder and jerked her head at Freya, clearly indicating that she should move. Freya did.

Taking a seat on Val's bed, Freya called her friend Aisha. It was well past time for a catchup, anyway, since she had been phoneless for weeks.

After several minutes of exchanging key information such as how Mr Fluffbum was settling in, how many lectures Freya had to attend, and how Aisha's family café was faring—not to mention why Freya hadn't called earlier—Freya dug into the trickier questions.

"So, aside from letting you know how I'm getting on, I had another reason for calling just now," she said.

"You've broken up with Karim?" Aisha jumped in before Freya could continue. Karim was Aisha's brother.

"What? No," she said. "I mean, we're barely going out anyway, what with him at uni in another city and all."

And that's really what's biting me, she realised. *The only time I've heard from Karim was when I asked him if he knew where I could get a phone. He hasn't rung me, messaged me, nothing. And for that matter, where is Lio? Usually in a storm like last night's one he'd swoop in before I had a chance to get lost. No wonder I'm feeling out of sorts.* She bit her lip. She didn't want to moan to Aisha about Aisha's brother failing to pay proper attention to her. *Stick with research.*

Aisha was silent for a moment. "You'll tell me if anything's wrong between you and Karim, right?" she said. "And remember, even if you and he don't work out, I'm always your friend."

Freya smiled into the phone, even as her nails bit into the palm of the hand not holding it.

"Thanks, Aisha. You're the best. For now, I need to know about any cults of Apollo over this way."

"That's not something I know much about," Aisha said. "Apollo's the Greek sun god, right? Big on medicine and healing and things. Lots of different messenger birds. Nothing too nasty, I don't think."

"Yes, that's what I thought," Freya said. "Mum never taught me anything bad about Apollonians. What about crows?"

"Crows, sure. There's some legend about Apollo getting crows to spy on his lover. Some people say a raven. Most of those legends are interchangeable when it comes to species. But while spying isn't exactly charming behaviour," Aisha said, "they're only another bird messenger, you know. Even if they're smarter than the average sparrow. Other than that, I don't know much. Why do you ask?"

Freya filled her in on the eventful night she'd had.

"Thank goodness you got through that," Aisha exclaimed. "It sounds to me like it could be a nasty hybrid situation. Apollonians are big on laws and rules, but crows are associated with the Morrigan, too."

"I'm not *sure* that the Morrigan's involved," Freya said slowly, although she had thought about the Morrigan's crow association, too. The Morrigan, a Celtic goddess of war, was known as a crow shapeshifter, but she couldn't imagine Ben bowing down to a goddess. Perhaps Aisha had it right with her hybrid idea. Although... if Ben really was a shifter, it could explain some things. Like how he escaped from the coal cellar he'd planned to imprison her in. She thought of the black feather in the gym, and the lack of footprints outside it in the snow—not to mention the broken skylight with its scraping of bird-claws. But he'd said he hated weres. Could Ben hate weres and still be some kind of shifter? Freya paced the two steps to the bed, turned, and paced back.

"Well, I hope not," Aisha said, unaware of Freya's thoughts. "It sounds like there's enough going on with possible Celtic thunder demis, Wodenites and who knows what else. Did you say your new friend had pony charms? Maybe she's got some Epona heritage. You know, the Celtic horse-goddess."

"I guess that's possible," Freya said, prepared to be distracted for now. "She's nice though, even if she does like to short-circuit nightclubs."

"That's a quirky skill," Aisha acknowledged. "Sounds like you're better off sticking with her than with the Apollonian, anyway. Although does Epona still do sacrifices? I'm sure I remember something about that. I'll tell you what, I'll ask my parents about cults over that way. They might know something."

That was a big concession, coming from Aisha. In general, she tried for as much independence from her parents as she could while still living at home. Freya knew from her own experience that Aisha's parents had their own ideas about things.

"Thanks, Aisha. I appreciate it. I'd better go now," she said. "I'll be in touch."

"What are friends' parents for? Look out for weres," Aisha said, and she hung up.

Freya rolled her eyes. Weres were the least of her troubles here.

CHAPTER TWENTY-ONE
SECOND BREAKFAST

After speaking to Aisha, Freya rang the train station to make sure the trains were running, given the erratic weather. She was assured that a train fitted with a snow plough had been out that morning, and trains should be going again shortly, although express trains were being prioritised.

"Typical," Val said when Freya relayed the information, including the timetable she'd extracted. "Some countries there wouldn't be any delay. So I've heard, anyway. That could be a myth. But at least the trains aren't totally cancelled. How'd you go on that research?"

"Not great," Freya admitted. "I'm making inquiries, though." *That sounds much more impressive than 'my friend's parents might know something'.* "But I still don't understand why Ben was targeting us after being a friend to your group."

"That's something we'll have to follow up," Val agreed. She zipped up Jemima's bag and handed it to her. "There you go," she said. "We'll see you to the train in a couple of hours. You'll have to wait that long for a stopping train. Now let's go eat, you'll need it."

Manuel knocked at the open door as Val spoke. "I will take her," he offered.

Val nodded approvingly as Jemima moved to join Manuel. Once Jemima had left, presumably to find a late breakfast downstairs with Manuel, Val turned to Freya.

"I'll need to call my dad this morning anyway, to let him know about the climbing gym issues," she said. "But I expect Jack has already rung in. So I'll ask him about any local cults too. What I'm most worried about is that Ben mentioned a mentor." She hesitated. "Also, I'm a bit concerned about Jemima getting in over her head if she really *is* an unknowing thunder demi. We should do what we can to keep her safe for now. Know any bindings?"

Freya shook her head, feeling more useless at every moment. "The only thing I know is how to call things, not how to bind them."

Val tapped her fingers on the edge of Jemima's bed. "Hmm. Well, calling could help. Usually, some sort of binding is involved in calling."

"I guess I do draw a circle," Freya said.

"Yes, that's a simple binding option. Hard to apply to a person who's moving, though. How did you go last night?" Val asked unexpectedly.

"Well... I had to do a summoning to find some iron to help us through the park," Freya said hesitantly.

"Excellent! And was there much thunder after that?"

"Well, yes," Freya said. "The iron was for help against barghests, though, not thunder. And actually, if I'd thought about it at the time, I'd have been quite terrified of lightning hitting us." She thanked her ancestors that she had arrived at her flat without being struck by lightning, despite carrying around a length of metal in a thunderstorm, and touched the teaspoon she'd stuck in her pocket that morning, in the hope that it contained enough iron to be a barghest deterrent.

"Ah." Val was momentarily at a loss. "I'd really thought iron might sort out Jemima's weather problem, too. Perhaps a binding ring of some sort, then. Salt would be good. That's a classic barrier material."

"No-one can walk around in a ring of salt," Freya protested. "And besides, even if you managed it somehow, how would you get Jemima to agree? It's not like she is a demi." She hesitated. "Or at least, if she is, she doesn't know it."

Val threw up her hands. "I've got to do something," she said. "I told her about the demi world when—yes, I know—I probably shouldn't have. But all the signs are there. I'm almost positive she's a throwback."

"No-one uses that sort of phrase anymore," Freya said. "It's rude." Inspiration from one of her biology lectures struck. "You could say she's got an unexpected recessive trait, though."

Val rolled her eyes. "I could, but no-one outside of uni—or even outside the genetics class—would understand me."

"Since you're talking to me, and I'm at uni with you, that's not a big problem," Freya pointed out.

"Let's stick with her being a probable unidentified demi, then," Val said. "One who needs some protection for her own good. Can you imagine if she encounters more thunder snow while she's on the train?"

"That wouldn't be great," Freya agreed, envisioning snowdrifts and train derailments. An idea struck her. "I know! What about those solid salt crystals, the pink ones? They can be carved, right? Could you get a ring carved out of salt crystal? I mean, I don't know if it would work to protect Jemima against her own gods, but it could be worth a try."

"Brilliant!" Val grinned at her. "You know, there might even be something like that already made in one of those crystal shops in the high street. We can drop by on the way to the train station, assuming there isn't any more of that crazy weather."

Freya pushed aside the curtain to look out of the window. The sky was grey and heavy with clouds, but there wasn't any more snow coming down. On the street, most of what had fallen overnight was already turning to slush, although the view was still mostly white.

"Do you think Jemima will be alright by herself on the train?" Freya asked. "I mean, her dad's just died. She must be rather upset."

Val tugged at the end of one of her corkscrew curls thoughtfully. "Maybe one of us ought to go with her, at least as far as that station where she said her mum would meet her. But I've got lectures this afternoon." She turned her gaze on Freya. "Why don't you go?"

Freya screwed up her nose. "I don't have any lectures, but I can't go. I'm completely broke." *Again. And here I was thinking life would be so easy with a student allowance.*

Val's forehead wrinkled in dismay. "Oh. That's right. And so will I be if my dad's climbing gym is out of action." But her smile returned as fast as it had fled. "But, hey! I'm not broke yet. I'll get you a ticket on my card and claim it as a gift." She picked up her phone and tapped out numbers faster than Freya's eyes could easily follow. "Right, done," she said after about a minute. "You're booked on a return to Chesterfield this afternoon. Hope you like adventures."

"Is it the same train that Jemima is going on?" Freya asked doubtfully.

"Of course it is. I booked Jemima's train for her too, though she'll continue all the way to London once she's met her Mum. Just be glad it's a train and not a bus. There are accidents up and down the motorway, according to the news. It's not the best day to have to travel."

"Thanks for the encouraging words," Freya muttered.

Val shrugged. "You should be fine. Let's go down and eat, too. I could do with a second breakfast."

"Is that allowed?" Freya asked, wondering at Val's cavalier attitude toward food.

"Probably not, but I've seen plenty of others do it, so why not me, too?" Val beckoned for Freya to follow her out the door and led the way to the dining hall.

Freya felt awkward and out of place, but she followed rather than stay by herself in someone else's room.

The aroma wafting out of the large room was an odd mixture of baked beans, tinned tomatoes and burnt toast. It wasn't especially appetising, but Freya was hungry enough not to care. A cup of tea didn't fill her belly for long.

Val led her to join a queue of students filling their plates. She wasn't confident enough to fill a whole plate with food, but she took toast and spreads, and once again followed Val to a table where Manuel and Jemima were already eating. Even cold, slightly floppy toast tasted good to Freya's tastebuds. She tried not to inhale the jam-covered bread *too* fast.

"You're all set for the lunchtime train," Val told Jemima. "Freya will go with you as far as Chesterfield. Your mum's meeting you there right?"

Jemima nodded. "If she can make it through the roads, she'll be there."

Manuel paused with a forkful of food halfway to his mouth. "I can come with you if you need me to," he said, perhaps reiterating something he'd said earlier.

"No, you already told me that you have tests today. You can't travel all this way to attend university and then skip the first lot of tests you come across," Jemima told him. "Though it's kind of you to offer."

Manuel finished his mouthful while she spoke, then patted her arm. "I will be here for you on your return then," he said. "I hope you do not have to be away for long."

Jemima looked down at her plate, which was almost untouched. "I hope it won't be long," she said. "But it's so unexpected. It might take some time to sort out."

"I understand," Manuel said. "Please, let me know if you need support while you are in London. I do not have tests every day."

Jemima gave him a wan smile. "Thanks for the thought."

Freya focused on her plate, feeling like she was intruding on a private conversation. She noticed that Val hadn't butted in for a change. Instead, she was busy adding spoonfuls of sugar to her porridge. Val looked up, saw Freya watching her, and grinned.

"It's only edible when it's half sugar," she said. "Are you sure you only want toast? It's a slow train to Chesterfield." She pushed a second, as-yet untouched bowl of porridge towards Freya. "I usually get through two. But you can have my second one if you want it."

"You must have a super-fast metabolism," Freya said. "Didn't you say this is your second breakfast already?" Val didn't *look* like she regularly ate two large breakfasts.

"Yes, but the first breakfast was mostly coffee. Go on, have the porridge."

Freya accepted it, but only added half as much sugar as Val had done. It still tasted surprisingly good. She'd finished scraping the sides of the bowl when Jemima stood up abruptly, making her chair scrape loudly—not that the sound made much of an impact in the rowdy atmosphere of the dining hall.

"I'm going to give my excuses for the tests, then go to my room until it's time to head down to the train station," Jemima said. "There's no point in hanging around here."

Freya and Val exchanged glances.

"We'll tag along to the station when it's time." Val said. "We can carry your luggage."

"I don't need company," Jemima said stiffly.

"That's OK, we'll walk behind you if you don't want to talk to us," Val said, ignoring the implicit message that Jemima wanted to be alone.

"May I come with you till it is time to go?" Manuel asked more politely.

Jemima hesitated, then nodded. "Yes, you can tell me the chances of my train getting there on time, based on whatever the current prediction model is."

Manuel smiled at her. "I will have to look that up," he said, "but it sounds like a useful model to learn." He and Jemima headed for the stairs that led to the upper floors where their rooms were located.

Val caught Freya's eye and made a gagging expression. Freya suppressed a grin. It wasn't fair to mock Manuel's gallant mathematical efforts, but it was tempting.

"Come on," she said to Val. "We can at least help Jemima with her luggage, as you said. And given yesterday's weirdness, there's probably safety in numbers. Crows are usually diurnal, you know." She shivered. There had been a lot of crows ignoring their nature last night.

Val rose and headed for the stairs again, apparently unbothered by the thought of crows. Of course, she had only had the one late-night crow encounter. Freya followed her out. While she was grateful for breakfast, the noise of the dining hall was getting to her. Life on the coast hadn't prepared her well for large crowds.

"So long as Ben doesn't show up with a bow and arrow again, I'll be happy," Val said, choosing the stairs rather than the lift. "I really did think better of him. Apollo's descendants are usually all happiness and light, y'know? Or else obsessed with justice." She grimaced. "I suppose justice depends on where you stand. From what he said last night, it sounds like he's got in with the wrong sort of puritans."

Freya paused on the landing between blocks of stairs and nodded slowly. "I never heard anything bad about Apollo before," she agreed. "Although, I have to say I haven't had good experiences with weres." She hesitated, not sure how to carry on with causing offence.

"Don't tell me you're anti-were," Val said, giving her a sharp glance before starting up the next flight of stairs.

"I..." Freya didn't continue. *What can I possibly say that will put me in a good light, from Val's point of view? I certainly don't want to be like Ben, shooting people. When in doubt, say nothing.*

Val waited on the next landing for Freya to catch up, and raised her eyebrows, clearly waiting for a response.

"Manuel seems nice enough," Freya said weakly.

Her statement must have placated Val, because she went back to talking about Apollonians, taking the stairs slowly. "I've heard the lawyers—demi-lawyers, at any rate—have a secret organisation. I wonder if Ben is in with them somehow. I never heard that they disliked any section of the demi world more than others, though. It's usually whoever can pay, wins."

"Weres should be fine with lawyers, then," Freya couldn't help but say. "At least the ones I've met are never lacking in resources." They reached Val's floor and started down the corridor.

"There are plenty of weres down on their luck," Val said. "Same as any group of people. Ben's not one of those, though. I wish I knew who is pushing his buttons, so we could neutralise that threat."

She reached her room and unlocked it, waving for Freya to enter first. Jemima's door, next door, was firmly closed.

"I hope you're with me on that, no matter what your experience of weres."

"Definitely," Freya agreed. "You or Jemima, or even Manuel, could have been killed last night. That's not the university experience I'm looking for. Look, there's some time before Jemima's train. I want to research a bit more about what's going on with Ben."

"Do it," Val said. "I'm going to revise my notes. In bed. With my eyes closed. You can use the desk." Pushing off her shoes, she sat down on her bed.

"Thanks," said Freya drily. "Good luck with the revision."

She stood still for a moment, pondering what she'd learned from Aisha. Not a lot, really. Perhaps it was time to use some of the skills she was supposed to be acquiring here at uni.

"Actually, I think I've just got time to go look up a few things at the library," she told Val. "Don't let Jemima go without me." Val grunted in response and pulled her blanket over her face.

Perhaps she is feeling that bump on the head after all, Freya thought. *Oh well. Rest should help her. And I should be OK in daylight, I think. If the crows stay away.* Hefting her bag, she left the student halls of residence and set off towards the library, taking care not to slip on the increasingly slushy snow.

Chapter Twenty-Two

A Research Trip

The library was crowded with other students making the most of the heated space. Freya made a quick search of the library catalogue at the front desk before heading for one of the stacks that she assumed was less well-used. There weren't quite so many students there, at any rate.

Checking the numbers on the backs of the books, she soon found the mythology and occult section. Like most mundane resources about the supernatural, the books she found held a lot of apocrypha, but there were elements of the reality that Freya knew tucked in here and there.

Many of the myths were familiar from her childhood, tales that her mother had told her. *Maybe I should have enrolled in the classics instead of science,* Freya thought. *I would barely have had to study at all. But then what would I do with a mythology degree?* She put back the book she was looking at. It had only contained the usual information about the Greek God Apollo, stories of music and nothing more. *Perhaps I should be looking up grimhounds instead. That's probably the most common word for barghests. But the barghests didn't seem to have anything to do with Ben. Not like those crows.* Scanning the shelves, her eye was caught by a small book on Celtic mythology. *That might be good for information about the Morrigan or Taranis.* She set it aside to read later.

She skim-read several more tomes, flipping through chapter headings and first paragraphs. There was a lot of theorising based on pictures on urns and statues, but nothing on the descendants of the gods. *So much pontification. What did they think happened to all those godly offspring?* Freya put back yet another collection of Greek and Roman mythology, then spotted a slimmer volume entitled simply 'Apollo'.

"That's more like it," she murmured. The librarian who had shown Freya and her fellow students around had been insistent about the importance of quietude in the library, so she kept her voice low.

At first, she skimmed the new book, too. But a paragraph caught her eye, about Apollo having two main attributes, and she settled in for a more thorough read. The well-known side of Apollo was everything she had been told about: Apollo was god of music and dance, god of the sun, god of poetry, all symbolised by Apollo's lyre. Less well-known, according to the book, were Apollo's darker traits, symbolised by his bow: a god of distant death, terror, and awe. One whom only some of the other gods could speak to. Freya shivered, remembering Ben with his bow and arrows last night. Distanced death indeed.

She read on, and the book informed her of Apollo's love affairs, which always ended badly for the recipient—Daphne turned into a tree to escape him, Cassandra punished with truth-telling for rejecting him, Coronis shot for being unfaithful, as reported by a crow.

"So that's how the crows fit in," Freya said to herself. "Not exactly a winner with the girls, was he?" She remembered Cassandra, of course. That was a well-known tale. And dryads claimed to descend from Daphne, or so Freya's mother had told her.

She flipped the page to find another chapter entitled "Apollo the shepherd".

"Sounds innocent enough." Most of what she read suggested Apollo could have been a shepherd's god, called upon as a source of music to pass the time, and to keep the wolves from the sheep.

"Oh." *Is that what it is? Does Ben see himself as protecting the human world from wolves—werewolves? I wonder if he makes music in his spare time, too? At least that attribute of Apollo is innocuous.*

She closed the book. She'd check this one out to read at home too—and took a step back to see if she could spot any more books on Apollo. She bumped into someone who must have approached silently while she was engrossed in the book.

"Oh, sorry!" she exclaimed, turning around and clutching the book to her chest.

The man she'd stepped into held up a hand to forestall further apology. "No need to apologise," he said. "You must have found that section very absorbing. Are you one of my history of law students?" He didn't step back.

Freya shook her head mutely, wondering why he would think that. She wasn't *in* the law section. It looked like she'd bumped into a lecturer. Although he only appeared a few years older than herself, he carried a slim, expensive-looking laptop case, wore a suit, and had a University ID card dangling from a lanyard around his neck. He had blond hair in a similar style to Ben, but was clean shaven.

"I don't take law," she said. *If only he'd give me some personal space.* She took a step back, but then there was nowhere further to go; the bookshelf blocked her.

"No? Pity." said the lecturer. "I can't tell, you know, half my students never turn up to classes. But I can see you would be an attentive student."

Freya couldn't see how he could tell that. She didn't like the way his attention was focused on her. His gaze roved over her. She dropped her own gaze from his face to his ID card. Focusing on the card, she saw the words *postgraduate* beside a name. Not a lecturer then. She felt slightly relieved. A postgraduate student was a student all the same, not someone to tell her off for being in a section outside their specialty. Not that anyone would, surely? She was suddenly unsure. Even if he wasn't a lecturer, he was too close, oily in his advances.

"I've got to go now," she said, backing away on an angle. She bumped into the bookshelf. *Trapped by books, this can't be right.* The man followed her. *Too close.*

"You won't mind if I come as far as the checkout," he assured her.

Yes, I will, Freya thought, but could not quite say. She turned towards the lighter area beyond the shelves and rushed out.

She retreated to the checkout desk as fast as she could without running—another crime in libraries, apparently—but found the postgraduate student still at her side when she got there.

She gave him an irritated glance. Why was he bothering her? As she checked out the book, she heard a familiar voice behind her.

"Why, if it isn't the new girl? Doing some background checks, are you?" Laughter followed.

Freya's blood ran cold, a bolt of terror lancing through her.

It was Ben. He'd obviously made his way out of the coal hole somehow, and he was wearing clean clothes, almost as formal as the postgrad's suit. Only a few bruises and scratches on his face were left in evidence of his evening's activities.

The postgrad turned around. "Ben! I *thought* you might know this girl. What do you think?" He seemed to be glad to see Ben.

Maybe they're in league somehow, Freya thought in wild surmise.

Ben looked Freya up and down, a sneer marring his features.

"I think she's definitely *not* the right sort for our group. Even though she's not a fan of weres. Besides, Val, you know, the climbing girl, already has her hooks in."

Freya looked at Ben in disgust. She thought she might be in danger of wearing a sneer herself.

"I wouldn't want to be in any group with you after the way you treated your friends last night," she said hotly. "Was it you who damaged Jemima's rope last night? You had a climbing rope with you when you turned up in that alley."

"Oh, a sleuth," Ben jeered. "Paul, this one thinks she's clever."

The postgrad, whose name must be Paul, laughed aloud. Ben joined in, until Paul made a quieting gesture.

"I would like to assess her myself, Ben. You're not in the big leagues yet, no matter how much promise you have."

Ben's face became thunderous, but he didn't say anything, simply crossed his arms and waited.

Freya looked back at the postgrad, Paul. "Do you know what Ben did? He almost killed one of—of my friends—in a climbing gym." *I think. I don't have real evidence.* She stumbled over her description of Jemima, uncertain of her friendship position. But she *wanted* to be friends. She decided that was close enough and continued her diatribe. "And he shot another person. With an *arrow*. That's practically barbaric!".

The post-grad, Paul, shook his head at her, smiling as though she were a cute but misbehaving kitten trying to bite its owner's fingers.

"It would be barbaric if he was shooting at a person. But if he was putting down a were—,"

"I was trying to," muttered Ben.

"Then it's simply justice, meted out at an appropriate distance," the postgrad continued, ignoring Ben's comment. "I'm sure you can understand. If not now, then certainly when you've finished reading that book. You see, Ben and I are in the fortunate position of being heirs to an illustrious ancestor. Ben here is at the start of his training, and obviously, I am considerably more advanced. The thing is, humans need to be protected from wolves, in whatever forms those wolves take. They always have needed protection. But these days, it's much harder to identify the wolves. Heredity has so many pros and cons, don't you know? Those who inherit wolf blood sometimes go under the radar for *years* before our organisation uncovers them. We're primarily concerned with protecting the dominant species, the rightful inheritors of the earth. You'll find some useful contact details in the references." He smiled at her, eyes crinkling at the corners in an appallingly normal way.

Freya's eyes widened, and she looked at the book as though it had grown horns.

Probably safer than looking at Paul that way. "You've read this book?" she asked, not wanting to debate the ethics of shooting people or weres at any distance. She suspected they'd hold differing views.

Both Ben and Paul nodded.

"But of course," Paul said. "It's the standard text for all disciples of Apollo. I thought that's why you had picked it up. But perhaps it's not for you, as Ben suggests. It's not everyone who can meet the exacting standards of a god. There are many false prophets, and if you are acquainted with the girl Val, you have met at least one of them."

"I'm pretty sure Val isn't preaching anything," Freya said. "And that still doesn't explain why Ben targeted Jemima."

Paul looked at Ben. "Did you have a reason?"

Ben smoothed a renegade strand of hair back off his face, revealing a solid purple bruise.

"She was consorting with weres," he said. "It's better to stop that sort of thing before it gets too far. It only leads to more weres." He glanced at Paul as though to judge the effect of his statement. Paul nodded approvingly.

Freya couldn't help but gasp at the injustice to Jemima. "How is that OK?" she said. "And if weres are the problem, why not target only Manuel?"

Ben shrugged. "She turned me down. She deserved what was coming to her. Besides, I'll get the were sooner or later." He turned to Paul. "Can you believe they're importing weres now? It's disgusting." Then he returned his attention to Freya. "But you've got better taste than Jemima, I'm sure. What are you doing this evening? Care to come over for a drink? I've got some rather good vintages in my room."

Freya shuddered. Ben was clearly some sort of pathological creep. She considered returning the Apollo book on the spot, but that might mean missing out on important information. Plus, she'd have to spend more time in the same building as Ben and Paul, which wasn't a healthy plan. Still clutching the book, she backed away from both Ben and the postgrad, then realised that she'd probably better watch where she was going, and stopped.

"No thank you. I don't want to join you," she said. "No matter my views on weres." She turned and stalked out of the library. Their laughter echoed in her ears as she escaped.

CHAPTER TWENTY-THREE
A DAYLIGHT ENCOUNTER

Freya burst out into a grey and brooding day, which felt disappointingly mundane. The remaining snow formed white edges on the grey pavements and melted in droplets from the trees. She made her way back to the halls of residence much faster than her outward journey. Still, by the time she entered the halls again, she had lost a lot of her initial panic. The person on reception recognised her and gave her a nod as she signed in again. Upstairs, she found Val awake once more, discussing train timetables with Jemima and Manuel. Manuel was gesturing with one hand, keeping his wounded shoulder still.

At least Manuel doesn't seem seriously injured, Freya thought. She'd all but forgotten his shoulder wound from last night. *I should have offered to clean the wound at least. Maybe Jemima did.* Seeing him made her feel guilty about her feelings against weres.

"So, I've been to the library," she said, trying to be casual.

"Did you find anything?" Val asked.

"I didn't find something, I found someone," Freya said. "Ben. Ben was there. And a postgrad who was in some sort of group with him."

Improbably, Val brightened. "You found a cult?"

Freya rolled her eyes at Val's response. "You're not supposed to sound glad about it," she said. "But yes, I think I found a cult. If two people can be considered a cult. And a book about it, perhaps." Pulling out the book about Apollo, she waved it at the group, leaving the Celtic mythology book aside for the time being.

Jemima paused in the act of zipping up her bag and looked up. "That's a book on Greek mythology," she said. "Not a cultist manual. You guys have some weird ideas."

Val snorted. "So says the one who thinks a maned wolf got out of a zoo," she said. "Don't you think there'd be headlines in all the socials if that had happened? Never mind," she hurried on. "You need to get on that train. We'll sort out whatever's going on here so you can carry on with uni as soon as you're back."

"Good idea," Jemima said. "I'm off. Anyone who's coming with me, come now."

Val declared that she had time before her lecture to walk them all to the station, and Manuel had an hour until his test, so it was a similar group to the previous night who set off down the hill.

"Did you do anything to Ben?" Val asked Freya.

"No! I was trying to find out about whatever organisation he might be in, not attack him," Freya objected.

"Pity. My head hurts this morning," Val said.

"I think his head does too, if it's any consolation," Freya said, remembering the careful way Ben had stood, and the purple bruise on his face.

"Less consolation than you'd think," Val muttered.

The footpath narrowed, and Jemima and Manuel drew ahead of Val and Freya.

"Perhaps Manuel should go on the train with Jemima," Freya said, observing how closely they were walking together.

"Nah, Mr Maths has a test, remember? Besides, a were can't deal with demi effects. Not so easily, at any rate."

"And what sort of demi are you?" Freya asked boldly.

"One who doesn't want to see an untrained near-mundane throwba— I mean, recessive gene holder," Val looked sideways at Freya as though to see the effect of her change of words. Freya ignored her and looked straight ahead. With an exasperated sigh, Val continued. "I don't want to see Jemima hurt, that's all. And I think you're best placed to protect her. What we really need is a way to neutralise her demi abilities, so she can live her life the way she's used to. Speaking of which, here's that shop." They were passing the crystal shop Val had alluded to earlier.

"Just a moment, Jemima," Val called.

Jemima looked back impatiently, but when Val said she had an urgent errand, she paused by the stone stairs leading up into the shop.

"There's plenty of time before the train," Val assured Jemima. "Come in with me, Freya."

Freya looked at the dull sky and decided it was unlikely to turn thundery in the couple of minutes Val had suggested it would take in the shop. She followed the other girl inside.

Inside the shop, dream catchers, candles, bowls of polished stones and feathers on strings adorned every surface and descended from the ceiling in drifts.

Mr Fluffbum would have a field day in here, Freya thought, looking at a wafting series of dangling feathers. She half wished her cat was with her to enliven the place. Gentle chiming music played from a speaker somewhere. It was all a world removed from her rough coastal upbringing.

How can I be homesick and glad to be somewhere new at the same time?

Freya looked around. Val headed straight to the counter, where she entered into earnest conversation with the shopkeeper. She turned towards Freya after a short discussion.

"They don't carry salt rings," she said in disbelieving tones.

"They'd dissolve in the sweat of your fingers," the shop assistant interjected. "It wouldn't be worthwhile making them."

Freya and Val looked at each other.

"A dissolving ring wouldn't do much good," Freya said.

"So much for that idea," agreed Val.

"Let's make sure Jemima gets on her train, anyway." Freya turned to leave the shop. As she walked down the steps, she was surprised, given how few people she knew in this city, to see a familiar person approaching.

Kessler, the demi who'd sold her a phone—was it only yesterday?—paused as he reached Freya.

"How's the new phone, then?" he asked in a friendly manner.

Freya's hand automatically went to the pocket containing her phone.

"Fine, thanks," she said inanely.

Kessler's eyes went to Val, exiting the shop behind Freya. Val was clutching a large piece of pink rock salt.

"You're not going to try making a ring yourself, are you?" Freya asked in surprise.

"No, but this stuff is supposed to be good for clearing influences and whatever, anyway. That's what the shop girl said." Val hefted the piece of salt, then offered it to Jemima. "Here you go. Bereavement gift."

Jemima looked between rock salt and Val in bewilderment. "Thanks, I guess. I'll... try to fit it in my bag."

Freya could see Jemima was holding back; perhaps a scathing remark about unscientific thinking was on the tip of her tongue.

"If you're trying to clear the air, I've got a few things that might help," Kessler offered. "Last night's storm was something else." He gave Freya a loaded look.

He knows about Jemima, she thought. *But how could he?*

"We're walking Jemima to the station," she said aloud. "We can talk on the way if you'd like. We've got a train to catch."

Kessler nodded amiably. "That works for me," he agreed. He waved at the little group. "I'm Kessler," he introduced himself. "If you need phones that last, I'm your man." Assorted greetings flowed his way.

Shaking her head at how much of an opportunistic salesman he was, Freya started walking. Kessler swung into step beside her, and Val closed the gap between her and Freya. As before, Jemima and Manuel strode ahead, Jemima taking two steps for every one of Manuel's.

"So, you're in the market for protection, is that correct?" Kessler asked in a low voice.

He's more perceptive than I realised.

"How do you know?" Freya asked, dropping back further by slowing her steps. Val dropped back with her.

"I keep an ear to the ground," Kessler said. "Last night was very busy, supernaturally speaking. Also, a flock of crows woke me up when some of them banged into the windows of my apartment. They're not usually out and about at night, so I put my head out the window and saw a very interesting scene."

"You don't live in that alley near midtown, do you?" Val asked sharply.

"Certainly, I do," Kessler replied. "And I saw an apparent mundane, *far* too many crows, a prat with a bow and... you. All of you."

"Oh."

"Quite so," Kessler said. "When I listened to the prat going on, I realised you must have run afoul of one of those nasty side-shoot associations. There are always some who take a darker path, you know." He paused. "But what really puzzled me was the weather. As I am sure you can imagine."

"That's why we're in the market for protection," Val said. "One way or another, we'll deal with the cultist, who you call the prat. But..."

"The apparent mundane wants to stay a mundane," Freya said, eyes on Jemima. "She doesn't know about demis, or weres—well she didn't, until last night—doesn't even *see* the supernatural if there's a mundane explanation. But her dad just died, and there's a lot of thunder about." Not sure that she should be revealing personal secrets to a mobile phone dealer, however well-informed, she hesitated before adding, "Her first name is Tara. I wondered if she was a descendant of that Celtic thunder god."

Kessler pursed his lips. "Taranis, eh? Well, I suppose it is possible."

"So, can you protect the mundane from the supernatural? Or is that more than the 'clearing the air' that you were thinking of?" Val pressed.

Kessler walked for a few minutes without speaking. They passed the alley where the crows had harried them last night—presumably where Kessler's apartment was also situated—and Freya glanced in warily. A single crow was perched on top of the building. It gave a caw and flapped off as they went by. Freya gave an involuntary shiver.

I hope that one's not a messenger of any sort. But what would it tell Ben, anyway? Students walking in town? Not exactly privileged knowledge. She wished she'd had a chance to read the rest of the book about Apollo, but it was still in her bag. Perhaps she'd have a chance on the train.

"So," Kessler said suddenly. "I think I can help your mundane. Are you quite sure she wants to stay in that category, though?" he asked, raising an eyebrow. Jemima and Manuel were walking very closely together.

"Perhaps something temporary would be good," Freya said. "Just so that she doesn't call down a thunderstorm on herself while she's, er, grieving her dad."

"And so we don't get stuck in a month's worth of snowstorms," Val added. "What?" she said when both Kessler and Freya stared at her. "No-one needs winter out of season."

"I suppose not," Kessler said. "It just sounded a little callous."

Freya was glad he'd said it, but Val only laughed.

"We have enough issues with the weather as it is," Val said. "Without storms of grief. Anyway, you think you can help. How?"

Direct and to the point. I guess that's Val.

A tram rumbled past, creating thunder of its own. Kessler waited until it had passed before speaking.

"I assume she needs something now," he said. "Or at least as soon as her current good mood evaporates."

Freya nodded.

"Did she say she's had problems with storms before?" Kessler asked.

"Not really," Val said, "though she's taking a meteorology course, so maybe she has."

"*Everyone* has had trouble with the weather," Freya said.

Val laughed. "Probably. Or complained about it, at least."

Jemima looked back at them, perhaps wondering what was making Val laugh. She frowned, and the sky darkened.

"All right. She could be manifesting late, I suppose," Kessler said hurriedly. "I'll have to duck back to my apartment to make something, but I'll catch you up. You're headed for the train, yes?"

"That's right," Val agreed. "Jemima needs to catch the stopping train to London. And it needs to get there, so no thunder snow on the way. Freya's going to go with her as far as Chesterfield."

"I'll do what I can." Kessler turned and loped back up the hill towards the alley which contained his apartment.

"Let's hope he really can help," Val said. "And that Ben doesn't show up."

CHAPTER TWENTY-FOUR
A NECKLACE

The group had nearly reached the station when Kessler caught up with them, panting slightly.

"Sorry," he said. "I had to do a little desktop blacksmithing to make this work." He held out a simple necklace made up of glossy, round, dark grey beads. They looked metallic. "It's much easier to make protective circlets as necklaces than rings," he added. "No size issues, you see."

"Huh, I didn't think of that," Val admitted.

"Thanks," Freya said. "How does it work?"

Kessler tapped the side of his nose. "Trade secret," he said. "But I'm sure it will work for a few weeks at least. There are other things that can be added, but I don't usually work with stones, so I didn't have much on me. I prefer electronics," he said. "Like phones. There are less ethical issues with phones."

Jemima, still ahead, paused at the entrance to the station, close enough that she would be able to see the departure boards inside. She flung her arms around Manuel and he patted her back a little awkwardly. Freya thought she might be crying—and who could blame her? Freya didn't know where her own dad was these days, but she'd be hugely upset if he died without her even getting to see him.

"I am so sorry I cannot come with you," Manuel told Jemima as Val, Kessler and Freya caught up.

"It's better you don't," Jemima said.

"Give her this," Val hissed, gesturing for Kessler to hand over the necklace.

Manuel looked taken aback, but his hearing was clearly excellent. He gave a sort of shrug and held out a hand for it. "Will it help her?" he mouthed over Jemima's head.

"Yes," Kessler said. "And it will also do no harm."

Freya felt an inner tension ease that she hadn't acknowledged existed. *Karim vouches for Kessler too, she remembered. He's an ally.*

Manuel's nostrils flared briefly, and she was reminded all over again that he was a were, but he took the necklace, released Jemima gently and stepped back. "Here," he said. "Your friends got this for you." He examined the necklace closely, then offered to put it around Jemima's neck.

"Oh. If I must," Jemima said, looking anxiously at the departures board, which advised that the London train was fast approaching.

Manuel draped the necklace over Jemima. It closed itself with a magnetic snap. It was probably only Freya's imagination that the necklace flashed briefly copper-coloured. Jemima relaxed a little, and a real smile lit her face. "Thanks. It looks pretty." She patted it, and then Manuel's arm. "See you when I get back," she said. "I'll call you."

"Keep that necklace on at least till you get home," Val urged.

"I guess." Jemima glanced at her watch. "I have to run now, though. Freya, I think Val said you are coming with me part of the way?"

Thank goodness that message got through, Freya thought. It would have been dreadfully embarrassing to be a chaperone without her say-so. "Yes," she said aloud. "Just until you meet your mum. Then I'll take the next train back."

"Great," Jemima said. "Let's go."

They hustled through the crowded station, ignoring several food and drink purveyors to reach the stairs that led to the station's overbridge.

"Not this one, not this one," Jemima muttered as she passed the stairways leading down to the platforms.

"That's the one, isn't it?" Freya pointed at the next staircase along.

"Yes." Jemima gave Freya an abstracted smile.

I hope that necklace is just suppressing any demi abilities she might have and not her intelligence as well, Freya worried.

Next moment, however, Jemima brought Freya into focus.

"Don't mind me, I'm upset, that's all," she said. "Let's get that train."

They raced down the stairs, arriving on the platform right as the door alarms started bleating.

"Go, go!" encouraged Freya, increasing her stride length from 'hustle' to 'hurtle'. Jemima did the same, and they fell through the train's nearest door as it started closing. Panting, they walked along the carriage looking for seats, holding onto the backs of the occupied chairs as the train jolted its way out of the station. The train was surprisingly full, but eventually they found two free seats and fell into them.

"That was a bit close," Jemima said. "I'm always late for trains."

"I don't remember the last time I was on a train," Freya said. "I took the bus to get here."

"Oh, I hate buses," Jemima said. "All those extra stops, and they go so slow! Plus, I can't read on buses, so there's no way to use the time to study."

Freya grinned. *That was more like the Jemima she'd met... was it only yesterday?*

"How do you cope with climbing, or walking, even?" she asked. "That's even slower. And no good for study."

"Climbing usually feels faster. It's the adrenaline, I guess. But yeah, walking can get boring. Though I can think about things while walking. Then again, I like some slow activities—like birdwatching. It's a bit like climbing though, there's so many little things to pay attention to in the moment, that you don't notice the time. Whereas when I'm travelling, I want to be done before I've left." Jemima shrugged. "Not that I've done much travelling, just between Mum and Dad's places, since they split." The corners of her mouth dragged down once again. "Guess that won't be a problem anymore." She blinked rapidly.

"Where does your mum live?" Freya asked hastily, trying to alleviate the other girl's pain by focusing on less difficult topics. Even if Kessler's necklace stopped Jemima accidentally summoning another storm, it wouldn't be good for her to dwell on her misery all the way to London, surely.

Jemima looked out the window as the landscape whipped past. The train had reached full speed. Freya followed her gaze and realised that there was no snow visible anymore, only autumnal colours on the rolling hills they passed. The thunder snow must have been very localised.

"Like I said earlier, she's out in the Peak District." She glanced at the phone she held loosely in one hand and swiped away a notification. "She's taking the bus in to meet me at Chesterfield." Her lips compressed briefly, though whether in pain or mirth, Freya wasn't sure. "Apparently the bus has been dug out of a snowdrift. I guess that storm spread a bit further than the city, even if we can't see it here."

"Will she get to the station on time?"

"Let's hope so."

They fell silent again, until Freya, uncomfortable with the awkward silence, said in slight desperation, "Perhaps we should study? You're in my bio class, aren't you?"

Somewhat to Freya's surprise, Jemima agreed with alacrity.

"I'll need good grades. I'll probably have to apply for a scholarship for next year," she explained. "Dad was the one paying my fees. But it's not far to Chesterfield by train. Why don't we quiz each other on the last few lectures? That way, we don't have to unpack."

Freya decided not to mention that the only books in *her* bag were the treatise on Apollo and the Celtic mythology book—nothing that would help them in biology. "Sure."

By the time the twisted spire of Chesterfield's church came into view—still standing despite all that the increasingly volatile weather had thrown at it—Freya felt like she knew the contents of their last few biology lectures backwards. Also, that she'd prefer to focus on plants than on the gruesome biology of animals. At least there hadn't been a hint of thunder, not even on the occasions that Freya had known an answer before Jemima.

"Thanks, Freya," Jemima said as the train began to slow with a screeching of brakes. "It really helped having you here. Will you be alright getting back?" She stood up, shouldering her bag, then picked up the hunk of rock salt in one hand. Jemima had been unable to wedge it into her packed bag even with Freya helping by holding the edges closed while Jemima pulled on the zip.

"I'll be fine," Freya assured her, steadying herself on the worn top of the train seat. The fraying threads of its fabric betrayed its many years of use as an impromptu handhold. "Let's make sure your mum is here before I switch trains."

The platform was empty.

"She's probably just running late," Freya said in an attempt at reassurance as she peered out the train door. Although Jemima was wearing Kessler's necklace, there was a distinctly thunderous feeling to the air. She stepped onto the platform. Despite the lack of snow here, it felt chilly outside the train.

"There's a few minutes before the train starts again. Can you see if anyone's coming down through Crow Lane?" Jemima asked. "That's the station entrance road. I'll stay here in case she's in the loo or something. That way if the train sets off, I'm still on it and you can head home."

"But what does she look like?" Freya objected.

Jemima fiddled with her phone for a moment. "Here," she said, turning the screen to face Freya.

Freya nodded, doing her best to memorise the picture Jemma showed her. "OK, I'll have a quick look. There's half an hour before I have to catch the train back north." She had no idea where Crow Lane could be, but assumed that she'd find it if she followed the exit signs. She darted through the station hall, dodging people as she went. No-one was heading into the station from the road—which did in fact bear a sign stating that it was Crow Lane. At that moment, a crow wheeled overhead, cawing. *I hope it's a regular crow, and not one of Apollo's messengers. Or a Morrigan-associate.*

Freya looked around quickly then ducked back inside, as much to escape the notice of the crow as because she hadn't seen anyone resembling Jemima's mum in the lane. Checking the departure boards inside, she saw that the south-bound train had only a couple of minutes left before it was due to depart. She plunged through the crowds to reach the platform, feeling the burn in her legs from the hasty exercise.

Luckily, I've kept up with my running. Even if my legs hurt, I can still breathe easily.

Jemima was standing in the door of the train, keeping it open despite its beeps of protest.

"Did you see her?" she asked anxiously. Then her gaze lifted from Freya to focus on something behind her.

Freya turned around as she heard running steps. A small, middle-aged woman with greying hair as short as Jemima's, ran towards them, an array of bags jouncing with every step.

"Mum, can't you ever be on time?" Jemima said in an affectionate, if exasperated tone.

A whistle sounded, and from somewhere in the distance a man's voice said, "Stand clear."

Jemima and her mum both ignored the sternly voiced instruction, hugging in the open train door. Freya looked on wistfully. *Imagine if my family was like that, hugging on arrival.*

The whistle sounded again, the impatience of the whistler showing in its stentorian blast.

"We'd better get on, love," Jemima's mum told her, gathering up the bags which had slipped while she hugged her daughter. She looked over her shoulder at Freya. "Thanks for looking after Jemima." Then she hustled aboard. There was a last-minute flurry of bag rearrangement. Something clunked near the edge of the platform.

Probably the train doors unlocking.

"See you soon, Freya. And thanks!" Jemima called as the doors closed behind her at last. The train eased away from the platform with a series of hisses and groans, and Freya was left standing alone.

CHAPTER TWENTY-FIVE
LEFT BEHIND

As the train receded into the distance, the air felt lighter somehow. Perhaps Jemima's feelings had been leaking a little, despite Kessler's necklace. Freya gave herself a mental shake. She had to change platforms to catch the train back... home, she supposed it was now. Mr Fluffbum would be annoyed at being left alone for so long, and she had assignments and tests to study for, as well as those mythology books to read. She yawned and rubbed her face with her hands. A bit more sleep would be good, too. Most of last night had been taken up with dancing, climbing, or walking, one way or another. If she got back soon enough, she could curl up and read a book on the sofa with Mr Fluffbum. She had a phone to download books onto again, after all. She felt her lips curl up at the corners as she contemplated the idea. *Yes. Time to relax, with no demands from anyone.*

Freya resettled her rucksack into a more comfortable position and started walking towards the stairs. As she did so, a splash of pink caught her eye. The rock salt crystal that Val had given Jemima sat on the rocky surface between the tracks and the edge of the platform.

Oh no, what will Val say? I can't leave it there. Freya stooped to pick up the piece of salt. As she did so, there was a rush of wind around her head. A pair of crows plunged towards her, wings batting at her, beaks and claws perilously close to her eyes. Straightening up with her fingers closed around the rock salt, she instinctively held it in front of her face. The next crow to swoop at her bumped into the salt and cawed in an offended tone. Despite her fright at being attacked by birds—again!—she smiled a little.

Who knew a crow could sound insulted?

The crow in question flapped to the ground and glared at her out of first one black, glossy eye, then the other. Freya waved her salt-holding hand at the other crow, and it too backed off warily, opting to perch on the edge of the platform roof and peer down at her.

"Look," she addressed the birds, hoping no-one would notice her doing so. Perhaps they'd think she was crazy and avoid her, anyway? But she didn't want to be thought crazy. Somehow, what was fine in the dark was unacceptable in daylight. "Look," she said again. "I've got nothing against birds. I usually like them. Except when they're attacking me. Please, leave me alone."

Not exactly an inspiring speech, Freya thought. *But who gives inspiring speeches to attacking crows?*

Cautiously, she started walking again. The crows followed her, hopping along the platform and on the roof, but didn't swoop at her again.

"That's right," she muttered. "Just following without attacking is OK, assuming you don't report to someone like Ben." The rooftop crow made a muttering sound. "He's not worth it anyway," she added. "I bet he doesn't feed any of the crows that give him messages." Another caw. Was this one inquisitive? Freya mentally catalogued the contents of her rucksack. Surely, she had some emergency supplies in there... Yes. She paused long enough to find one of the flapjack bars she *always* had in her rucksack, even as a penniless student. Opening it, she crumbled some of the sticky, oaty snack into pieces and surreptitiously scattered it along the edge of the platform. It would be embarrassing to be arrested for littering. With caws of delight, the two crows descended on the crumbs. Freya made good her escape, racing down the stairs to the subway that connected the platforms.

A hurried glance at the departure boards that were positioned at the base of each staircase told her that the northbound train was approaching, so she continued up the next set of stairs, arriving just in time to enter her train. She hit the close button on the doors hastily. As the doors closed behind her, she saw a startled-looking pair of crows flapping away from the train. *Wish I'd remembered that flapjack last night. We could have avoided being attacked by crows entirely. I wonder if being fed would have fended off the barghests?*

Freya spent the short trip back reading the books she'd borrowed. She started in with Apollo. Most of its contents were standard Greek mythology fare that she'd learnt as a child, along with all the other information about gods and other supernatural creatures. There were a few sections that emphasised lesser aspects of Apollo, such as his association with mice and plague. She shuddered, thinking how much worse things could be. At least Ben was only fixated on keeping the 'flock' safe from wolves—where the flock was people, and the wolves were werewolves. She just hoped there weren't other rogue Apollonians out there, perhaps in laboratory positions, or in armies, or in government, rather than doing law degrees. A dark-focussed Apollonian interested in plagues and working in a lab would surely be more dangerous by far than a mere lawyer, in terms of their ability to harm lots of people. Probably. Although being a law student hadn't stopped Ben being active with a bow in a way that was surely illegal, and had definitely harmed Manuel. For that matter, how had Ben managed to harm Jemima? Freya was sure it was Ben's doing that Jemima had fallen in the climbing gym, but she had no way of proving that. Just because she thought she'd seen a crow exiting the gym through the skylight, didn't make Ben the culprit. Although... She remembered the way the rope had looked dark in Ben's hands, before Jemima started her climb. Had that been more than simply her imagination? That same rope had frayed shortly afterwards in what her friends assured her was an entirely unexpected manner. She needed to know more about Ben's capabilities, and whether he was a descendant of Apollo, the Morrigan, or worse, both.

Freya flipped through the book to the index section, wondering what the postgrad, Paul, had meant about the address that might be there. A bookmark fell out as she did so. She snorted a little—she'd expected to see something much more permanent—perhaps the home institutions of the scholars who had written the book, or a sacred site listed as a reference, or suchlike. Perhaps she had more imagination than her erstwhile persecutors. Still, she examined the bookmark carefully. The front had a picture of a... she squinted. Was that a badly drawn bow, or a lyre? Perhaps some artistic version of both, sort of twisted together. So far, so Apollonian. The back was blank, but had words pencilled on it. She peered at the words. They were a little smudged, but it looked like... yes, it was the address of a high-end residential building, one whose adverts Freya had dismissed as too expensive and unsuitable for cats, in her search for somewhere to live while she was a student. She wrinkled her nose. Could a building like that really be the centre of an entire divergent cult of Apollo? One way or another, she felt like she would be finding out.

Luckily the book was reasonably short, so she had time to glance through the Celtic mythology book too. It was organised alphabetically, so she was able to skip to the section on

Morrigan—*hmm, generally a dark goddess, incites warriors to battle, associated with Samhain, which is Halloween. That could fit with Ben I suppose*—and then to move on to Taranis. There was less on Taranis than there was on the Morrigan. Freya was only able to reaffirm what she already knew, that Taranis was an ancient Celtic sky or thunder god, whose symbol appeared to be a wheel. She switched to her phone in frustration. That didn't further her search much, although she did find a reference to an old drone system which bore the god's name. Perhaps if Jemima's dad had been involved with that, he had some importance in the demi-world. It was a bit far-fetched, though.

More likely that he was a direct descendent of Taranis, Freya decided. She turned her thoughts back to Ben and his possible association with the Morrigan or Apollo. Or both. She sighed. Life would be so much simpler if heredity wasn't so mixed up.

Freya arrived back in her northern university town, Sheffield, with surprisingly little fanfare. No crows flew threateningly over the station when she disembarked, and no friends were waiting near the water feature outside the station. She tried not to feel offended—they hadn't arranged to do so, after all. She had somehow expected to see... someone she knew. She made her way home with plenty of time to feed Mr Fluffbum and make herself a cup of tea. The cat begged for something *other* than the dry kibble she had on hand, turning up his nose at the bowlful of pellets and rubbing insistently around her ankles.

"Sorry, Mr Fluffbum," she told him, bending down to give him a pat. "You'll have to wait till next week for variety in your diet, unless Lio turns up. I'm surprised he hasn't already, with the storm we've had."

Her cat stopped rubbing her legs and leapt onto the kitchen windowsill, where he stared longingly at the sky.

"Yeah, I wish he'd show up too. But I'm not going to delay a brew by waiting for him."

She peered into the packet of tea. There weren't many tea bags left; she might have to resort to foraged herbal tea sooner than later. Meanwhile, she dunked one of the remaining tea bags into her cup of water for a few seconds then set the bag aside to dry out for a second use. Mug in hand, she settled down, as planned, on the sofa.

Freya awoke with a start sometime later. Her phone, left balanced on the arm of the sofa, rang with an unfamiliar sound. She hadn't yet set the ringtone. She fumbled for the phone, in the process disturbing Mr Fluffbum who was curled up near her head. The cat glared at her and leapt off the couch, stalking out of the room without a backward glance.

"Hello?"

"Freya, it's Aisha. You haven't replied to my text. I thought you would want to hear what Dad said as soon as possible. Actually, you probably don't want to hear everything he said because he really did go on a lot. But the upshot was that yes, there is some weird cult going on over where you are. And you should definitely avoid crows and don't join archery clubs."

"Oh, hi Aisha," Freya said when she could get a word in edgewise. "Thanks for the words of warning. It's a bit late on the crow front, but since I have no intention of joining the archery club, I'll stick with that." She looked around for Mr Fluffbum, but didn't see him. A flash of movement at the window drew her eye, but was gone before she could identify it. *Probably just a bird.*

Aisha laughed. "Yeah, I don't know how you'd avoid crows, anyway. They're everywhere. I figured I'd give you the complete rundown. Not that there's much more—only that, yes, there is more than one branch of Apollo's descendants, and not all of them are good guys."

"I don't think that's news either at this point," Freya said. "I've been reading about Apollo." *No-one can see me blush because I fell asleep doing so,* she reminded herself. "There's a bunch of stuff in the book I got from the library, but I also met the Apollonians there, and they more or less told me I'd find something in it."

Freya pictured Aisha rolling her eyes in the short silence that followed.

"I thought you wanted me to do the research," Aisha complained. "Did you get away from those guys all right? And was there?"

"Was there what?"

"Something in the book."

"Oh. Yes, there was a bookmark with an address on it for somewhere near the uni. Some fancy apartments or something. I'll go have a look at it later. Or maybe tomorrow," Freya amended, looking out the window and seeing how dusky it was getting outside.

"Yeah, don't go there at night. And Freya, don't go alone, either. It sounds like things are riskier there than even I thought they would be."

Mr Fluffbum reappeared, leapt up onto the couch and curled up by her feet. His fur brushed against her bare skin, surprisingly cold.

Freya found herself nodding. "Yeah, I wasn't expecting to be set on by so many different things on a night out. But actually, most of them weren't aiming at me. Except perhaps the crows, and I think I've got an edge on them now that I know they can be bribed with food."

Aisha laughed, but quickly grew serious again. "Be careful around the Apollonians, won't you? They're descended from a major god. They might have all sorts of powers."

Freya tapped her fingers on the arm of the sofa. Mr Fluffbum stood up and stretched, then eyed her fingers as though contemplating pouncing on them.

"They're not the only ones with great ancestors." *Even if I've never felt that my powers lived up to expectations, as a descendant of Freya and Dionysus.*

"Maybe not, but you should still be careful."

"Yes, mother hen," Freya said, laughing again. She sobered quickly. "Honestly, Aisha, that's why I asked you to help with the research. I just want to be a normal student. You wouldn't believe how hard it is to concentrate on assignments with this stuff going on."

"Let's get it sorted out then, so you don't waste your loan," Aisha said. "Did your book have any gems of knowledge about how to defeat the descendants of Apollo?"

Freya shook her head, forgetting they weren't using video chat. Power was expensive, and video used more of it.

"Not really. There was a bunch of stuff about how he always stuffed up his relationships. I can see Ben being like that, I guess. I think he was trying for a relationship with Jemima, one of the students I've met, but she wasn't having any of it. But I don't see how that helps me." Freya frowned, thinking of how much trouble Ben had been causing for Jemima. She really didn't want that sort of ire directed at her.

"Yeah, especially since this Ben is a descendant, not the god himself. I mean, I'm not exactly like Bastet, either." Aisha named her own deity ancestor.

"Not even close. You don't wear a cat's head," Freya teased her friend. "Seriously though, it sounds like I have to make it up as I go along. Knowing someone's ancestry doesn't tell me about *them*."

"Too true," Aisha agreed. "But at least you have an idea of where they're coming from."

After a few more minutes of conversation that didn't really get anywhere, Freya ended the call. It was too late for a trip out tonight, but thanks to her afternoon nap, she wasn't feeling tired. She grinned ruefully. She might just have to work on her assignments, like a regular student.

CHAPTER TWENTY-SIX
MISSING PERSON

Freya awoke the next morning feeling like it was a holiday. She stretched luxuriously, wondering what made waking up feel so good today.

It's a Saturday. No lectures. And my assignments are all done. She'd stayed up late to get things finished, only slightly hindered by Mr Fluffbum's attempts to sit on her keyboard.

She picked up her phone. It still had battery left over from yesterday, even though she'd forgotten to set it to charge last night. Kessler's phones really were good. There was a message from Jemima, saying she'd arrived safely in London and would be back after the weekend, unless it turned out there was more to sort out than it looked like at first glance.

That's one problem sorted out. Or put aside. Now I just have to work out how to stop a misguided couple of Apollonians from attacking me or my friends for the rest of the time I'm studying. Simple, right?

It didn't feel anything like simple. In between assignments, she'd been juggling ideas about Ben and his co-cultist—or leader?—Paul. The book about Apollo had given her ideas, but none concrete enough to turn into a plan. Really, the one thing that kept tugging at her mind was the idea that Apollo was a failure when it came to relationships. But she didn't know Ben well enough to know if that was really a weakness for him. Plus, the Morrigan didn't seem to *have* any weaknesses, and if Ben was any sort of hybrid demi, he could have inherited powers from both the Morrigan and Apollo. Both deities had crow associations, so it wouldn't be easy to separate them. Of course, Ben's postgraduate friend Paul had mentioned Apollo, so maybe Freya should keep things simple for herself, and focus on the Greek god rather than the Irish goddess.

Perhaps... perhaps I should think about Apollo's good side after all. Maybe Ben simply needs a healthier outlet for his demigodness?

She picked up the book on Apollo and leafed through it again. She couldn't think of a way of subverting his attitude to werewolves. But maybe if he was occupied with something more fulfilling than damaging climbing ropes and shooting his erstwhile friends with arrows, he'd be a safer person to have around. She tapped the lyre-shaped drawing on the front of the book. If Ben truly was a descendant of Apollo, then he was probably into music, poetry, or both. Although maybe he'd only inherited the inability to form healthy relationships.

No, I've got to hope he's not all bad.

She started scrolling through the contacts on her phone. It was time to see if Val had any connections in the music industry.

But before Freya could call Val, the phone buzzed in her hand. She almost dropped in it surprise. She'd received so few calls since arriving, and she didn't recognise the number.

Who could it be?

Answering cautiously, Freya was surprised to find herself speaking to Kessler.

"Freya, you'd better rally your friends," Kessler snapped.

"Wha—"

"I just saw your South American friend being bundled into a van by that Apollonian who's been causing you trouble," he went on urgently. "It's lucky I was looking out my window and saw it happening."

"You couldn't stop it?" Freya asked.

"I'm one person, and I was on the second floor," Kessler pointed out. "I make electronics and occasional jewellery, not offensive weapons."

"Oh. Um, sorry," Freya said. "Do you know where they went?"

"No, but I did get a photo of the van's plate number. We should be able to get something from that."

"Right. Er. Can you start looking into that while I alert the others?" Freya had no idea how to track a plate number. It was rare enough for someone to have a private vehicle these days.

"Will do. I thought you'd better know as soon as possible," Kessler said. He rang off before Freya could say goodbye.

She stared at the phone a moment in blank astonishment.

Manuel, kidnapped? Apparently, she'd underestimated the extent of Ben's evil intent. She shivered, remembering Ben's accuracy with a bow and arrow. She only hoped Manuel was found before anything worse than a fast-healing shoulder wound happened to him. She picked up her phone again. It was time to rally the troops.

CHAPTER TWENTY-SEVEN
AT HOME FOR VISITORS

Kessler arrived not long after that. Freya had felt a little uncomfortable about inviting him over, but she'd decided that dealing with Ben was more important than being shy, and Kessler had some useful skills, if his success with Jemima's necklace was anything to go by. Not to mention he'd been the one to report Manuel's kidnapping. Really, she couldn't *not* invite him.

"Come in," she told him. "The others will be here soon."

Val appeared at Freya's door a short time later. Val had brought along the cold-hating Nesh.

Is it really a good idea to involve mundanes? It seems churlish to turn him away at this point, though. At least Jemima is out of town; we'd probably be up to our ears in snow otherwise. And there's hardly room for more people in here.

"No Lin?" Freya asked, not that she wanted another body in the room, but remembering Nesh had been interested in the other girl she'd met with this group.

Nesh looked glum. "She said she had other things to do. Seems she wasn't impressed with me looking after Val after all."

"Oh. Bad luck."

"Told you it wouldn't work," Val said.

Mr Fluffbum, who had been winding around Freya's legs in the hope of more exciting food, disappeared back into Freya's bedroom with an irritated twitch of his tail.

"Was that your cat?" Val asked. "He looked cute."

"He is," Freya agreed. "He just doesn't like crowds." *Thank you, Mr Fluffbum, for saying with actions what I can't politely say aloud.*

Val didn't appear at all abashed. "I thought we should have someone from the men's floor of the halls," she said.

Freya hadn't even known that was a thing, but she nodded as though in understanding.

Freya closed the door behind them all. Nesh made himself comfortable on the floor since Kessler was already taking up most of the sofa. Val leant against the door frame, leaving Freya to choose between standing, sitting on the floor beside Nesh, or perching on the edge of the remaining sofa seat. She hovered in the doorway, indecisive. She wished she had enough tea bags left to offer some around; it would give her something to do.

Maybe I can come up with something.

She glanced through the kitchen window. Her flat had a rosebush by the back door; the flowers themselves were over for the season, but a few deep orange rose hips waved at her as she looked.

"Just a moment," she said, and darted to the back door. She set the kettle to boil while she collected the rosehips, then poured the boiling water over them in the largest pot she owned.

Rose hip tea. Problem solved.

She re-entered the living area and offered her makeshift tea. Kessler and Val accepted some; Nesh refused.

"How come you didn't come dancing the other night?" Freya asked Nesh, the person she knew least well.

"Not my sort of music," Nesh replied easily. "I prefer to make my own." He grinned. "Besides, Val always goes climbing after dancing, and I can't be having with that sort of thing."

Val snorted with laughter; Freya wasn't sure if she was more amused at Nesh's borrowing of the local phrase or at how correct he was in his analysis of her evening plans.

"Lucky you didn't come, what with the snow and all," Val said.

"Too right. That would *really* not have been my thing," Nesh said. "Much too cold." He ran a hand over his tight black curls. "So, what was it you wanted us for so urgently?"

Freya cast around for a place to start. It was much harder to know what to say with a mixed audience. "Well, Val and Manuel were injured the other night. And Jemima had a climbing accident that could have killed her. You know that, right?"

Nesh nodded. He had looked after Val; of course he knew, Freya reminded herself. "So, the person who injured them has a bit of... an obsession, I guess. He's into Apollo, the Greek god." She hefted the book, which was still sitting next to the sofa.

Nesh and Kessler both peered at the book. Kessler shrugged.

"That's the god who's all about himself, right? Music, poetry, that sort of thing." He sounded bored.

"That's right. But the problem is that the person—"

"Just say Ben, Freya," Val interjected. "They need to know who they're dealing with."

"Wait, *Ben* hurt Val?" Nesh sounded outraged.

How come he didn't know that yet? Perhaps he wasn't as close to Val as she'd thought.

"Yeah, though I think I was an innocent bystander," Val said placatingly.

"Maybe so. Because now he's taken Manuel somewhere. Kidnapped him, I guess you'd call it. Kessler saw it happen. And given that he tried to kill Manuel the other night, I'm really worried about Manuel's safety now." Freya waited impatiently as the room filled with a hubbub of voices. "Alright, so yes, Ben has some odd ideas," she said over the others. "But we need to do something about Manuel."

Everyone turned to look at her, and she felt a blush sweeping over her cheeks.

"What do you mean, Freya?" Val asked. "I've got no idea where Ben might have taken Manuel. Especially not if that postgrad you mentioned is involved. Isn't it more a matter for the police?"

Freya bit her lip. How to explain that she didn't trust the police, anywhere? Even if she'd chosen this university town for its supposed lack of weres.

Kessler broke into the silence, saving her from the awkward moment. "I reported it to the police when I saw it," he said. "They told me they'd look into it. But what if he's in another form?"

"That's just the sort of thing he would do if he felt he was in danger," Val said. "And if he's shifted, the police won't recognise him. They're all mundane around here, right?" She aimed that question at Kessler.

"Right. That's why we have so many other, ah, types, in this city," he agreed, with a cautious look at Nesh.

"I love the variety here," Nesh said, clearly feeling put upon.

"Me too," Kessler agreed, giving Nesh a lazy smile. Nesh looked away, and Kessler's smile faded.

"That's why we're all here," Val put in. She leant over and patted Nesh on the shoulder.

"So... do we try and find Manuel ourselves?" Freya asked. "I don't want to be the one to tell Jemima he's disappeared, when she returns." She took a sip of her rosehip tea. It didn't have the caffeine kick of black tea, but the warm liquid was a welcome distraction from trying to be the leader.

"It would be much better all round if we find him before that," Val agreed. "So, Kess, what else can you tell us?"

Kessler tapped his fingers on his knee, one-two-three, one-two-three.

"I didn't see all that much," he admitted. "I was working on my latest project for uni when I heard a yell down in the alley. I looked out the window and recognised Manuel from walking with you lot to the train station the other day. But by the time I got downstairs, that archer guy, I think you called him Ben, had already got Manuel into a van." He looked down at his hands, which were cupped around something. "I phoned in the number plate. But it turned out to be a rental vehicle and the rental company wouldn't give me any details. Privacy, you know. All I got was this." He held up a black feather.

The group exploded into words.

"But why didn't you—"

"What is that supposed to be?"

"Couldn't you have—"

Val overrode the babble with her louder voice. "It doesn't sound like we've got much to go on from you, Kessler, but at least we know what happened. Otherwise, we might not have known he was missing till next week. Everyone, quiet now and let's think about what we might work with."

Much to Freya's relief, the noise subsided. As it did so, a thought niggled at her. *What was it?*

"Manuel spent most of his time either studying in his room, or drinking and climbing with you and Jemima," Nesh pointed out. "The rest of us didn't really know him well."

"He joined the salsa club, didn't he?" Val asked.

"You'd know more about that than me," Nesh said. "I only went the once."

"Yeah, I know, long enough to discover you've got two left feet," Val teased gently.

"Long enough to know it's not the scene for me," Nesh countered.

"Right, I'm sure that was the *real* reason," Val said.

Given Manuel's predicament, Freya was surprised that Val had time for humour. But Val hurried on, so perhaps it was simply her response to stress.

"Anyway, the salsa club meets in one of those rent-by-the-hour dance studios, there's no way Ben would stash Manuel there."

"There was something..." Freya began.

"Spit it out then," Val commanded.

Freya didn't much like being commanded. She gave Val a hard glance. But Manuel needed their help.

"I was thinking about something I found in that book about Apollo," she said. "There was a card in it, with a local address. For some apartments, much posher than halls. I know Ben's in the same hall as you. Has anyone checked there?"

"We only just found out Manuel is missing, Freya. We haven't checked anywhere," Val pointed out.

"Right. Sorry. Maybe that should be the first place we look. But the second place might be those apartments. They had Apollo in the name. Or actually Phoebus, but that's just another name for Apollo. I thought perhaps that postgrad Paul might live there. Or the society they're a part of might have headquarters there, or something."

"Break out the ginger beer," Nesh muttered. "We're looking for Timmy."

Val gave him an irritated look. "It's not Enid Blyton, you know," she said. Then she snorted. "But you're not so far off with Timmy."

Freya rubbed her temples. Surely, Val was going beyond what was reasonable in talking about shifters like that in front of Nesh.

"Well, we've got two places to check," she said. "Who's going where?"

"You're the only one with the Apollonian apartment address," Val said. "How about you and Kess go check it out. I'll go back to the halls with ginger-beer boy here. Check in by phone in an hour, perhaps?"

"It's Kess*ler*," said Kessler. "But fine. Lead on, Freya."

"I'm only agreeing if you never call me ginger-beer boy again," Nesh told Val. "Some things are beyond the pale."

"Oh, be a spoilsport then," Val muttered.

She didn't repeat the offending nickname, Freya noticed.

Within moments, the flat had emptied. Kessler moved to the door and put his coat on.

"Shall we go?" he said.

Freya bent and patted Mr Fluffbum's head as he reappeared from the bedroom and sidled around her ankles.

"I'll just feed my cat," she said. "Then yes, let's go." She hesitated. "Maybe bring that feather."

CHAPTER TWENTY-EIGHT
HIDDEN MEANINGS

Kessler wasn't impressed with Freya's suggestion that they walk all the way to the inner-city apartments.

"I'll pay your fare if you're skint," he said impatiently when Freya explained her reasons for not taking the bus. "I'm certain that timing is important."

She nodded. "Thanks. The quicker we get there the better."

The bus trip was silent; there were too many other people on board to make a conversation about kidnapping a possibility. Kessler alternated between straightening the bent barbs of the feather and scrolling on his phone. It didn't seem like *he* was worried about bird mites. Freya looked out of the window, feeling a vague sense of rejection even though she could understand why Kessler wasn't talking.

At least the bus is heated. Although much of the snow had melted, the day was still chilly.

"What might we do with the feather?" Freya asked when they got off in the city on a road lined with high-rise buildings and containing a rather desolate nature strip.

Kessler glanced at her, a cool, considering look. "I haven't decided yet. But there seem to be a lot of crows associated with Ben. If he's any kind of crow-were, we may be able to use it to locate him."

"But he hates weres," Freya pointed out. "Surely he couldn't be one himself?"

Kessler shrugged. "People can be all kinds of strange."

Freya laughed without mirth. "I suppose that's true. How about we go look at the apartments, and if we need more directions, we try that idea with the feather."

"Very well."

It wasn't far from the bus stop to the apartments indicated on Freya's bookmark. She looked up at the high-rise residential complex with some dismay. It was on one corner of a busy intersection and looked forbidding.

"How are we supposed to find anyone in there? Would Ben really have dragged Manuel in without someone noticing?" There were university buildings across the street, and some sort of warehouse with wide, shuttered entry bays. A couple of the shuttered doors held a small pattern near the bottom. Freya vaguely assumed that they belonged to a fine arts department.

Kessler turned around in a circle, slowly, apparently assessing the situation.

"I know your address is those apartments," he said, with a nod to the building in question, "But if I were trying to hide someone, I would probably use the warehouse. With a big van like the one I saw, you'd be able to back right up to one of those doors."

Freya looked from the apartments to the warehouse. She didn't really want to intrude on either building.

It would be crazy to get this close and not investigate, she told herself firmly. *Really.* Despite that, she looked longingly towards the bus stop. It would be so easy to absolve herself of responsibility. After all, she didn't even like weres. And it was Kessler who had seen Manuel being taken. On the other hand, if not looking meant someone died—even if that someone was a were—then she'd better suck up her reluctance and do it.

"Shall we start with your feather?" After all, if they could eliminate one building with something so simple, they should.

"I suppose we can try," Kessler agreed. But he looked around doubtfully. Although the day was chilly and grey, there were a lot of people on the street. "Not here," he added.

"Let's look a bit closer at the apartments anyway," Freya said reluctantly. Kessler was right that the street wasn't the best place to start waving around feathers and whatever else he needed to locate a possible crow shifter. "After all, Paul, Ben's postgrad friend, did sort of point out the address." She led the way into the lobby. There was a stairway on one side and a bank of letter boxes with apartment numbers beside it, but no names. The other side held a lift and a reception booth, currently unmanned. Both access points had keylocks on them. Another open stair led up to a glass-walled room which even from the ground floor, Freya could see was empty. "Looks like a dead end," she said, trying and failing not to feel relieved that they couldn't get in.

"Not necessarily," Kessler said. He held up the feather. "It's a bit more private in here, so long as no-one comes in or out." He fiddled with his phone a moment, placed the feather on the face of the phone and held it away from him, then pressed the screen. Some sort of harp music started playing loudly from the phone, every plucked chord making the feather vibrate.

"What is *that*?" Freya asked.

"Lyre music, of course," Kessler said with a grin. "An Apollo special." A particularly loud arpeggio made the feather spin on the phone. A gust of air swept into the lobby as someone opened the door, and the feather flew to the ground, spinning as it did so. Kessler cursed and lunged for the feather and his phone.

"Can I help you?" asked a steely voice. A tall, thin woman wearing a large and colourful turban had entered the lobby, and slid into the vacant seat as Freya stared.

"Er... we were just looking for a friend," she said, since Kessler seemed too busy with his feather to answer.

"What apartment number?"

Freya hesitated. The bookmark hadn't included an apartment number, only the name of the building.

"I'm not sure," she admitted. "His name is Paul."

"Surname?"

Freya bit her lip. She couldn't remember the postgrad's ID card well enough. "I don't know."

"In that case, you'd better contact your friend yourself. I can't let just anyone in," the woman said. She adjusted her turban, and Freya's eyes widened as she saw a tiny snake's head emerge from behind the woman's ear.

"Let's go, Freya, we can catch up with our friends another time," Kessler said loudly.

"Yes, let's." Freya was at the exit door before she finished speaking.

"Just a moment," the receptionist called. Freya paused, her hand on the door. The turbaned woman ran her finger over a clipboard and gave a sharp nod. "There's a note here for someone of your description. Name, please?"

"Freya," Freya said doubtfully.

"Yes. Here you are." The woman held out a small pink post-it note. Freya approached the desk and took the note as soon as she was close enough to do so, then dashed out to join Kessler outside. A Medusian receptionist was more than she was prepared for.

Back on the street, Kessler shook his head.

"I don't think Ben was in there," he said. "At any rate, the feather landed pointing back out this way."

"Thank goodness," Freya said. "We wouldn't have got far in there anyway. Did you see that woman's hair?"

"I was too busy watching the feather to pay attention to hairstyles," Kessler said. "But I haven't seen one yet that was so bad it stopped entry."

"Hmm. Well, never mind. I got a note from her. I think it's from Paul. Or Ben, I suppose. There isn't a name." She held up the post-it note, the sticky edge tacky against her finger.

There were only a few words on the note.

You'll find your friend with the fishes.

"It's rather sinister, but it doesn't sound like they took Manuel to the apartments. Where else do we look? I can't imagine where 'the fishes' are. Any idea?" Freya decided that since Kessler hadn't seen it, it was easier to pretend she hadn't seen the snake under the turban.

"Like I said before. That warehouse over the road. Unless it's a gangster reference, like in those old *noir* movies."

"I suppose we'd better look then." *And let's hope there aren't Gorgons running the warehouse.*

CHAPTER TWENTY-NINE
DISCOVERY?

The pattern on the warehouse doors turned out to be out to be a couple of fish curling around each other.

"Manuel could actually be here," Freya exclaimed. But every door was locked. Before Freya could give up the whole expedition as a failure, Kessler pointed out the service door.

"That one's got an electronic lock," he said. "Give me half a minute." He pulled a small roll of tools out of his pocket and selected something that looked like a fancy screwdriver. He pressed it into the lock, twisted the end, pressed a button and twisted again. Then he removed it and placed the quill end of the feather in the lock instead, and turned it. "Voila," he said, as the door opened.

Trying not to feel useless in comparison to Kessler's display of competency, Freya switched on the flashlight function on her phone and entered the building.

Inside, it looked like the large space was filled with silent machinery. Not fine arts after all.

Unless it's steampunk? Freya's flashlight revealed large hulking shapes, some covered with cloth and others gleaming dully under a coating of dust. An antique smell of motor oil and wood filled her nostrils.

"This is amazing," Kessler murmured, laying a hand reverently on one of the machines. "Like something out of the 19th century."

"This is spooky," Freya whispered back. "Any idea how we find out if Manuel is in here?"

"Casablanca style," Kessler said. Then, perhaps realising that Freya didn't know what he was talking about, he elaborated. "We check everywhere and hope not to get disturbed by the enemy."

Freya shivered, although it was no colder inside than outside. "Let's get started then," she said aloud, and set off purposefully to one side of the warehouse, checking under and behind banks of machinery as she did so. Kessler set off in the other direction, taking a similar approach from what Freya could see.

Several minutes later, they reached the end of the warehouse. Kessler looked at Freya and shook his head.

"No luck. I was dead sure he'd be stashed in here."

Freya shook her own head. "He's not here. But I can't help but feel that we've been missing something. Let's go back to the front and double check." They made their way back, switching sides to check that neither of them had missed anything. But there was no-one in the warehouse.

"I don't know," Freya said, standing between Kessler and the street as he re-locked the door. "Where else could 'with the fishes' mean in this town? And why would Paul or Ben tell me Manuel's whereabouts, anyway?"

Kessler finished with the lock and leant against the door. "Perhaps they're not as keen on doing away with people as we thought," he said. "Perhaps they just want to scare us. As to the fishes, I guess there's a few fish shops around," he said. "If you wanted someone kept on ice you'd go to one of them. Except that they'd call the police on you if you did. Hmm. I suppose the other place to find fish is in the river." He clicked his fingers. "Yes! That could be it!"

"I'm new here," Freya reminded him. "What could be it?"

"The tunnels," Kessler said. "There're dozens of underground rivers in this city. There's even one under the station where a couple of rivers meet. It wouldn't be my choice of place to visit, but if you wanted to stash someone out of sight, it'd be perfect."

Freya nodded slowly. "You're right. But if there are dozens of tunnels, how do we find the right one?"

Kessler rubbed his chin.

"People are usually lazy," he said. "Why don't we start with the closest one? It's only a couple of blocks from here."

Whilst not in the least wanting to enter an underground river, Freya knew he was right. They had to look. "Lead on," she said with a sigh. "I'll message Val while we walk."

The nearest entry to the underground river system turned out to be a small park on the edge of a stream. On a more summery day it might have been pleasant. Several winding paths made the slope down to river level more accessible, and despite the chill, a few people were sitting by the riverside. Buddleia bushes—still holding a few bunches of late-blooming purple flowers amongst their grey-green leaves—overhung the river, almost hiding the entrance to a tunnel.

Freya paused on the lowest section of the park, just above the river, which was more of a stream than anything else. She checked her phone again.

"Val and Nesh haven't found anything at the halls," she reported. "Val's on her way here, but Nesh isn't coming." She tapped on her phone nervously. *Why would they tell us where they've stashed Manuel? And how did they know I'd visit the apartment building?*

Kessler shrugged. "Probably just as well," he said. "I've heard the ceiling's pretty low in those tunnels, and Nesh is a tall one."

"So is Manuel," Freya pointed out.

"We're assuming he didn't have much choice in the matter."

"True." Freya gazed uneasily at the tunnel entrance. It looked dark and uninviting. Was it even safe in there? What else lived in the tunnels? And how would the local river deities react to being confined in such a place? "Have you been in?" she asked.

Kessler shook his head. "Not my kind of thing. I prefer to keep my feet dry. Electronics and water don't mix well."

"Freya!"

Already uneasy, and unaccustomed to having her name shouted in public, Freya almost dropped her phone in the river in surprise. But it was only Val announcing her arrival. Freya slipped her phone into a pocket and forced her shoulders to relax.

"You startled me," she muttered as Val descended the slope in leaps that reminded Freya of a show pony. The other girl reached the lowest level in a scatter of small stones and a gasped greeting.

"Any luck? There was no sign of anything wrong at the halls."

"We haven't found Manuel yet. But Kessler thinks he might be in the underground tunnels, the river system. Because of the note we found, and because we haven't found him anywhere else."

Val's eyes widened, although Freya had already said more-or-less the same thing via phone message.

"Maybe he's in the Megatron," she whispered dramatically.

Freya felt the hair rise on the back of her neck. "What's the Megatron when it's at home?" she asked, trying to ignore the feeling.

"It's a sort of manmade cavern where the rivers meet underground," Kessler said. "If he's in there I hope he's a good swimmer. It's supposed to be deep water."

"Just as well most of that snow's already melted," Val said cheerfully. "Otherwise, it'd be too deep for us, too." She looked from Kessler to Freya. "We going in?"

"Yes," Freya said, despite her misgivings. "I think we have to at least check the more accessible parts." She took the final step into the river. Frigid water rose to her ankles, invading her shoes. "Hello again," she muttered, in case the water spirit was listening. Then she ducked under the buddleia and entered the darkness.

CHAPTER THIRTY
UNDERGROUND

At first there was space to walk without ducking her head. Green light filtered in through the vegetation.

"Manuel?" she called, in case he was somewhere nearby. Her voice echoed back to her, amplified by the curved brick ceiling. There was no other reply, so she kept walking, water sloshing with every step. Behind her, she heard the splashes as Val and Kessler also entered the stream. After only a few metres it was too dark to see properly. She rather thought the ceiling was closer than it had been. "I'm going to use my phone light now," she told them, turning her head back towards the entrance to minimise echoes. An inadvertent sideways step revealed a deeper channel, which helped a little with headspace, but also meant more of her got wet. *Frigg.*

Val was close behind her, but Kessler had hung back. He stood silhouetted, with a hand actually touching the ceiling; it must have lowered faster than she had thought.

For once being short is an asset. She tried not to think about how old the tunnel must be.

"I'm not sure I can do this," Kessler said. His usually calm voice held a wobble. "I'll... keep watch from here."

Although she wasn't enjoying the sensation of being underground, Freya took heart from Val's presence.

"We won't go far in," she said. *If it's not just me, I'll be OK down here. Even if Kessler stays here. We don't have to go all the way. Just far enough to make sure Manuel's not in here.* She had no desire to find the Megatron Val had spoken of.

"Let's get on with it then," Val said impatiently.

Freya took a last look at the daylight behind her, then resolutely turned to the darkness, tapping on her flashlight app. The light revealed an even lower pitched ceiling ahead. There would be enough room to breathe, but it looked like she and Val would be getting wet. *More* wet.

"Manuel had better be in here." Freya bent her head low and held her phone above the water. Dark green slime covered the curving brick ceiling, and she winced away from it. Then again, she didn't know what was in the dark water surrounding her to waist height, either. *Just otters, right?* Her foot slipped on a stone and she stumbled closer to the water's surface.

"It's the perfect place to hide someone. Especially if Ben thought he had to hide someone from a were," Val pointed out. She followed close behind Freya, her breath loud in the enclosed space.

"He didn't, though," Freya said, stepping more cautiously. "I mean, no-one else we know is a were. Are they?"

"Probably not, but I don't see why Ben would know that," Val said.

"How did he know Manuel was? And why did he try to kill Jemima?" Freya countered.

Quiet, watery, trickling sounds filled the pause that followed.

"Maybe he's just an evil bastard," Val suggested at last. "Not everyone is all peace and light."

Freya laughed without really wanting to. The sound bounced off the close walls of the tunnel and she quickly stopped.

"If only." She rubbed her aching neck with one hand. "I hope the ceiling rises soon." Step after sloshy step, Freya followed the underground river. *The walls aren't really pressing in,* she assured herself. She pointed her flashlight towards the ceiling anyway, just to make sure. There was less algae up there, but that only served to draw her attention to the weight of earth that must surely be above her, held back only by ancient Victorian brickwork. *Ignore it.*

"Anything to see up there?" Val's cheerful voice helped her to ignore most of her qualms.

"Only bricks." Freya forced herself to copy Val's tone and kept splashing forward. Happily for the crick in her neck, the low section eventually ended, and she stepped out into a steep-sided vault that was open to the sky, although high brick walls constrained the river's flow. Buddleia bushes hung over the walls, obscuring much of the sky.

Freya looked around carefully for any signs that a were-maned-wolf and his captors had passed this way. It was hard to pick anything out given the glass bottles and assorted broken bricks that were stranded in the shallow muddy edges. However, while she rolled her shoulders and tilted her head from side to side to ease her tense muscles, she spotted a tuft of reddish fur on the lip of the next tunnel. *Too high for regular foxes, surely.* Up at street level she could hear voices as students called to each other. A crow flew overhead, barely visible as a dark shape through the scrappy bushes that overhung the vault. Freya hastily strode towards the next tunnel. She didn't want to be spotted by crows, not the way they'd been acting lately.

"We'd best keep going," she told Val as the other girl emerged. She pointed to the fur. "It looks like we're on the right track." Taking a deep breath, she stepped into the next section of tunnel. At first it was much the same as the first: low-ceilinged, curving brick, cold water trickling around her legs and unidentifiable lumps decorating the shallower edges of the stream. However, after a while the tunnel opened up, the ceiling rising, although it didn't get any lighter. Scanning with her flashlight app, she saw that several tunnels opened out of the space she was in. Which way should they go? She could do with Kessler and his way-finding feather now. As she stood and waited, a deep rumbling noise filled the air. Dust sifted down from above as everything vibrated. Freya stared wide-eyed at the ceiling, before blinking dust out of her eyes. It sounded as though a train was passing right above her.

I can't wait to see daylight again.

"Woden's eye, that sounded way too close," Val said, her cheerful tone a contrast to her words, when the noise dissipated. "We must be right under the station."

"Yes," Freya agreed. She shuddered at the thought of all those heavy carriages and engines going overhead. "Any idea which way to go now?" There were no handy clues of fur this time. She stepped closer to one tunnel to peer into it and kicked something solid. "Ow!" She angled her light downwards to see what she'd hit with her foot. It was roundish, and hard. She picked it up. She thought it was some sort of ceramic, though it was hard to be sure in the dim light. "For that matter, any idea what this is?"

"It's a crucible, isn't it?" Val said. "You know, for making steel and stuff. Didn't you see them in the intro to the city video they made us watch? That one's a bit on the small side, though. It's hard to imagine it's big enough to be useful for anything."

Freya nodded. She hadn't expected to see such a thing in an underground river, but Val was right. "Perhaps Kessler would appreciate it? It's an engineering sort of thing, right?"

Freya didn't see Val shrug, but she could imagine it.

"You can take it back to him if you like," Val said.

Freya stuffed it into a pocket, but she was distracted from the crucible, because her light showed a glimmer on something dark floating downstream.

"The feather!" As she watched, the black feather floated down the leftmost tunnel. The water in that tunnel seemed to be a little shallower, too. "Let's follow it!" *I don't know if Kessler sent it for us, but it's not like we have any other guide at this point.*

She ducked her head and entered the tunnel. Splashing behind her assured her that Val followed. At least, she hoped it was Val. The floor of the tunnel sloped downwards, and Freya was obliged to follow. The shiver she felt was caused by more than the cold water.

I hate it underground, she realised with sudden clarity. *Why did I ever come down here? For a* were*! Insanity.*

"Val?" she asked uncertainly, turning to look behind her.

"Still here," Val assured her, although her voice was further away than Freya would have liked.

Freya clenched her fists, trying to convince herself that she was fine, and took a few more steps forward. Since she *was* here, she might as well do her best to find the were in question. The sound of trickling water, which had never quite gone away, intensified. Something flapped past her face, and she couldn't quite suppress a shriek. Instantly, the space above the water was alive with wings. Flashing her light upward again, Freya saw hundreds of bats flying in a tall, vaulted chamber. Right in the middle, huddled down in water nearly up to his neck, was Manuel.

Chapter Thirty-One
Stand-off

To begin with, Freya couldn't do much about Manuel. She was too busy ducking away from the flurry of bats, while trying not to get any more of herself into the water than she could help. *They're as scared as I am,* Freya reminded herself. That didn't stop her heart thundering when a bat got caught in her hair and she flinched away from its tiny scrabbling claws.

"Out you get," she said aloud, hoping her voice would make other bats avoid her. She hated the tremor in her words. *You're supposed to be a scientist in training, not an easily flustered mundane.* Deliberately breathing out through her nose, slowly, she switched off her phone's light.

"What'd you do that for?" Val's voice echoed in the large chamber, and Freya felt more than heard the additional panic in the bats, puffs of air hitting her face as the bats fluttered here and there in the semidarkness. Val pointed her phone light downward after one skewbald flash at the ceiling, which erupted with bats.

"I'm trying to let the bats calm down," Freya whispered as loud as she dared. "Manuel's here."

"Operation success!" Val half-whispered, but her triumphant tone was obvious.

A horribly familiar slow clapping stopped anything Freya might have said in reply.

"I honestly didn't think you had it in you to go underground to save a were." Ben's voice came from beyond Manuel. Freya almost dropped her phone in combined shock and terror. What was Ben doing down here—and what trap might he have rigged for her or her new friends?

She gripped her phone tightly and, turning the light on again, scanned the huge chamber—keeping the beam low this time to avoid stirring up the bats any more. A flash of blond hair glinted in the light.

There he is. Beyond Manuel, Ben stood in another tunnel entrance. Presumably he'd entered the tunnel system some other way and waited for them. But why?

Fear glued her tongue to the roof of her mouth for a moment. *Talk. Don't let him take over the conversation.*

"You've really got it in for weres, don't you?" Freya said lightly, trying to keep judgement and fear out of her voice.

Ben laughed, a low chuckle that didn't stop the bats from settling back into their roosts.

They must be clinging on to rough bits in the bricks, Freya decided as she risked a glance at them before returning her full attention to Ben.

"I told you before. Weres are a blight on the world. If we demis are ever going to stop hiding our powers, we can't present ourselves to humanity as a bunch of half-animals." There was a sneer in his voice as he described weres.

"But we're not trying to reveal ourselves," Freya objected. *Now I've gone and revealed myself as a demi. I guess he already knew that though. Somehow. Apparently, I'm still lagging in the demi skills department.* If she hadn't been almost vibrating with tension, she'd have sighed at that continued lack. After summoning various water deities over the last few years—especially after negotiating with a sea goddess for her sister's life—she'd thought she finally had a grip on her own powers. But it seemed that she was still missing some basics. She took a deep breath. *Don't let yourself get sidetracked. We need to get ourselves and Manuel out of here in one piece.*

"That's all you know," Ben jeered. "I for one am not going to spend my life hiding."

"Not hiding is not the same as killing off innocent people," Val pointed out reasonably, sloshing through the deepening water to stand beside Freya.

Ben snorted. "I'm not talking about people."

Manuel whimpered, apparently too far gone in fear to speak up for himself. Freya rather thought he must be tied up, or surely, he would have made an escape by now.

Not surprising he's terrified, if he's been stuck down here in the dark all this time.

A chill ran through Freya, and not only from the water she was standing in. Val had been right. Some people were just plain evil.

"Well, I'm a person, and so is Freya. We won't argue over the niceties, Ben. Point is, what are you planning down here?" Val's voice rose as she questioned Ben, and the bats responded by leaving their roosts to flap in a cloud around the high-roofed chamber. Freya crouched low, heedless of the water that soaked her to the waist (although she held her phone higher; losing her light source in here was beyond imagining) and she saw Val do the same.

"Just the elimination of an invasive pest," Ben declared, ignoring the cloud of bats. "I wasn't expecting two of you to come after him—or rather it—but since you're both obviously were-lovers, I don't see you holding a place in the new world order my organisation is planning. But of course, it won't be anything to do with me when a flash flood sweeps unsuspecting and unauthorised tunnel explorers to a watery death."

Ben's words at first gave Freya chills of terror. But as he continued, a germ of hope unfurled inside her.

He doesn't know! He doesn't know what my abilities are. But... can I even use them here? There's nowhere to draw a protective circle, nothing to use as a thyrsus. Just Val and me and Manuel standing in a river.

"What flood is that, Ben?" she asked in an encouraging tone.

"You're not planning to replicate that nineteenth century flood, are you?" Val said, doubt entering her voice for possibly the first time since Freya had known her. "Hundreds of people died back then."

Freya wasn't sure what flood Val meant; non-mythological history was not her strong suit—but she knew there were huge dams in the hills and moorland that rose to the south and west of the city. She couldn't imagine the devastation that one of those rupturing would bring. But Ben denied the suggestion.

"You and that beast—," he pointed at Manuel, who was being surprisingly, or perhaps sensibly, silent, "—are not worth that much effort. No, Paul's arranged something a little closer." He grinned unpleasantly. "Why bother with a dam when an industrial spill will do the job?"

"Wouldn't a flood in here wash you away too?" Freya pointed out logically.

"You must think I'm stupid. Obviously, he won't instigate it until I give him the signal," Ben said. "And there's no reason to stick to plain water." He hefted a phone then put it back in his pocket.

Val glanced at Freya. "Do we think he's stupid?" she said in a stage whisper.

Freya bit her lip. She wanted to laugh at Val's throwaway line, but she was too worried about what Ben might do in response. And what did he mean about plain water? Water was enough to drown anyone. Instead, she started pacing out a circle, hunched over to avoid the bats, not going any closer to Ben in case he took it as a threat—he probably had that bow and arrow stashed nearby—and circling around Val. She couldn't see a way of including Manuel in her circle. He was too close to Ben.

"Got you worried, don't I?" Ben said. "Going back the way you came won't help."

Freya thought there should have been more uncertainty in his tone. But she was certain that it was better that he didn't suspect what she was doing, so she ignored him and completed her circle. She put her hands in her pockets in case anything handy was in there. Her questing hand found soggy, crumbling cat treats, a pencil with a broken lead, and some hawthorn berries she'd planned to turn into something edible later. There was something heavy and rounded as well: the crucible she'd picked up earlier. Well, that didn't seem useful. It wasn't even metal, to keep away the barghests. Although, with luck those were gone, or at least kept at bay by the metal rails of the train tracks, somewhere above her.

She pulled out the hawthorn berries. They probably wouldn't help, but it was worth trying anything. She repeated her circle, this time dropping haws as she paced, and humming under her breath. She didn't dare to sing aloud, but at least she'd connected with this river's deity before.

Help me, she thought fiercely, as though thought alone would work to summon a deity. *If only.*

As she completed the second circle, Ben snapped at her.

"Stand still! And stop that awful noise."

Perhaps the humming hadn't been as quiet as she thought. But even as she stopped her pacing, she saw the water level around Manuel begin to rise.

Oh Frigg, what if it goes too high, above his head? He must be tied up, or surely he would have just walked out of here. It's bad enough, trying to summon a water deity without a protective circle. I don't even know which deity it is here anymore, there have been so many tributaries adding to this watercourse.

Despite her misgivings, the water swirled improbably, following the circle she'd paced out, rising higher and higher in a vortex around her and Val. Oddly, the water level fell in the centre of her circle.

"What have you done?" Ben snapped. "I haven't given the signal yet."

Over the sound of rushing water, Freya heard his phone ringing. He must be trying to contact his accomplice, Paul.

"Now that is some serious energy," Val muttered in Freya's ear. "Give me a few seconds more and I'll short out his phone."

"I'm not controlling this," Freya whispered back. "But go ahead and do it."

Val gave her a thumbs up, then began turning in a circle in the opposite direction to the vortex that surrounded them. The wall of water was almost high enough to shut off their view of Ben, and Freya couldn't see Manuel at all. She *could* see brown, furry bodies swimming in the vortex: otters. They seemed to be enjoying the unexpected water action, diving though the edges of the whirlpool and popping in and out of it. Then some maximum must have been reached, because all the otters abruptly swam to the crest of the circle of water, and disappeared off the other side.

"Hurry!" Freya told Val. As Val lifted her arms towards the bat-covered ceiling, the entire cloud of bats ceased their panicked flapping and flew directly towards Ben, perhaps fleeing the roost that had become too dangerous to inhabit. Ben cursed, and Val brought her arms down with decision. Instead of a flash, this time the light vanished. Freya cried out in surprise as her phone tingled in her hand, but managed to hold on to it. Ben shouted too, some incomprehensible words that could be Greek or Gaelic for all Freya knew. His voice rose in a crowlike shriek.

"Now!" Freya yelled to the river deity who must be imbuing the vortex with its power. "Flow to the sea!" *It always helps to work with a deity's natural inclinations.* She flung her own arms wide, scattering cat treats and haws into the yawning darkness. And the water responded, gushing away from Freya and Val, away towards the far-distant sea—which meant towards Ben. Freya staggered as the suddenly strong current pulled at her, and grabbed hold of Val's arm. She rather thought Val was holding onto Manuel. Still the water flowed, drawing them one step at a time towards the place where Ben had stood. She had lost sight of him with the loss of light. The sound of water seemed to mingle with the sound of wings, and if it wasn't impossible, Freya would have been nearly certain there was at least one crow in the tunnel with them.

Unexpected waves hit her as the wall of water ricocheted off the curved brick walls of the chamber, taking her mind off impossible crows. Brick dust filtered down in sheets as the tunnel took more of a battering than it must have done in decades. Freya stumbled one way then another, trying to keep her footing and her phone.

Then, without warning, the vortex collapsed. The water level fell once again, draining away through the tunnel where Ben had disappeared. It should have been quiet, but somebody nearby was gasping, coughing and spluttering as though struggling to draw breath.

"Just a mo," Val said, pulling her arm from Freya's hand. Freya took the opportunity to tap at her phone. Miraculously, it was still working. At least, it restarted, and Freya was able to tap the flashlight app again. A second later, welcome light flooded the chamber. They were only an armlength away from Manuel, who was the one doing the gasping. Val stood beside him, using what looked like a sliver of rock, or possibly a rusty bit of metal, to saw industriously at the zip ties which had held his wrists and ankles together, preventing him from escaping. There was no sign of the bats, the otters, or of Ben.

Chapter Thirty-Two
The Return

The return trip felt faster, despite Manuel holding them back to inchworm speed. Apparently, he'd been in the tunnels for hours, after being blindfolded, cuffed, and shoved through the underground waterways. Being tall, he'd received several blows to the head on his way in, where ancient bridges lowered the ceiling height. He complained of tingling limbs and lack of sensation, no doubt the effect of being held in one position for so long. But he also expressed gratitude, enough to embarrass Freya.

"I can't believe you found me," he repeated several times. "I can't believe I'm alive."

"Well, thank Kessler. It was his suggestion to look down here," Freya told him. "I didn't even know this place existed." *I wish I still didn't know. How am I going to get through three years of uni knowing there are water deities underfoot practically everywhere in the city? Of course, first I have to escape these tunnels in one piece. And make sure that Ben is well and truly dealt with, or I might not make it three weeks.*

Val and Freya linked arms with Manuel to help steady him against the current, which was much more noticeable when going upstream. Perhaps the instruction Freya had given the river deity was also increasing the usual trickling pace of the stream, because the water level remained higher than it had been.

So long as it's not Paul's industrial accident, whatever that might be. Unidentifiable objects banged into their legs from time to time, startling them. Freya didn't hit her foot on a crucible on the way back, but she fingered the one in her pocket. Perhaps Kessler would like it. Or if Ben did reappear despite the river deity's help, she could throw it at him. *Tempting.* She felt better with a potential weapon in her hand.

They reached the first open stretch of river without incident. But this time, crows ringed the walls of the pit-like enclosure. When the three of them appeared, the crows lost no time in diving-bombing them. Freya found herself torn between lobbing the crucible at a crow or attempting to call the river deity. Neither seemed like a great option. There were too many crows for one thrown item to make a difference, and if she called a river spirit without a protective circle again... well, she'd obviously have no protection. The chances of them surviving another unprotected encounter with a river deity seemed slim, no matter how helpful the first one had been.

Taller than both girls, Manuel was more exposed to the crows' sharp beaks and claws. He ducked his head with a cry of pain as one scored his forehead.

Val decided their course of action by yanking Manuel further on, back underground, jerking Freya along too. Deciding that into the next bit of tunnel was probably the best way to get away from the attacking birds, Freya flung her free arm over her head—bumping aside a sharp beak as she did so—and lurched into the dark opening.

Manuel's harsh breathing was louder than Freya's or Val's, but as the ceiling forced them into a lower and lower stoop, Freya was thankful they'd evaded the crows so easily. She hoped the birds couldn't follow an underground river and meet them at their final exit. At last, the roof of the tunnel rose higher. There was someone waiting for them several metres inside the tunnel, but Freya could tell at once that it wasn't Ben—his silhouette was shorter than Kessler's. Kessler was rather further into the tunnel than Freya had expected given his earlier reaction to being underground. They paused to catch him up on events, although Freya was keen to see daylight again, and Manuel leant towards the light, clearly yearning to be out of the tunnel.

"You found him!" Kessler exclaimed. "You all right, mate?" he enquired of Manuel.

Manuel rocked a hand to indicate 'so-so'. "Better than I was," he said. "But I am not going to feel the same way about swimming in future". He glanced around at the curved brick tunnel. "Or masonry."

"I thought you were waiting outside?" Freya asked suspiciously.

"I was," Kessler confirmed. "Until some weirdo with a tank on the back of a truck turned up and started feeding a hose down the bank—one of those big industrial ones. I wouldn't have come in here then, either, except that there was a huge flock of crows hanging around the truck. I remembered what happened to you lot the other night and decided to seek shelter before something similar happened to me."

"A crow attack or an assault?" Val asked.

"Either."

"Ben didn't turn up?" Freya said.

"No, only the crows. I think they're gone now. I was just inside the tunnel, but I could hear them flapping around before. I sent an anonymous message to the police about the truck, just in case it would do some good. Then I heard a siren and decided not to hang around in plain sight. I heard you coming and thought I'd better see how you got on, since it was my idea to come down here at all."

"Well, you were on the right track," Freya said. "I'm worried that Ben might return. It's hard to know what happened to him in there."

"It'll be fine," Val said, confident once again. "You hit him a good one with that river."

"Let's hope so," Freya muttered. She put her hand in her pocket and encountered a hard lump. "Oh, right. Kessler, I don't know if this is something that interests you. Val said it might be a crucible." She handed over the heavy bit of ceramic. Kessler put away his phone and accepted it, tossing it in his hands to get a feel for its heft.

"Thanks. That might come in handy."

"Running water is well known to remove magic," Manuel said suddenly. "That is why I was still stuck there, you know. I could not change shape, even if I wanted to. Maybe the same is true of Ben."

"I've seen plenty of water that holds power," Freya objected. "But I'd be happy if it were true."

Val put an arm around Manuel and one around Freya.

"What we really need is to get Ben to focus on something else," she said. "Any idea how we do that?"

"Yeah," said Manuel. "We go to the pub."

CHAPTER THIRTY-THREE
A CHANGE OF HEART AND MIND?

When the bedraggled group finally exited the tunnel, the first thing they saw was Paul, being held against a truck by a pair of policemen. Freya paused in the tunnel entrance, shielded by buddleia bushes. The truck and tank Kessler had mentioned were still at street level, above the stream by a few metres, but a third uniformed officer was inspecting them, and the hose attached to the tank was safely reeled up. Freya spotted a big chemical hazard sticker on the back of the truck and shuddered. If her biochem lectures had taught her nothing else, they'd taught her to recognise that sign. Whatever was in the tank shouldn't be going into a waterway with people, otters, or indeed any form of life nearby.

"Let's keep going as though we know nothing," Kessler suggested in a low voice. "Just students off to the pub, like Manuel suggested."

"Yeah, they'll probably want to check the tunnels, maybe test the water, by the looks," Val whispered.

"Wait till they take Paul away," Freya suggested. She didn't want to get involved with law enforcement, even though she'd done nothing wrong. So many times in the past, the police had been run by weres. There were nods of agreement all round. They waited while Paul was led out of sight. The moment the police officer by the truck rounded its far side, Manuel seemed to find a bit of extra energy, and they hurried up the hill, leaving only wet footprints to show their passing. Spits of rain promised that those prints wouldn't show up for long.

Once on the street and away from the river, Freya felt a vast sense of relief, despite being cold and dripping with water. *Hopefully just water.* She decided not to speculate on what else might have been in the water they'd been wading through. Not corrosive chemicals, at any rate. Thank Frigg Kessler had averted that fate.

"I've had an idea about how we might deal with Ben if he turns up again," she announced.

"Well, you tell us your idea once we're all sitting somewhere warm," Val said. "I need fortification after that effort."

"Yes, it's been a draining experience," Kessler said slyly.

Val groaned. "If that's all you have to say, you can stay behind."

"Sorry. I guess next time we make a plan we need some in-sewer-ance."

Freya smiled at their banter. She hadn't realised Kessler was the type to make puns. Perhaps he needed to let off steam after being underground.

"We don't change his mind *forever*," Freya explained to the reassembled group. They'd adjourned to the student halls to wash and change into dry clothes before returning to the pub. Freya suspected they wouldn't have been allowed in the door, otherwise. Val had called Nesh and begged him for extra clothes again, so the cold-hating student had joined them.

"Explain, Freya." Val commanded. Manuel shivered in three layers of Nesh's clothes and clutched a mug of coffee. Freya had given in to temptation and bought herself a hot chocolate for a ludicrous price.

"Kessler's necklace for Jemima gave me the idea. Assuming Ben turns up again—I'm guessing he will, and the river won't take him very far downstream, especially since it merges with the Don." *And that wasn't a river I called on.* "We work on a short-term change in his mindset and hope that the change sticks. It'll buy us time, at the very least. Maybe time enough to complete our degrees. And also, we stick to what he likes—Apollo. In case he's actually a Morrigan descendant too, we should work around Halloween, since that's a big day for the Morrigan, and it's not far off. There're a few Apollonian festivals in October too, but none of the dates quite match up." She shivered. Her research into Apollo had turned up more than one 'festival' that hinted at human sacrifice. She felt inordinately lucky that the postgrad, Paul, had been carted off by the police.

"Interesting idea," Kessler said. "I'm not a miracle worker, but I'm game to try."

Freya gave him a quick smile, grateful for any drop of encouragement, and sipped at her hot chocolate, a luxury she'd felt the need of.

"I thought we could try and get him to focus on Apollo's more admirable traits. You know, the music, or poetry. That's why I asked Val to bring anyone musical she knew. And we could use Kessler's technomancy to help get him to refocus," she said.

"I'm an engineering student and occasional phone seller, not a techno-what-have-you," Kessler said. "But I'll help if I can, of course. Can't have my customers getting attacked in the streets," he joked.

"I don't know that I want to socialise with Ben, knowing what I do now," Nesh complained.

Val gulped down the last of her coffee and leant against Nesh. "Freya's trying to make it safer for all of us," she told him. "It would be better if we don't have to worry about Ben doing unexpected crazy things."

Nesh gave her a considering look.

"Better is good, I guess," he said. "Especially if it means less snow."

"It would be much better," Manuel agreed. "Better if he went away altogether, of course. But I would be happier if I did not have to stress over him stalking me every night."

"So, we can agree on that," Freya said. "Though I don't know that snow comes into it. I don't think he's behind the snow. What I thought was that maybe Kessler could make another necklace, or circlet, or something, but specifically for Ben. We think he's already going to be less connected to his power once the river's done with him. So, while he's feeling that way, Nesh, or someone musical, anyway, could get him involved in—"

"A band," said Nesh. "I bet he'd like to be a lead singer. Or perhaps a base guitarist. Or I know, a viola player."

"Yes," Freya agreed, although she wasn't sure why he'd added the viola comment. "Something that would take up his spare time and energy, but would also keep him away from the rest of us." She gave Nesh an apologetic look. "I don't know anyone like that, though, so that's why we need you."

She looked around at the group. Val nodded enthusiastically. Manuel looked unconvinced, arms crossed, but he had the most to lose. Nesh brushed his hand over his hair repeatedly. Kessler had a phone out and was tapping away industriously. He looked up and gave a sharp nod.

"It's probably best to outsource the band idea," he said. "I don't think we wish to keep our enemies close in this case. Fortunately, there's a local band competition starting soon."

"What if he only likes classical music, or jazz, or something?" Freya asked, suddenly feeling like her idea had more holes than a rusty sieve.

"Then we find him a friend in the music school. There are all sorts of chamber orchestras and so on, you know," Val said.

"I know some people in a swing band," Manuel added unexpectedly. "But I do not think I want to foist Ben on them."

"It sounds like the first step is to find out his musical tastes," Kessler said. "Assuming he does turn up, of course."

"I'll do that," Nesh offered. "Probably better coming from me, anyway."

"And I will see what I can make to sever a connection to Apollo, and perhaps the Morrigan too," Kessler said.

"I don't know if severing is what we need," Freya said. "Refocus, really. After all, we need him to get into music as a distraction from hunting wolves. And music is very Apollonian." She grimaced. "The Morrigan seems a bit more than we can take on. Battle frenzy, death and so on don't sound like something that's easy to refocus."

"All the more reason to sever any connection," Kessler said.

"Do I want to know about this wolf-hunting?" Nesh asked. His tone was only half-joking.

"Probably not," Val told him. "It's a bit metaphorical, anyway."

"Just this once. I'll take your word for it," Nesh said. "But only because all the wolves I know of are in zoos."

"So, er, that's it, really," Freya said. "Music, connections and redirection." She hesitated. "Do you think it will work?"

Kessler tilted his head a little, obviously considering. "I think it's worth a shot," he said. "No guarantees."

Val said, "Of course it will."

She's always so confident. Kessler's probably got a better handle on it, but no-one else has come up with an alternative.

"Right then. Let's give it a try," Freya said.

Chapter Thirty-Four

It's a Kind of Magic

The next few days sped by in a blur of classes, assignments, and taking turns at watching Ben, who turned up two days after the tunnel escapade, seeming very subdued. Freya was rather disappointed that the river deities she'd called hadn't put him permanently out of the picture, but also relieved. She didn't want to be responsible for taking a life. That would make her no better than Ben.

She didn't spend long dwelling on her problems in the city. She'd found some woodland walks leading out through the valleys which contained more than enough vegetation to supplement her pot-noodle diet. That much-needed hot chocolate had wiped out a few meals' worth of funds. The woods replenished her cupboards, and helped to take her mind off the problem of Ben. Mr Fluffbum often walked out with her, drawing startled looks from other ramblers.

"It's a funny sort of dog," one said, aptly expressing the expressions of most of them. Freya didn't know what to say to that, so she shrugged and gave a sheepish smile, which seemed to be all that was expected.

But the evenings were growing shorter, and Freya found she didn't feel quite as safe out at night as she had by the coast, even with a nail or teaspoon tucked into a pocket. Especially not when Samhain, or Halloween, rolled around.

Too much practical mythology, Mum, she thought to herself. So that afternoon she joined Val in the pub after lectures instead. The pub had been decorated with a few carved pumpkins and some old-fashioned hollow turnips, but any big celebrations were taking place elsewhere.

She found Nesh and Manuel already gathered there, sitting outside in the scruffy beer garden as usual. She wondered what they'd do in winter. It wasn't like there were gas heaters anymore to make sitting outside in winter comfortable, not since the North Sea wells had been pumped dry. Her mum had told them about such things, back when her dad had been spending so much time in pubs. She looked around at the flattened grass and struggling shrubs, and the view out over a road, wondering if this was the sort of thing he'd been used to. But her dad was long gone. All *she* had to do was make sure she didn't follow in his footsteps, and she was sure that she could avoid that. Especially if she stuck with lime and soda.

"Anything to report?" Val asked Nesh casually, swinging a leg over the bench part of the wooden picnic table. Freya settled in opposite her, wrapping her cloak around herself a little more closely.

"Ben and that Paul fellow, y'know, the postgrad, have been to concerts pretty much every other night," Nesh said.

"Woden's eye, Paul must have sweet-talked the police into releasing him," Val groaned.

Manuel had understandably avoided Ben, but he too had seen the pair of them going out, to poetry evenings.

"I don't think they need their appreciation of music increased," Nesh said. "They go to more musical events than me already. I wish I could afford that many concerts." He took a sip from the drink that was sitting on the table in front of him. "Maybe that postgrad is subsidising them, but I didn't think postgrads made much money either."

"Depends how many extra tutorials they teach," Val said authoritatively. Somehow, Val always knew more than anyone else about how things worked. "You said the postgrad thought you were in his law class, didn't you, Freya? He probably gets enough from that to attend a few concerts with a plus-one."

"I wouldn't mind if attending concerts was all they did," Manuel said. He rubbed the spot where Ben's arrow had hit him. His immersion in the river hadn't helped it to heal.

"Be glad he wasn't a disciple of Eros or Aphrodite," Val said, laughing. "You'd have more problems than just an arrow-wound, then. "

Freya smiled too, thinking of the chaos they would have encountered if Ben had been using the arrows of one of the gods associated with love, rather than the proud and distant Apollo.

"That really would have been worse, wouldn't it?" she agreed. Then she sobered, thinking of how nearly fatal Ben's actions had been. "Probably."

"They take their allegiance to Apollo very seriously, don't they?" Val observed, wrapping her gloved hands around her drink.

"I don't know if Ben actually wants to be hanging out with that Paul chap," Nesh said suddenly. "He doesn't look as happy as you'd expect."

Freya tilted her head, surprised at the comment. "That's... sort of encouraging."

"Yeah, I reckon if he's got an incentive to be somewhere else, he'd take it," Nesh added.

"Any word from Jemima?" Freya asked, thinking of Ben's other victim.

"Still in London," Val said. "Doing remote classes. She'll be back when she can. Apparently, there have been some complications."

Freya wondered what she meant by complications, but didn't ask.

At least there haven't been any sign of barghests, or thunder snow, since Jemima left. The weather was back to the usual autumnal mix of afternoon sun and scattered showers. Their table had an umbrella up, more to keep rain off than to cast shade.

"I hope Kessler comes in today," Freya said. "If Ben has any Morrigan association, then tonight would be the best night for action." Halloween was the day the Morrigan was most commonly celebrated, as Freya had found out when she'd finally returned to the Celtic mythology book.

Manuel stiffened as Ben himself entered the pub, making their vigil all too easy. Ben glanced their way and changed direction to sit morosely by himself at another table, his back to his former friends. There was no sign of Paul this evening. A stray beam of sunlight brightened his blond hair for a few moments before clouds dulled it once more.

"Phoebus Apollo indeed," Freya said under her breath.

"What's that?" Val asked.

"It means something like bright Apollo," Freya said. "It was in that book. Apparently, Apollo had some good marketing. Almost the opposite of the Morrigan, in some ways. Though they both have inner darkness."

"So much darkness," Manuel muttered.

"It's all about the words, isn't it?" Nesh said flippantly.

"I suppose that's why Ben's taking law," Freya said. "Words are important to lawyers, too."

"It's a shame he didn't stick to words last week," Manuel said. "I feel like we should be doing more than just changing his mind. What about retribution?"

"Consequences for his actions, you mean?" Freya asked curiously.

"Yes. I do not think he should be getting off so lightly," Manuel complained bitterly. He opened a packet of crisps he'd bought on his way in, tearing the bag open with jerky, angry movements. Crisps scattered across the table. "Val and I were injured. We could have been killed. Jemima too." His eyes fixed on Ben's back in a menacing glare. "It is only luck that no-one drowned in those tunnels."

"In my experience, those sorts of consequences never work out well," Freya said, thinking of her sister and the sea goddess who'd taken her. She wrapped her arms around herself. One day, she told herself, she'd try to avoid the supernatural altogether. Life must be so much easier for mundanes.

"We're trying for consequences that mean none of us get injured further," Val said placatingly. Absentmindedly, she picked up one of the scattered crisps and ate it. "And without getting ourselves in trouble, too."

Manuel nodded reluctantly. "I liked it better when I thought he was a friend," he said quietly. "And I was just a student of mathematics."

"Sure, we preferred that," Val said. "But there's no point in dwelling on the past. Mistakes were made, we move on. By the way, my dad's climbing gym is re-opening next week," she added. "I hope you'll all come."

There was a moment of silence, and Val's eyes narrowed. "Come on, guys, it just means we need to make sure Ben's not an issue by then. It will be perfectly safe."

"I'll come," Freya said. "But I might stick to the lower slopes, as it were."

Val smiled as though the sun had come out again. "Excellent choice."

Ben had his back to the group, and indeed had ignored them all week. That was probably just as well, because as of yesterday, Kessler had not yet come up with anything that he was happy with. Freya had been checking in with him daily. However, to her relief, Kessler chose that moment to saunter into the beer garden.

"You don't mind if I join you?" he said. He took a seat without waiting for an answer, placing a bottle of something in front of him. "So, I've been looking into your problem," he said. "It's apparently not cool to enforce your will on someone else. We had a course on it the other day."

"In *engineering?*" Val muttered disbelievingly.

"It's not all circuit diagrams and engines," he said cheerfully. "Anyway, I think I have something for you to try, which still passes my ethics test. To be honest, after the tunnels, I would do it anyway, ethical or not. I don't know how you'll get it on him, mind you." He took a sip from his bottle then began to peel off its label.

"I suppose that depends on what 'it' is and how big it is," Freya said, sticking to practical rather than ethical concerns. She toyed with her glass of tap water, turning it in slow circles and watching the vortex that formed in the middle. *Just like the moment before a water deity appears.* She stopped moving her glass, letting the water subside. They didn't need any more deities. Especially not tapwater ones.

"It's a sort of pendant, and it's small. I wanted to do a circle, but there wasn't really any way to make that work. Circlets aren't in fashion this year. This just needs to be hung on his clothing somehow—though if he takes it off, it will lose its effect," Kessler said.

"So, show us what you've got, and then we can figure out how to get it on him," Freya said.

Putting down his drink, Kessler pulled a small object out of his pocket. Freya had never seen him wear a rucksack like other students did.

Perhaps he's got some fancy recording phone, souped up according to his own specifications.

The object was shaped like a lyre, or perhaps a severely bent bow, fashioned out of some sort of metal. It looked like it was patterned in some way, but it also gleamed with a faint golden light. Kessler passed it around. When it was Freya's turn, she saw that it had tiny words etched all over it, almost too small for her to read. The letters were unfamiliar. There was even a crow etched on one side.

"It's pretty," she observed. "What does it say?"

Kessler smiled proudly. "It's a listing of the positive attributes of Apollo. In Greek. I used a magnifying glass and a Greek lexicon to get the words right. And I forged it in that bit of crucible you gave me, Freya. For a bit of local magic."

Val raised her eyebrows. "Impressive. Let's hope it does its thing."

"We still have the problem of getting him to wear it," Freya said. "Any ideas?"

Silence. Freya thought about the past few days. A crow wheeled overhead, then flapped to perch on the edge of the building that housed the pub, probably looking out for dropped bits of food. It gave its wings a shake to settle them, and a black feather wafted down, landing almost at Ben's feet. He stooped to pick it up and tucked it into a pocket. Then he tossed a crisp onto the ground. The crow swooped down and pecked it up, then looked expectantly at him for more.

"That's it!" Freya exclaimed.

The group looked at her inquiringly.

"Maybe he'd collect it if a crow gave it to him," she suggested. "We should use the crows, they're Apollo's messengers. Or possibly descendants of the Morrigan. Anyway, Ben obviously likes them. And crows like shiny things. I don't think I'd trust them to give up a shiny thing, of course. But if we tempted one close enough, then... I don't know, maybe attach this thing like a message to its leg? Then Ben would find it on the crow and take it off. Probably." She lost her excitement as quickly as she had found it. "Never mind, it's not going to work. Why would any particular crow go to Ben? And we don't know that he'd take it, anyway. Especially if he knew we had anything to do with it. Plus, we would have to catch a crow."

"No, wait, you could be onto something there," Val said. "The crow-catching part sounds dangerous, and maybe illegal, but if we find a crow that Ben feeds regularly—like that one..."

At the other table, Ben was feeding the crow more crisps.

"Then we could also feed it," Freya said. "The crows that went for me at the station in Chesterfield were bought off by food."

Manuel nodded. "It is worth a try," he said. "With strong gloves and glasses."

Kessler laughed. "It's a crazy plan. I like it. I've got safety gear you can borrow."

"Or we could just give it to that crow now," Val said. "No time like the present."

"That's risky," Freya said. "Won't he see it's from us, if we do it now?"

"Not if we engage our inner sneakiness," Val said.

Another crow glided down to join the first. Several more flapped in from somewhere nearby and perched on the roof.

"I *can* make another charm if the crow takes this one to its secret horde of shiny things," Kessler said. "But it would take a few more days. I do have to pass my tests and get my workshop hours in."

"I'd like to feel safe sooner," Manuel said. "Ben may have taken a few days off to enjoy some music, but he could start hunting again at any moment."

Freya nodded. The past week had felt like borrowed time. "He might have been taking a break, but none of us wants to risk him attacking again. I think tonight's the night." She opened her rucksack. She'd eaten the rest of the flapjack she'd fed to the crows in Chesterfield, but she had another bar remaining. Filling though the bars were, you had to be hungry to appreciate them. "Let's see if we can attract a crow," she said. "There's no shortage of them." She opened the bar, crumbled the contents, and tossed a little of it in front of her. She looked around. Some of the crows on the roof were definitely eyeing her offering with interest.

An offering... Now there's an idea! Deities do love offerings. She watched as a crow flew down and began to peck at the crumbs, never getting near enough for her to touch it. Nesh leant over and made a lunge at the bird, which promptly flew back to the roof. He cursed inventively, making Val chuckle. Manuel scattered some of his crisps near the table, then made a lunge of his own when a crow hopped over to investigate. He was quicker than Nesh, but equally unsuccessful, his chosen crow hopping just out of reach, and darting back in to grab a crisp before flying off with it. Kessler looked on with crossed arms, wearing an amused and possibly superior smile.

"Just as well," Manuel said defensively. "I've suffered enough from crows already."

"You're not doing it right," Val said. "You need to win its trust first, surely." She grabbed some of Manuel's crisps, ignoring his half-voiced protest, and threw pieces out in a line, starting further from her and leading in. A couple of crows flew down and pecked up the furthest pieces, but stopped warily a metre or so away from the group, turning their heads from one side to another as they assessed them—then flew back to the roof. Val harrumphed in an annoyed way.

"Wait," Freya said. "I think there might be a way to make this work. But... I'd have to do it alone. And not here."

Val rolled her eyes. "Really Freya, here we are trying to work together to fix a problem, and you want to go off alone? What happened to teamwork?"

Freya felt herself blushing furiously as everyone looked at her, but she held firm. "I think if I take Kessler's lyre-thing, and that salt you bought, Val, with a few other bits and pieces, I can get the lyre to Ben, without it seeming to come from us. So, teamwork, yes, but the type of teamwork where I sort out the delivery mechanism. I'd need you to get Ben somewhere near running water, though."

"Not that skanky river again," Val muttered.

"I'm fine with your plan so long as I'm at a distance," Kessler said.

Nesh had the least objections, perhaps because he hadn't been involved in Ben's attacks. "Fine by me," he said. "It's not like grabbing crows is working."

"How long will this take, Freya?" Val asked. "Dancing night is coming up fast, and I don't feel like ending up concussed in a coal hole again."

"We do it tonight," she said, hoping her confidence wasn't misplaced. "So long as we can get Ben to a river. Maybe that one in Endcliffe Park?"

We might have got lost in Endcliffe Park on the night of the thunder snow, but at least the water deity there is obliging. I don't want to risk trying to use the Don. That river's been through enough industrial toxicity to leave a lasting effect, otters or no. Although at least we're introduced now. Freya had taken advantage of the improved weather during the week to make herself formally known to that local river deity. She *hadn't* stood in the river to do that. Bad enough she'd had to do so with the Porter brook and the river Sheaf. It still seemed miraculous that she'd survived the experience with nothing more than a wetting. Her previous river encounters had been rather different.

Nesh grinned widely. "No problemo," he said. "There's a concert in that park tonight. I'll go scrounge a couple of flyers and drop them near Ben."

"Musical bait, that's awesome," Val congratulated him.

"Maybe bring something to feed the crows, too," Freya suggested. "Just in case."

"Good idea," Manuel said, feelingly. "I think I have had enough of crows *and* rivers."

CHAPTER THIRTY-FIVE
CROWBAIT

Freya finished her water—her wallet still hadn't recovered enough to pay for either soda *or* cider—and stood up. "I'll need the Apollonian thing, Kessler," she said.

He snorted a bit as he handed it over. "It's not 'an Apollonian thing'. It's a finely crafted amulet."

"In that case, I'll need the finely crafted amulet," she said with a smile. The amulet felt warm from the hands that had held it. She considered how to keep it safe for a moment, but decided that her pocket would do. "I'm going now. Do you think you can get him there while it's still light? It would help, I think," she said.

"I'll go get those flyers," Nesh said. "See what I can do."

Val lifted her glass in a salute. "And Kessler, Manuel and I will stay here and be obvious decoys," she said. "Though I still think we should have your back."

Freya nodded, appreciating the thought. "I wouldn't say no if you were somewhere nearby," she said. "Just not right by the bridge in the wooded bit, OK? In fact, if you could make sure no-one comes near me other than Ben, that would be great. If you leave after him, you can still be decoys."

"It's a plan," Val said. "Sounds much more fun than sitting around doing nothing."

Freya hurried away. She wanted to call the brook spirit before anyone else arrived, to get it onside for her plan. Now that the icy layer of snow had melted, she should be able to find more suitable materials for a thyrsus, and she thought that using the salt crystal to make a circle around herself might work better than her trainer-scuff-in-the-snow had done last time. She didn't want to risk another unprotected summoning. It wasn't that she didn't trust water deities... she caught herself in the lie.

No, it really is that I don't trust water deities. Even the ones that have been helpful.

She took the route through the botanic gardens, hoping for a pinecone. She didn't find one, but she did find a fallen spruce cone that she decided was close enough. There was no shortage of ivy winding through the fences and hedges on her path. She took a little from where it wouldn't show as missing and hurried on out, up the road that led to the park. Finally, on the edge of some trees where the gardeners hadn't been quite ruthless enough, she found some tall, sturdy fennel stems. She took the time to bind the spruce cone to the fennel, using the strong vines of ivy. She rather liked the resulting thyrsus. She gave it a gentle swish, like the wand it was supposed to be, and rather to her surprise, it held together.

Right, now all I need to do is summon a water deity, in daylight, without someone mundane seeing me.

She sent a quick text to Val and received a reply almost immediately.

So, Ben took a flyer and is on the move and they're ten minutes away. That's not too bad.

Looking around, Freya waited for some families to walk past on their way to the playground, and for a couple of students to head in the other direction, perhaps on their way home. Two crows flew overhead, but disappeared without swooping or otherwise appearing interested in her. When the coast was clear, she ducked into the woods that surrounded the brook. She found a stretch of earth which was clear enough to take a mark and pulled Jemima's salt crystal out of her rucksack. Somehow, she hadn't got around to removing it after last week's trip. Now, she used it to draw a clear ring around herself, then she took hold of her thyrsus and started singing quietly to call the spirit of the brook. Just as it had done previously, it appeared quickly and quietly, whirling round in a swirl of clear brownish water, then rising to a small peak which formed a face near the top.

Feeling more secure today, Freya explained what it was she wanted the brook spirit to do. Rather to her surprise, the brook deity at first refused to take the lyre-amulet as Freya asked it to.

"But it won't hurt anyone," she assured it. "In fact, it's to prevent us from being hurt."

"Otters must be safe," the spirit told her in its burbling voice.

"Of course!" she said. "Actually, it would be best if the otters weren't seen, anyway. So, if you or they could place the amulet so that only Ben can find it..." She waved the thyrsus again, wishing she knew better how to wield it.

The brook bowed its wavelike head. "Very well." It splashed back into its brook just as a loud group of people walked past on the nearby path. One or two of them glanced her way, but weren't unduly disturbed by a student standing by a brook.

I guess Val hasn't arrived yet after all. Or maybe there was no way of diverting that group.

She heard some sort of music strike up in the distance. Maybe that was the concert Nesh had mentioned. It sounded like a brass band.

When the group of people had gone, Freya noticed there was a small ripple of water heading towards her, pushed ahead of the brown head of an otter. She knelt down and held out the amulet to it, hoping that the water deity had sent this otter and she wasn't just handing over Kessler's amulet to a random wild animal. Her phone chimed at her. Freya hesitated, then pulled back the amulet and checked her messages. The otter lunged for the amulet, but missed, its sharp teeth grazing her hand.

"Fenris' teeth!" she cursed. The otter blinked at her. "Sorry. I'll be with you in a minute."

Why am I talking to an otter? I doubt it can understand me.

Val's latest message said Ben had headed for the train station instead of towards the park. Freya paused for a long moment, trying to figure out what to do next.

I guess I'll have to head there too and hope the river Sheaf will help me instead. But first, I'll need to explain to the Porter brook.

She hummed the same tune that had called the brook spirit to her before. The otter chittered at her in an annoyed way, then dived, water closing over its back like dark silk. Freya wrinkled her nose, but kept humming. Soon, the water of the brook dimpled and rose. Once the swirling water raised itself up in front of her, she outlined her difficulty.

"Help granted for help given," the brook told her.

"What does that even mean?" Freya asked.

"My otters need more fish," the brook burbled.

"Oh. I'm not really one for fishing. Umm. Would habitat improvement help?" Freya was sure she could manage to join a community group or something to make good her suggestion. Maybe she could forage for extra food while weeding. She only had a hazy idea of what such groups did. But although the brook was picturesque in the park, she was sure its history as a sewer and mill-driving industrial stream would mean there were stretches of it that still needed improvement.

"Yes. Help." The brook spirit unexpectedly swept up into a wave that washed the amulet from her hand, before once more dissolving into a regular stream.

Oh, no.

Freya's stomach clenched into a tight knot of anxiety. She'd lost the amulet.

She splashed into the stream, peering into its shallow waters in an effort to find the amulet. Golden sunlight glinted off the water as the sun finally sank below cloud-level, but she couldn't see Kessler's finely crafted effort. Freya felt as though the sun was mocking her as she searched in vain.

"Time to head towards the train station, I suppose." The others would wonder where she was if she didn't show up there soon.

Is there any point in showing up now? I've lost the key part of our plan.

In the end, Freya decided it was better to turn up without the amulet than to abandon her new friends. She jogged to the end of the park and was lucky enough to catch a bus heading stationwards after only a few minutes wait. Consulting her phone, she found she'd have to change buses to make it all the way to the train station. The unfamiliar city traffic was nearly at a standstill when she reached the appropriate stop, so she decided to run the rest of the way instead of waiting for the second bus. It was cheaper to run, too. And she needed to keep up her fitness, anyway. Especially if there were more weres than Manuel in the city. Her footfalls were heavy as she worried about what she'd face when she arrived, but she passed a lot of vehicles on her route, making her realise just how much later she would have been if she'd tried to bus the same way.

As a result of her efforts, she arrived at the station puffing and hot. On the plus side, she spotted Ben near the long, steel water feature, watching a busker pluck out a tune on a lap harp. Val, Kessler and Manuel were lurking near the station entrance, trying—and obviously failing—to look inconspicuous, with their huddled stance and frequent glances at Ben. At least it was growing dark now, so they didn't stand out as much as they might have done. Nesh was nowhere to be seen. Perhaps he'd gone to see the concert in the park himself.

Freya slowed to a walk to cross the courtyard.

"Great, Freya. You made it. I was worried he'd give up on the busker before you got here. What's the plan now?" Val said.

Freya looked around, trying to work out where the river was. She'd need it.

Our only hope is that the brook has transported the amulet. She wrinkled her nose. *Some hope. Though at least I know now that there is a river under the station.*

Crows perched on the many pitched rooves of the station, alert for any opportunity. The only water in sight was the artificial water feature. She spun around slowly, looking for the brook, which surely flowed this way, but only found signs for the Sheaf River walk, which informed her that the river was underground at this point, and that it was possibly not even the waterway she needed.

"I should have remembered!" she groaned. Even if the brook had transported the amulet, how would she be able to retrieve it in order to get it to Ben, when the water was all underground? *I should know better than to put my trust in a water deity.*

"What's wrong?" Val asked.

"Er. I think I might have to use the water feature," Freya said. "And that wouldn't work. Does anyone happen to know if it connects to the river? Although that rules out otters, I suppose."

Val's expression said that Freya sounded more than a little mad.

Hey, she's the one who gathers power at nightclubs, Freya reminded herself. *Madness isn't exclusive.*

"There's a bit of the Porter Brook daylighted over on the other side of the square," Kessler said. "If that's what you're after."

Freya's shoulders slumped with relief. Partial relief, anyway. She wouldn't have to re-enter the Megatron, and the correct stream was nearby. Still, the chances of getting the amulet back seemed miniscule.

"Thank goodness. I was worried the whole thing might be underground. And I am over being underground. I doubt Ben would go there again, either. We may need to distract the crows," Freya said. "Anyone got food? Or a fishing line?"

"Why, were you planning on going fishing for tips in the fountain?" Val asked. "Or catching birds on a wire?"

Freya laughed reluctantly, worry still squirming inside her. It was a long way between the park and the station. Would any water deity remember what it was doing over that stretch of darkness? "No. Just hoping that I'll find what I need in the water."

"You worry about water. We'll deal with crows," Val said. She conferred with Manuel, who ducked into the station and appeared shortly afterwards with yet another packet of crisps.

"Don't you think we should give the crows a better diet?" Freya asked. "I'm sure crisps aren't good for them."

Val paused in the act of opening the crisps and stared at her. "Do you want help, or would you prefer to lecture us on the help we're giving?"

Freya winced. "Sorry. I do appreciate your help. And the crows probably regard human food as a treat."

She looked up at the crows, then over towards Ben. The harp player had been joined by a fiddler, and a crowd had formed a wide circle around them, clapping in time. Freya squinted at the fiddler.

Is that Nesh?

She supposed that there was no reason for him *not* to provide the music they needed to attract Ben. And it sounded like he was playing an Irish tune, suitable for the Celtic Morrigan.

Should he be playing bouzouki for Apollo, instead? Somehow, she doubted that would be appropriate.

In many ways, the harp was the closest modern instrument to a lyre. It was probably the best cover she'd get, and it combined elements of the two deities she was concerned about. She jogged in the direction that Kessler had indicated, and came to a short section of water, walled off and flowing into a culvert that looked like it must run under the station. She and Val must have been inside there somewhere.

This must be it.

She fished the salt out of her bag and used it like chalk to etch a circle around herself.

If Jemima really likes this thing, I'll have to save up and buy her another.

It was hard to sing a tune at first, especially with the harp and fiddle in the background, but she managed to come up with a hum that resonated with the lower notes of the harp. It sounded pleasingly dark, like the Megatron itself. To her relief, the water formed into a whirlpool almost at once, pulsing along with the claps.

"Er. Hi. I mean, greetings. Or something. Do you have my amulet by any chance?" she asked the water deity, then held her breath as though she was six years old again, hoping for a miracle. For a moment, nothing happened. Then a furry brown head popped out of the side of the tall brown column of water. Astonishingly, she saw the otter had the amulet in its mouth. It twisted through the water, playing with the ripples that continuously poured from the water deity's form, then scrambled up the steep bank, its back humping and flattening as it ran. It released the amulet at the edge of Freya's circle, then raced back to the water. The amulet now had a dark feather woven through it. It looked like the crow's feather that Freya had picked up in the gym, and like the one that had floated downstream in the tunnels. As she stooped to pick it up, a burst of air blew Freya's hair across her face, half-blinding her. She felt feathers brushing her face as a flock of crows descended on the amulet. Freya flapped her arms at them, but they ignored her.

A screeching of metal on metal sounded from the station as a train pulled in, and a minute later, while Freya was still trying to dislodge crows, someone approached her from the station.

"Do you need a hand with those crows?" called a familiar, but not unwelcome voice, from across the square.

Jemima! But although Freya was cautiously glad to see the other girl again, that feeling was overwhelmed by the anguish of having lost Kessler's amulet a second time. What could they do about Ben without it?

Although the day had been clear, clouds massed overhead and underlying the caws of the crows, Freya thought she heard thunder grumble. Or was it the large black dog that Jemima brought with her, growling on its leash, that made the threatening sound?

Jemima let the dog loose and it bounded towards Freya and the crows. Freya gasped as the canine hurtled towards her, too scared even to scream. The birds rose in a flurry of wings and headed towards Ben and the buskers.

"Heel!" Jemima said sharply, and the dog wheeled away from the crows to stand obediently at her side. "I'll come catch up in a moment," she told Freya, re-attaching the lead to her dog's collar, and moving off in what looked like a wide circle around the crowd of people listening to the buskers.

Relaxing a little, Freya turned her attention to the crows, unsure if she should be furious or glad. After all, she'd been trying to get the amulet to Ben, and it was closer to him now. The flock descended near the crowd around the buskers, many of whom ducked or covered their heads. As Freya watched the birds, Val and the others ran up to her.

"Sorry," Val said. "You might be right about giving them something else to eat after all."

"Never mind," Freya said. "It looks like we've had the desired effect anyway." She pointed. One crow was still aloft, circling over Ben. As they watched, something small and shiny dropped from the crow's beak and landed on him. He flinched as it hit his shoulder, then picked it up. He turned it to and fro, examining it, then attached it to a chain around his neck, stroking the feather before turning his attention back to the music.

The crows flapped up into a giant wheel above Ben and the musicians. Freya's eyes followed them a moment before she snapped her attention back to Ben.

Is it going to do anything?

The music from the harp and the fiddle became suddenly tempestuous, as though expressing a battle between light and dark. Despite the small size of the harp, its player seemed able to conjure forth low, menacing ripples of sound. Or was it Nesh's fiddle, chugging those deep chords before leaping for the highest notes? Ben's expression seemed to change with the music, sometimes grimacing in pain and anger, sometimes smiling in awe or wonder. Freya caught glimpses of Jemima, walking her dog through some complex pattern as the buskers continued to play. People shied out of the way of the huge canine, but stayed in the crowd for the music. The sound of Nesh's fiddle soared with the crows before plunging into a grinding series of notes like a dirge. He drew out a final note, then stopped, leaving the harpist plucking a slow, ascending scale. On the final note, Ben crumpled to the ground, his face going slack as he fainted. The crows wheeling above him made a sudden squabbling, manic cacophony, then flew away.

Val offered Freya, then Kessler a high-five.

"Mission accomplished!" she crowed.

"Let us hope it works," Manuel said, gloomily. "I give it a 45 per cent chance."

Chapter Thirty-Six
More than Music

Freya hurried forward as Ben fell. But Nesh caught him before he hit the concrete: awkwardly, with his violin bow in one hand. That made Freya realise that she hadn't seen Ben carrying his bow and arrows at all since their underground encounter. Perhaps the running water or the water deities had done something after all. And it looked like Kessler's amulet had had an effect too. An immediate one.

Whoever the harp-playing busker had been, he didn't stick around to help his audience. Freya saw him striding away towards the station, stowing his harp into a bag as he did so.

Ben sat up as Freya arrived. He looked bewildered.

"I can't feel her," he muttered.

"Who can't you feel?" Freya asked—then wondered if she should have kept her mouth shut. It wasn't as though Ben had shown any desire to confide in her in the past, beyond sharing evil thoughts. But it seemed she needn't have worried.

"My crow. She's *always* there, in my head, telling me to do things, making me shift. Making me do terrible things. Making me agree with the things that Paul suggests. But she's not there now!" A slow grin spread over his face, making him seem younger, and a lot nicer than he'd ever acted in the past. His hand crept to the amulet around his neck, and Freya worried that he'd pull it off. But instead, he caressed it. "She's not there," he repeated softly. Then he turned his grin on Nesh. "Great music, man. You should do more with that."

Nesh spread his bow and fiddle to make a mock bow. "Glad you liked it," he said. "You play anything?"

Ben frowned, his grin fading. "I used to play harp," he said. "I haven't touched one for years though. That's why I came here when I heard someone mention there was a busker with a harp. It made me remember… how I used to be. Before I met Paul. Before my crow turned up." He grimaced as though in pain, or perhaps remembering painful thoughts. "Back when I was the kind of person I wanted to be."

Thinking of the sorts of activities Ben had been up to, Freya thought he deserved that pain. But still, the point of giving him the amulet was to get him to redeem himself, so…

"Maybe you should take up the harp again," she said. "And get better friends than Paul."

Ben tossed her an uncertain look, but he didn't reject the idea.

"Maybe," he said.

CHAPTER THIRTY-SEVEN
A BETRAYAL

The next few days were full of anxiety. Freya stayed away from everything but lectures at first, worried that Kessler's amulet wouldn't keep Ben tamed. But when Val caught up with her after another incomprehensible, late-afternoon biochem lecture, and suggested a visit to the pub, Freya felt it would be rude to decline. Besides, she'd missed having someone to talk to other than Mr Fluffbum. Cats and calls were all very well, but they weren't the same as spending time with people.

The usual suspects occupied a table in the beer garden: Kessler, Nesh and Nesh's friend Lin sat outside, well-wrapped in gloves and scarves because the weather hadn't returned to its warm October temperatures. A light drizzle threatened, but hadn't yet driven everyone indoors.

Val strode across the damp grass, waving exuberantly to her friends. Her energy once again astonished Freya. How was she always so enthusiastic? It was refreshing, but also possibly something that Freya could only cope with in small doses. Still, as an antidote to her recent lecture, it was perfect.

Nesh looked up with a grin. Lin was occupied on her phone, though she smiled politely. Kessler gave a laconic wave, then looked past Freya and Val. His eyes widened, but he beckoned.

Freya paused and looked over her shoulder to see who he was waving at. Ben had entered the beer garden behind them, and was standing uncertainly in the doorway. As she watched, Paul came up behind him and placed a hand on his shoulder. Ben twisted away, scowling. Curious to see how this interaction would play out, but also keen to avoid Paul, Freya hastened the few steps to the table and squeezed in between Nesh and Kessler. Kessler made way for her, though he did glance wistfully at Nesh before doing so. Freya pressed her lips together. She didn't want Kessler as more than a friend, but it still stung to have to wait while her new friend yearned after someone who clearly wasn't interested.

More secure in company, Freya looked over to Ben and Paul again. They were facing off in the doorway; each one with clenched fists and angry stances.

"You're acting like a child," Paul snarled at Ben, his voice carrying. "You knew you'd have to prove yourself when you joined. If you're not willing to do that, perhaps you should just leave."

"Children don't have to deal with the sort of stuff you've been throwing at me," Ben countered. "You told me we were saving humanity. Doing worthwhile things. But so far, it's just been me crawling around in tunnels and lurking in dark alleyways while you sod off to your club. And you know what? That stinks. That's not uplifting humanity, it's just doing your dirty work."

"Go Ben," Kessler muttered in Freya's ear.

"I didn't think he had it in him," Freya agreed.

"I'm not ready to start a cheer squad yet," Val said from across the table. "I still need an apology for that concussion. I only got a B on the test I sat after that. But even so..." She trailed off, clearly impressed with Ben's change of attitude.

Freya missed whatever Ben said next as a result of her friends' commentary, but it was hard to miss when he started shouting.

"I don't have to be some sort of were to be against harming people," he yelled. "But even if I was one, I would still be leaving. I am done with your damned society of Apollo. I want to go back to making my own decisions. With you, I've seen nothing but betrayal!"

"In that case," Paul said coldly, "you can consider yourself on your own. And see how you like it being on the wrong side." The postgrad deliberately turned his back on Ben and stalked out again.

Ben looked after him for a long moment, then seemed to realise that all eyes were upon him. He looked wide-eyed, defiant, but also rather lost.

Val gave him a thumbs up, at which he smiled weakly. Then he abruptly turned and exited the pub again, glancing around before disappearing in the opposite direction to Paul.

The group sat in stunned silence for a moment. Then,

"Ten to one he's a were," Val said. "My bet is on crow."

Freya nodded slowly. Ben surely was some sort of shifter or were, though possibly not in the usual way.

Chapter Thirty-Eight

Aftereffects

Jemima sighed and stretched as she put away her notebook. Almost every page was now filled with notes. "Is that the last lab I missed?" she asked Freya. She had been catching up on the biology notes from her missed classes.

"I think so," Freya told her. "You've seen all the lectures online. I'm sure you'll be fine for the test."

"I know. It's just I want to do well," Jemima said. "I'm still not sure I'll go back to rock climbing, though. Not indoors, anyway. And it's getting too cold to go climbing in the Peak District now."

"Val will be disappointed," Freya said lightly. "But she'll get over it, so long as you still go out dancing with her."

Jemima tilted her head to one side, considering. "And you're sure Ben's not going to cause trouble?"

"Mostly sure. He's switched programs—he's doing English lit now, instead of law. And he's joined a folk band. With Nesh. Apparently, they've got a gig lined up. Nesh is happy because Lin is going to see him in it. Kessler's unhappy because Nesh didn't invite *him.*" *Best of all, Paul the postgrad has moved on. Apparently, he got a job offer abroad and decided to take it after being reprimanded by the police.* But she didn't tell all that to Jemima. It had been hard enough explaining Ben's change of attitude.

"Do I know Kessler?" Jemima asked with a frown.

"Probably not," Freya admitted. "But he's a friend." *It's going to be alright here,* Freya decided. *It's still weird living on my own, but with friends, everything is better. So long as no-one's trying to kill me or them, that is.*

Thinking about the closeness of death made Freya consider Jemima's recent brush with it. She asked abruptly, "How did things work out with your family? In London, I mean?"

Jemima grimaced. "Weirder than I'd ever expected. Enough so that I was glad of you weirdos up here, for having introduced me to the crazy side of the world. I'll tell you about it. Sometime. Just... I'm not ready yet."

Freya restrained herself enough to nod understandingly, although Jemima's reply made her wildly curious. *I'm sure she'll tell us... at some point.*

"What do you do with that dog you brought home?" she asked instead. "I know they don't allow pets in the halls."

Jemima bit her lip. "That's kind of the weirdest thing of all," she muttered. "But—I guess you might get it. Look, I'll show you." She leant down and shuffled through the things in the satchel that she'd leant against her desk when they sat down to study, bringing out a rolled-up leash. Stamped on the loop at the end was a cartwheel pattern that matched Jemima's t-shirts. Jemima unrolled the leash, made sure the end was under her desk, then ran a finger over the pattern, whispering something under her breath. As she did so, a huge black dog appeared in the shadows under the desk. Its eyes glinted oddly where they caught the light. Freya gasped and shoved her chair back hastily, trying to put distance between herself and the canine.

"It's OK," Jemima assured her, though sadness tinged her voice. "It's completely under control now." She brushed her hand over the cartwheel pattern again, and the dog vanished.

Freya tried to slow her hammering heartbeat.

"You're right," she said aloud. "That is weird. But I can see how you're able to stay in halls. Convenient, really."

"Convenient, in a really inconvenient way. He doesn't like it when I keep him gone for long. I'm just hoping I can keep this going for the rest of the year. I'd already paid for a year of halls and I can't get that back." She finished rolling up the leash and stowed it away again.

"That must make things tricky," Freya agreed. "I suppose you'll have to take a lot of walks." She eased her chair back in. "Sorry I reacted like that. I'm... not really a dog person." *Or a barghest person.*

"It's all right," Jemima said. "I was more of a cat person before myself. And this thing is so illogical, it does my head in." □

"Yeah, the mundane is easier that way," Freya agreed.

Val appeared at the end of the stack of books. Freya waved a greeting to her.

"Are you coming dancing tonight, Freya?" Val asked.

Freya smiled, but replied in the negative.

"Take Jemima," she said. "I'll come next week, but tonight I promised my cat I'd put the heating on."

"You and your cat," Val grumbled. "You give him too much sway over your life."

Jemima jumped in to defend Freya. "Freya and I—and Manuel too—owe that cat our life," she said. "We'd never have got out of that park without him."

The park—and the thunder snow—seem so long ago, Freya thought. *So much has happened since then.* Given Jemima's sudden acquisition of a dog that looked a lot like the barghests that had been chasing her, Freya suspected that a lot had happened to her, too.

Jemima stood up. "I'll come dancing if we go somewhere different," she said. "I never did like that underground club you chose." She glanced at Freya and took a deep breath. "And I don't mean climbing. Just dancing, OK?"

Val gave a mock pout before her normal cheerful expression returned. "Fine, fine, I won't drag you to the climbing gym. Not this week, anyway. Besides," she added. "There's a big group booked in tonight, now that the roof is fixed. It's too busy for a lot of casual climbers. On the other hand, profits are up, and my fees are secure again."

Freya watched them go, then turned to pack up her own things. Over in English Lit, she saw Ben had his head down, writing something which seemed to involve a lot of crossing out and rewording. Across the library, she could see Manuel leaving the maths section, angling to join Jemima and Val. It looked like they'd all be going out tonight. But she was happy to skip the dancing this once. She had an offering to give, as well as Mr Fluffbum to appease.

She stopped at a fishmonger on her way home, grimacing at the smell. Given the limits on fishing since the fish stocks collapsed, there wasn't much of a selection in the small shop. She bought several of the smallest fish on offer. She had saved up especially for this. Taking the fish, she walked on until she came to the Porter Brook, where it left the park. She waited until the daily traffic of parents with prams, late joggers and students had passed, watching the water flow past her. At last, she spotted it—a sleek, brown-furred head, parting the water silently. A second head appeared, and the two otters chittered a greeting. Freya waved the fish at them, and they swam towards her. She laid down her offering on the edge of the brook and stood back. Of its own accord, the brook lapped over the fish, washing them into itself. The otters dived after the fish and were gone.

Honour is satisfied, Freya thought. She'd still have to see about finding a habitat restoration group, but the otters had their extra food. She wrapped up the one remaining fish and walked home to present her final offering: to Mr Fluffbum.

THE END

ACKNOWLEDGEMENTS

Thanks as always to my family, especially Isabelle and Elise who asked what happened to Freya between Storm Surge and Heat Wave. This book was supposed to be a quick novella to answer that question, but it grew into a full novel with a complete cast of characters, both old and new.

Thanks also to Grace Bridges, my editor (any remaining mistakes are my own), to my critique group: Anne, Annie and Susy, your questions helped this book to be the best it could be (and twice as long!), and to Keri for the ARC read.

It's been a long time since I went climbing in anything other than a tree, so thank you to SJ Pratt who checked my climbing technique and ensured my climbers were properly inducted.

I started this book while working with the Writers' Café Auckland Novel Writers Club – a great organisation for helping writers to actually finish a book (another one complete, thank you team). One of the Writers' Café mentors, Paul, passed away during the pandemic years, just before his own book was published, hence the dedication of this book.

Thunder Snow is set in a magic-containing, near-future version of Sheffield, UK, and is based on a combination of my memories and current maps. I am indebted to the makers of the map of 'lost rivers of Sheffield', available on the Sheffield forum, for information on the flow paths of Sheffield's underground rivers. If you'd like to travel the path that Freya takes underground, search Youtube for the Megatron! I have taken some small geographic liberties for storytelling purposes.

Thanks to John for suggesting the title; it led to me asking strangers on the internet what thunder snow *really* felt like as an experience. I hope I've conveyed some of that experience in these pages. I also made use of Sheffield City Council's climate predictions.

As always, there is a mix of fact and fantasy in this book. I hope you've enjoyed both aspects.

ALSO BY MELISSA GUNN

Weather Gods:
Flash Flood
Thunder Snow
Storm Surge
Heat Wave

Woodside Cosy Urban Fantasy:
Divination and Disaster
Seers and Salt

Short stories & novellas:
Treescape (First published in Magic and Mystery: A Limited Edition
Urban Fantasy Mystery Anthology)
Feels Like Heaven (in Aftermath: Stories of Survival in Aotearoa
New Zealand)
First Pav on Mars (in Pav Deconstructed, Pavlova Press)
A Gift of Coconuts (in Imagine 2200 2024 collection)
Sweet enough? (in Artificial Sweetener: Tales of AI: 100% Written by
Humans)
Hauraki Lament or a Song of Love? (in Tales of the Hauraki Gulf)

ABOUT THE AUTHOR

Melissa always planned to write books, but she trained as a scientist and climbed trees after squirrels first. She enjoys mixing fact with fiction and imagining what might happen if the world was just a little different. She also loves wildlife photography, but mostly finds that plants are best at staying still to be photographed.

www.ingramcontent.com/pod-product-compliance
Lightning Source LLC
Chambersburg PA
CBHW020653120726
47906CB00001B/249